TIMELESS

MW01286563

Summer
HOUSE PARTY

OTHER TIMELESS REGENCY COLLECTIONS

Autumn Masquerade
A Midwinter Ball
Spring in Hyde Park
A Country Christmas
A Holiday in Bath
Falling for a Duke
A Night in Grosvenor Square

TIMELESS *Regency* COLLECTION

Summer
HOUSE PARTY

Regina Scott

Donna Hatch

Sarah M. Eden

Interior Design by Heather Justesen
Edited by Jennie Stevens and Lisa Shepherd
Cover design by Rachael Anderson
Cover Photo Credit: Holly Madchen

Published by Mirror Press, LLC
ISBN-10:1-947152-05-X
ISBN-13:978-1-947152-05-2

TABLE OF CONTENTS

An Engagement of Convenience
by Regina Scott
1

A Perfect Match
by Donna Hatch
99

The Paupers' House Party
by Sarah M. Eden
217

An Engagement of Convenience

By Regina Scott

OTHER BOOKS BY REGINA SCOTT

A Rancher of Convenience
The Bride's Matchmaking Triplets
The Bride Ship
The Courting Campaign
The Wife Campaign
The Heiress's Homecoming
The Rake's Redemption
An Honorable Gentleman
The Lady Emily Capers Series
Uncommon Courtships Series
The Marvelous Munroes Series
Spy Matchmaker Series

DEDICATION

To Kathryn Merry, for choosing to be my friend again after lo these many years, and to the Lord for providing friends to comfort and cheer.

CHAPTER ONE

Chapworth Grange, Somerset, August 1816

Why did they always have to elope at midnight?

Katherine Chapworth smothered a yawn as she waited under a neatly trimmed chestnut tree. Hugging her pink flannel dressing gown to her frame, though the summer night was warm, she kept her gaze on the Grecian folly that marked the edge of the lands belonging to Chapworth Grange.

It was always the folly, too. No, wait, Clementia's besotted beau had attempted to scale a ladder to her window. How he had thought to carry her down the wooden rungs, Kitty had never known. In any case, the top of the ladder had broken the glass, and Clementia's scream had been enough to wake the household—and the dead in the churchyard nearby—and Kitty's work had been done.

But Clive Bitterstock was a different sort. He'd been sniffing around her youngest cousin, Lucy, for the better part of the Season. His family, though not wealthy by any standards, was respectable. He was said to be prudent, thoughtful. Very likely Kitty could convince even Uncle to see the young man as a decent husband for the sixteen-year-old Lucy.

1

So why elope?

"Circle around the back," she advised Bollers, who was waiting with her, and the tall, strapping footman stalked off to the side of the stone building and began to worm his way through the shrubs that clustered there. Thank goodness most of the staff heeded her requests with respect and deference, for all she was only at the grange on her uncle's sufferance. As the chaperone for the Chapworth family for a decade, she'd safeguarded the reputations of all six of her cousins before they'd married. Once Lucy wed, she'd be done.

And she was a little concerned about what happened then.

The breeze brushed an auburn lock past her eyes, and she pushed the errant curl up into the mobcap she wore at night. Nearby, footsteps crunched up the graveled path from the lane to the church. The sound was as loud as gunshots to her listening ears. A shadow darted toward the stairs, running up to the graceful white stone columns. Inside the folly, a light sprang to life to reveal her cousin, dressed for travel, lantern shining in her gloved grip.

Time to put a stop to this. Kitty strode to the bottom of the steps, the lawn of her nightgown flapping about her legs. "That's far enough, Lucy."

Mr. Bitterstock stiffened, but her cousin gasped, clutching the chest of her pretty lavender redingote. Everything about Lucy was pretty and delicate, from her pale blond hair to her petite figure. She reminded Kitty of a Dresden shepherdess, fragile, frozen in time.

"Oh, Kitty," she said, hand falling. "You gave me such a fright. I thought you were Father."

"Be thankful I am not," Kitty replied, "or I might have come armed."

Beside her, Mr. Bitterstock began to draw himself up, gathering a head of steam like one of the new locomotives.

Kitty moved to cut him off. "This is an ill-advised venture. Kindly return to the grange, Lucy. Now."

Lucy blinked big blue eyes. "But Kitty, I love him."

"And I love her," Mr. Bitterstock declared, puffing out the chest of his paisley-patterned waistcoat. She supposed he had to posture somehow. He was not terribly imposing, being of middling height with brown hair combed to one side of a narrow face and sharp blue eyes. But she knew Lucy found his tenor voice delightful.

"How sweet," Kitty told him. "Request her hand in marriage like a proper suitor, and stop making me stay up late."

She thought she sounded rather forceful. Waspish, even. Like Mr. Bitterstock, she had to do something to enforce her rule. She wasn't much taller than Lucy, and her brown eyes could look soft and sweet, or so she had been told. Confidence in playing chaperone was key.

But her stern demeanor was not enough to dissuade Mr. Bitterstock. He put his arm about Lucy's waist. "Now, see here," he told Kitty, eyes as cold as the stars that dotted the night sky. "You cannot stop us. You're nothing but an old raisin, shriveled on the vine. The only reason you're interfering is you cannot abide to see other people happy."

The comment cut, but she wasn't about to let him see it. "Oh, stand down, puppy," Kitty returned, wondering what had happened to Bollers. "Raisin I may be, but at least I have the sense God gave me. What of you? You claim to love Lucy, yet you're willing to steal her away from the bosom of her family, risk her safety by driving through the night on roads unknown to you and your team, and deny her the one shining moment of a young woman's life: her wedding day."

Lucy's lower lip trembled. "I did so want a pretty wedding gown, Clive."

"Don't listen to her," Bitterstock warned, tightening his hold on Lucy's waist. "She's trying to trick us."

"If you consider truth trickery," Kitty allowed.

He scowled at her. "You're a bully, madam, but I wager you wouldn't stand so tall before a real threat." He stepped away from Lucy and raised his fist.

Kitty stared at him. He'd strike her? None of the men she'd confronted before had done more than protest. Where was that blasted footman? Bitterstock stomped down the stairs, head lowered like a bull's and mouth set. He expected her to run, to cower.

She would do neither.

She braced herself, feet pressed into the gravel, ready to dodge or throw up her arms to block him if she must. He reared back his fist, and a hand materialized out of the darkness and seized it before the pup could make good on his threat.

She thought surely Bollers had arrived, but the arm attached to that hand and the broad shoulders above it had better lines than the footman's and were clothed in a fine green coat. Where the footman wore a powdered wig, her rescuer had hair the color of darkest chocolate and eyes to match. Besides, she would never forget those handsome features, arranged as if by a sculptor's hand. The sight of the face that had haunted her dreams for a decade rocked Kitty more surely than any blow.

"I wouldn't do that if I were you," he said to Bitterstock. "I have it on good authority that she bites."

4

Quentin Adair watched Kitty Chapworth wash white. How odd that the first person he should meet on returning to Chapworth Grange was the last person he'd seen before being exiled from it ten years ago.

"Adair," she said, her voice a ghost of the one she'd been using on the young man beside him.

"In the flesh," he promised. "And whose elopement are you attempting to ruin this time?"

The young man wrenched his hand from Quentin's grip. "That is none of your concern, sir. You have no right to interfere in my affairs."

Another movement caught Quentin's eye. A tall, imposing footman wrestled his way out of the bushes and tugged down his coat before going to stand self-importantly behind Kitty.

"I believe a gentleman has every right to intervene when a lady might be in danger," Quentin replied to the young upstart in front of him. "Indeed, I think it the duty of every gentleman or lady, wouldn't you agree, Miss Chapworth?"

"Quite," Kitty snapped, sounding more like her usual determined self. The footman standing at attention behind her likely had helped her regain her composure. The fellow would have been more menacing if his black coat hadn't been speckled with leaves and his powdered wig askew.

"Although Mr. Bitterstock seems to have forgotten the rules of good Society," Kitty was continuing. "A gentleman courts a lady properly and seeks her family's permission before marrying her."

Was she attempting to remind Quentin of his failings? The

little blonde in the folly must have had other ideas, for she hurried down the stairs. "That's true. But we were concerned that Father might refuse if he knew the state of Clive's finances."

Kitty made a sad moue. "Pockets to let? And how exactly were you planning to support your wife?"

"I am persuaded we would survive," Bitterstock grit out.

"Sadly, I am not," Kitty said. "You have two choices that I see, Mr. Bitterstock. You can return to the grange, speak to my uncle in the morning, or you can leave now before I have the keeper set the hounds on you."

The fellow blanched. "You wouldn't dare."

She tsked. "And a poor judge of character as well. Mr. Adair here can attest to my single-mindedness when it comes to protecting my family."

"Vicious," Quentin agreed. "I'd run now if I were you."

He gaped.

"I shall give you until the count of three," Kitty said. "One, two . . ."

Bitterstock turned and pelted down the lane.

"He left!" the little blonde protested. Quentin thought the footman smothered a laugh.

"Alas, yes," Kitty told her. "I'm terribly sorry, dearest, but he was a fortune hunter. A man who refuses to speak to your father generally has something to hide."

Even after ten years, he felt the comment like a slap to the cheek. He had given his attentions freely, pursuing this woman and that, never raising expectations too far before moving on. When he'd finally thought himself genuinely in love, he'd known he was blighted by circumstances. The black sheep of the neighborhood, the wastrel who preferred horse racing and gaming to duty. Yet he'd dared to love the most beautiful lady in the region, had begun to plan a future together. The woman in front of him had made him realize that future was doomed and changed his life in the process.

"But Kitty," the blonde said, a sob hitching her soft voice. "What shall I do?"

Kitty took the lantern from the girl's trembling hand and patted her arm. "You will go on, dearest. Better tears now than a lifetime of regret. Go back to the grange. It's time we all slept. Tomorrow will be brighter, I promise. Bollers, would you escort Miss Lucy?"

The footman stepped forward. With a sniff, the girl started back toward the house.

Quentin thought Kitty might follow, but she turned to him. Amazing how sharp those brown eyes could look when leveled his way.

"What are you doing here?" she demanded.

"I came home to see my father," he replied. "I couldn't sleep and decided to take a walk to clear my mind."

"At midnight?" In the golden light of the lantern, her coffee-colored brows rose in question.

He shrugged. He wasn't about to confess that he'd been watching the grange from the folly for several days now, noticing who came and went. By the number of carriages arriving, it was clear Sir Thomas was hosting a house party. A shame Quentin would never be invited. Nothing would suit him better than to keep an eye on the crafty codger up close.

"As I said, I couldn't sleep. But I'm not sorry I arrived when I did. You were in rare form."

She dropped her gaze and tugged on the sash of her

dressing gown with her free hand. The wrapper was plain flannel without a scrap of lace or embroidery to embellish it. Yet it outlined her curves as surely as satin.

"Yes, well," she said, cheeks coloring as if she'd noticed his regard. "Thank you for your help. I imagine you would prefer it if I simply bid you good night now."

He ought to prefer that. He had hoped never to lay eyes on her again. She had been witness to the worst moment of his life. She was related to the man who had made himself Quentin's enemy. He ought to have nothing further to do with her.

But there was one question he wanted answered.

Quentin put out a hand to stop her from following the footman. "After all this time, have you nothing to say to me?"

She eyed his hand on her arm, then raised her gaze to his face.

"Yes," she said, eyes tearing. "I am so, so sorry."

CHAPTER TWO

There, she'd said it. She'd wanted to beg his pardon for ten years.

She'd thought about their last meeting so many times. She'd been Lucy's age, awash with the excitement of her first Season. Her parents had been alive then, and they'd been honored when Sir Thomas had invited Kitty to join her cousins at the grange before heading to London.

Even then, Uncle had been the more prosperous, commanding brother, with Kitty's father being a mere country rector. Her life had comprised of helping her mother see to the good of the parishioners and dreaming of one day having her own home with a husband who loved and appreciated her the way her father loved her mother. To think, she'd actually trembled with delight knowing she'd be tutored in the mysteries of popularity by her oldest cousin, Eugenia, the reigning belle.

With golden hair and emerald eyes, the willowy Eugenia kept a long line of suitors dangling, like the train on a ball gown. Eugenia inspired sonnets, duels at dawn. In the eyes of the *ton* and her family, Eugenia could, quite simply, do no wrong. Kitty certainly thought so.

It had been a marvelous, magical Season, even if there were

9

moments Eugenia seemed out of sorts having Kitty underfoot. For a time, she had even earned the attentions of the most sought-after bachelor in their county, the son of the family who owned Rose Cottage, whose lands marched next to the grange. Every unmarried woman for miles around had been pining for Quentin Adair. That silky brown hair, always tousled as if he'd just finished racing his thoroughbred against the wind. Those dark eyes, so brooding, so intense. The effortless grace with which he moved, as if every man was so blessed in power and physique. At church services in the village and at the local assembly, each lady sighed, hoping he might smile in her direction.

How Kitty had preened to be seen on his arm. It seemed as if they could converse about anything, that their minds and hearts were perfectly attuned.

But it hadn't lasted. Like a butterfly, Quentin had fluttered off to the next flower. It was the way of Society, Eugenia had cautioned her. Looking back, Kitty could see that his attentions toward her had been no greater than what he offered any other young lady. She'd set her sights on finding another suitor. Surely next Season would see her dreams of marriage come true.

Then she had taken a stroll about the grounds at a house party not unlike this one, only to come upon her incomparable cousin by the folly, apparently struggling in a man's arms. Kitty had been stunned.

But not silent.

"Help! Help!" she'd cried, hoping to alert one of the footmen who always hovered about. "Unhand her, you ruffian!"

As Kitty had dashed toward the couple, Eugenia and the man had broken apart to stare at her, and in that instant, Kitty learned that her cousin was not the lady she seemed. For not only did Eugenia appear to be enjoying the gentleman's embrace, her eyes sparkling and her skin glowing, but the gentleman who held her was none other than Quentin Adair.

As voices grew in volume in the distance, Quentin had seized Eugenia's hand. "Come away with me. We'll find someone to marry us."

Kitty sucked in a breath. So it was love. She'd never seen a fellow look at a lady with so much passion, as if she were his entire world. She wanted to reach out to him, tell him he'd chosen the wrong woman. But if he truly wanted Eugenia, who was she to get in the way? She stepped back, waited for her cousin to dash off, and tried to think what she would say to keep her uncle and his staff from pursuing the happy couple.

Eugenia placed the back of one long-fingered hand to her brow, green gaze drifting toward the summer sky. "Oh, that you would ask me to abandon my family, my sisters who are so dear to me. That, sir, cannot be love."

She was posturing when she should be running. What was wrong with her? Kitty glanced back toward the house and spotted a hoard of men dashing toward them, summoned by her cry.

Quentin seemed oblivious to the impending danger. Indeed, a frown darkened his handsome face.

"Are you toying with me?" He took a step back Eugenia as if he couldn't believe it. "You accepted my kisses, my ring. Did you think it all a game, madam?"

Eugenia glanced at Kitty. "Well, certainly it is a game. And I always win."

Kitty felt cold all over.

As Sir Thomas and his footmen barreled up to the folly, Eugenia ran to her father to collapse in his arms. "Oh, Papa! He is a brute! He hurt me! I don't know what I would have done if Kitty hadn't come upon us."

Kitty wanted to sink down under the flowers that edged the graveled walk. This was wrong. Eugenia might protest all she liked, but the only hurt Kitty felt was radiating from the man opposite her. That, and the pain building inside her as she realized what her cousin had done.

"Brute, is he?" her uncle growled. At his nod, the footmen surged forward to grab Quentin. Kitty opened her mouth to protest, but Eugenia reached out and pinched her arm. Those emerald eyes promised retribution if Kitty should so much as speak a word. And once more Kitty was stunned.

But not silent.

"Uncle, stop!" she cried, pushing forward.

They paid her no heed. The footmen forced Quentin to his knees, stripped off his coat, and pinned his arms to his sides while he glared at Kitty's uncle.

Uncle was in no way intimidated. "I'll teach him to mind his manners," he threatened. "Taughton, my riding crop."

Kitty closed her eyes now against the memory. While Eugenia had held Kitty in place as if determined to make her watch, Quentin Adair had said nothing while Uncle struck his back and shoulders, again and again, until the lawn was striped by red. And when it was over, the footmen had dragged Quentin home while Uncle ordered his father to take him somewhere Eugenia and her family might never lay eyes on him again.

And Kitty had been too young and heartbroken to know

how to intervene. As it was, when her parents suggested she could go back to London with Eugenia next Season, she had refused. And then fate had taken the matter from her hands.

Now Quentin shrugged a pair of shoulders that seemed to have grown even broader over the years. "You needn't apologize. You did me a favor."

Kitty stared at him. "A favor? Because of me, you were whipped and exiled to . . . to . . ."

"Jamaica," he put in helpfully. "Yes. And I can tell you there were many days I cursed you, your cousin, and your entire family. But toiling under the hot sun taught me to stand on my own feet, and I made a success of my family's sugar plantation. I am convinced none of that would have happened had I continued with the life of gambling and romancing I'd led in England. I doubt even marrying the once-fair Eugenia would have changed me. No, because of that dark day, I am a better man."

She wanted to believe him. How wonderful that something good should come from such pain. But finding him here, now, made no sense.

"And you have truly returned merely to see your father?" she asked.

He nodded, boot scraping at the steps. "He is unwell, but the doctor says he should recover."

She was glad to hear that. His father was a quiet, unassuming man who had always seemed a little in awe that he had lent a hand in birthing so magnificent a fellow as Quentin. Uncle was forever badgering him to sell his property so the grange estate could expand. She admired anyone who would stand up to Sir Thomas.

"I should leave you to your walk," she said. "Welcome home, Adair."

She turned, then hesitated, surprised to see that Lucy and the footman had nearly reached the grange. Another moment, and Kitty would be the one who needed a chaperone.

"Kitty."

Her name stopped her movement, and she glanced back at him. His eyes were narrowed, as if he studied her.

"I'd like to speak to you further," he said. "Would you have time to slip away in the morning, meet me here?"

Slip away to the folly to meet Quentin Adair? How romantic!

How ridiculous.

"Sir Thomas is hosting a house party," she explained. "I have responsibilities."

He cocked his head so that a lock of that exquisite hair caressed his forehead. "Please?"

"Do you do that on purpose?" she demanded. "Perhaps practice in front of the mirror?"

He straightened. "What?"

He probably couldn't help being so impossibly perfect. "Never mind. Suffice it to say neither of us will be well served by meeting like this. I must refuse."

"Of course." He inclined his head but not before she saw something spark in those dark eyes. "Never let it be said that a Chapworth would consort with an Adair."

Kitty stiffened. "Oh, consorting. Is that what you had in mind? And here I thought it was merely a simple conversation. Had I known we would be consorting I would surely have given you another answer. Perhaps the cut direct?"

He chuckled, and the sound eased the ache inside her. "Forgive me. I simply thought because of our past association . . ."

She should be more solicitous of his wishes. She felt as if she owed him, though she had been unaware of Eugenia's jealousy until the end. No matter his claim that she had done him a favor, justice had been denied. What was one conversation against that? Perhaps she could break away for a short time.

With Lucy and a footman or two in tow.

"Very well," she allowed. "I will endeavor to be here at nine tomorrow morning. You will have to be satisfied with that."

Satisfied, she said. Quentin shook his head as he started back toward Rose Cottage, his family's estate. Since that day when Eugenia had turned on him, the only thing that had satisfied him was the success of the plantation in Jamaica. Now that was in jeopardy, and all because of Kitty's uncle.

The moon turned the stone blocks of the two-story house silver as he approached. Surrounded by roses, his ancestral home could only be called a cottage compared to Mallery Manor on the north and Chapworth Grange on the south. Still, no matter how lovely the sight, he found himself missing the brilliant sun, the balmy breezes of the island.

If only he could convince his father to leave England and join him.

In deference to the old man, he slipped in through the terrace doors, knowing the Aubusson carpet would swallow the sound of his footsteps. Still, he hadn't even crossed the

15

withdrawing room before a flint was struck, illuminating the face of the man sitting in the armchair by the empty grate.

"Still keeping your own counsel, I see," his father mused.

His voice was more sad than condemning, as if he had somehow failed in his duty to raise Quentin properly. Quentin took a seat in the wingback chair opposite his father's.

Alastair Adair had always been a slight fellow, sure of nothing save his love for the son his dear wife had died birthing late in their marriage. Now his hair was nearly white, his slender frame beginning to bend. Years of worrying about Quentin had taken its toll.

"I am done with midnight assignations," he assured his father. "I merely wanted one last look at the grange before retiring."

"Ah." His father smiled as he turned to light the lamp beside him, brightening their corner of the simple withdrawing room. "No more secret trysts with lovely ladies?"

Kitty came immediately to mind, though their meeting could hardly be called a tryst. Of all the young ladies he'd met over the years, she was the most memorable, and not because she'd been the one to bring her uncle's wrath down upon him. No, Katherine Chapworth had been different.

Oh, she'd had the same wide-eyed excitement about her Season as any young lady making her debut. But where they flitted and fluttered from one beau and ball to the next, Katherine had been calmer, deliberate. It was as if she considered the worth of each person she met, then either cherished or dismissed them, depending on the goodness of their character. Her head might have been in the clouds, but her feet had been solidly planted on the ground. Small wonder Sir Thomas had asked her to chaperone one of his girls.

A shame Quentin had not understood her worth then. Eugenia had played him well, determined as she was to show up her cousin and keep her undisputed place as reigning belle. Still, he could not lay all the blame on her. He'd been the one to flit from one lady to another. She'd merely taken advantage of a nature he had now outgrown. He was glad that when he had encountered one of the denizens of the grange, it had been Kitty.

"She must be special to put that smile on your face," his father commented.

Quentin leaned back. "Kitty Chapworth was at the folly, foiling an elopement."

"Miss Lucy's," his father said with a nod. "Chapworth's youngest seems to have attracted quite a following, much like her older sister."

But without the calculation. Lucy Chapworth seemed to have been sincerely attached to her swain, so much so that she'd needed Kitty's sharper eye to see the fortune hunter within.

"It would do my heart good to see you settled, Quentin," his father said. Now his voice sounded weaker, and he added a cough for good measure.

"You fool no one," Quentin told him. "You are not dying, Father."

"Yet," his father predicted, hitching his crimson dressing gown closer.

"Not for some time, if I have anything to say in the matter."

His father sighed. "Sir Winston and Sir Thomas think otherwise. In the last fortnight, they have both renewed their offers to buy Rose Cottage."

"Sir Winston will understand when you refuse," Quentin answered. "And as for Sir Thomas, I believe I have found a way to circumvent his plans to ruin us."

His father leaned forward, eyes dark in his pale face. "Be careful, son. You know what happened last time Sir Thomas considered you a threat."

"I will never forget," Quentin replied. "But this time, I will get the better of him, Father. I promise you that." And it might just be that Kitty Chapworth could help.

CHAPTER THREE

O f course, slipping away the next morning to meet Quentin was not as easy as Kitty had hoped. Lucy, having lost her current love, slept late in consolation. And Kitty was needed to mediate ever so many squabbles.

Somehow, over the last ten years, she had slipped into the role of chatelaine to her uncle—directing staff, ordering his schedule, managing his correspondence—all while chaperoning her cousins. She was rarely thanked for her efforts. Indeed, most of the family assumed it her duty. That morning, she had to confirm the meal plans for the next two days, see about switching Mr. Cadberry to another room because he claimed the northern exposure left him bilious, and send to the village for more chocolate because Miss Gaffney could not start the morning without at least three cups of the melted sweet. So, it was shortly after nine before she could return to the folly, and then only with Bollers as company.

The youngest and least experienced of her uncle's footmen, the newly hired Bollers tended to act before thinking. That was all right with Kitty. She preferred to do the thinking herself.

Quentin was waiting at the folly, prowling back and forth

among the columns like a leopard in a cage. His black coat and buff pantaloons only added to the illusion.

"Forgive me for being late," Kitty said, lifting her gray lutestring skirts to climb to his side. "Duty."

He eyed the footman, who took up residence at the foot of the stairs as if prepared to defend the folly from all comers. "And I see you brought reinforcements."

"Only to preserve propriety," Kitty assured him.

He lifted a dark brow. "I thought you were serving as matron chaperone to your cousin—Lucinda, if memory serves."

Kitty nodded. "She is the youngest of Eugenia's sisters. She was only a child in the nursery when you left. But I am hardly a matron. I never married."

She thought he might comment on the justice of that—the woman who had denied him marriage to his true love was denied it as well. But he merely smiled.

"Ah, that explains things. I had a suspicion that the intelligence of English gentlemen had plummeted since I left."

He was being kind. She knew her worth on the marriage mart. "They were intelligent enough to know an impoverished orphan would not suit."

"Orphan?" The teasing tone left his deep voice. "Your parents passed on?"

She could only nod. "Shortly after you left. Carriage accident. I was an invalid for months, one leg terribly twisted. What funds they left me went to pay for doctors and treatments. Even now, my leg aches when it is cold. I was fortunate Uncle gave me a place."

"A place, or a position as a servant?"

Was that anger she heard now? She chanced a glance up at him. He was frowning, but she couldn't be sure of the reason.

"I have a home and a role in the family," she told him. "If it seems at times I have ceased to be visible, I find I cannot mind. Indeed, in light of Sir Thomas's temper, some might consider being a nonentity a blessing."

His frown only deepened. "And have you no thought you might be meant for more?"

Her temper flared. "Easily said, sir, when you have freedom, funds to travel, a father awaiting your return. As it is, Sir Thomas has determined that when Lucy weds, I shall be sent to live with an elderly cousin who resides in Dartmoor. No more Society, no more helping young ladies avoid despicable cads— just gentle snores and bleating sheep." Oh, but she would say something vile next. She clamped her mouth shut to prevent the bitter words from spilling out.

He offered her a commiserating smile. "Perhaps she will leave you a fortune."

"As she too lives on Sir Thomas's mercy, doubtful. No, he is congratulating himself on saving the cost of a nurse, you may be sure of it. I replied to some ads for governesses and companions in *The Times*, but no one has responded."

From the grange came the sound of laughter. Kitty glanced out of the folly to see that some of the gentlemen staying for the house party had ventured out onto the lawn. Very likely they were preparing for the bowling she had arranged for later that morning. But she could not chance that one might stroll close enough to see Quentin.

"You should go," she said. "My uncle tenderly nurses his

21

grudges. I couldn't bear it if you were whipped again on my account."

"If you are invisible, what danger can there be?" he asked.

Oh, that smile would be her undoing. He still wielded it as deftly as a sword.

"You never know," she threatened. "My uncle might surprise us both and insist that we wed to protect my reputation."

He started. "Kitty, you're brilliant!"

"Yes," she agreed. "So go, while you can."

"No, no." He reached for her hand and held it against the wool of his coat. "Don't you see? It would serve them all right if you agreed to marry me."

Even in the shadows of the folly, Quentin could see that Kitty was staring at him. "Marry you? You're mad!"

Perhaps. He'd been told that often enough over the years. But this time he knew exactly what he was doing.

"Think about it," he urged. "You say your uncle intends to remove you from Society, that the others no longer see you. Engage yourself to me, and I guarantee they will wake up and take notice."

"But not in a way I would like," she protested. "Uncle may well call for his crop again."

"He called for his crop because Eugenia claimed I had attempted to harm her. It will be a different matter when your uncle sees how devoted we are. And your good opinion of me could sway him to see me in a more favorable light."

She was shaking her head so violently he knew he had blundered. He cocked his head. "Unless you think it would upset Eugenia."

She waved her free hand. "Eugenia is married and living in the north of England with her baronet husband and nine children."

"Nine!" Whatever he'd imagined for his perfidious former love, it was hardly that.

"And she still managed to keep her face and figure," Kitty said with a sigh. "There is no justice."

"Rarely," he agreed. "But we have a chance to make our own. Your uncle has not been the best neighbor to my father. I'm sure the animosity stems from that day with Eugenia. It troubles my father deeply. A friendship between our houses would surely ease his mind."

She regarded him, auburn brows tight. He kept his look eager, compassionate. She had no need to know that something more drove his suggestion.

"Being engaged to you, I will be able to join the house party," he pressed. "In such proximity, I can win your uncle's favor, and I'll help them see the vibrant woman they're overlooking. Or do you wish to die an unlamented spinster?"

She raised her chin. "I wish to die an old lady with no regrets of wasting my life. And I was on the way to achieving that. I have been fruitful, sir, since you left. Every lady in my family has married well and married for love."

Except her. She seemed to have convinced herself her infirmity and lack of funds would prevent her from making a match. Or perhaps her uncle and his not-so-charming daughters had drummed that opinion into her. Eugenia was likely as determined as her father to hold a grudge.

"As you said," he murmured, "there is no justice. Help me make it just for us both, Kitty, at least for a little while. Think of how much fun it would be to be part of Society again instead of living in the shadows."

She made a face as she pulled back her hand. "You may think your words honeyed, sir, but I can see through the treacle to the hard truth within."

He stilled. Kitty Chapworth had always seemed quiet, but the first time he'd looked into those wide brown eyes, he'd known she had depths few appreciated. Had that clever mind seen through him now?

"And what truth is that?" he asked as if the answer meant little to him.

"Do you think nothing of my reputation?" she challenged.

Her reputation. Of course. The chaperone would consider that above all else.

"Jilt me as it pleases you," he told her. "That is the lady's prerogative, after all. Who knows? Perhaps another man will step in to take my place."

She put her hands on her hips. "And what if I hold you to your word?"

He grimaced. "There's always Jamaica."

She dropped her hands and stepped back. "Rogue. You know how to tempt, I can see that. Can you imagine the look on Uncle's face if I introduced you as my betrothed?" Her laugh was bright and pure, like sunlight piercing the clouds.

Quentin smiled. "Then you'll do it?"

"I don't know." Her fingers twisted around each other as if

24

they were as tangled as her thoughts. "You'd have to be convincing. Very convincing. Can you truly make them think you love me, of all people?"

"Why not? Surely you have had other suitors since I left."

Her silence said otherwise.

"Kitty." He took her hand again, her fingers stiff in his. "I promise you the most devoted, besotted betrothal. No one will doubt my admiration for you. Every one of them will have cause to rue the day they made light of you. You can retire to your moor with your head high, if it comes to that. Please say you will go along with my plan."

Her gaze searched his face as if she could see more than the earnestness he'd erected. He willed her to agree. She could not know how cruelly her uncle had pressed his father, how he'd undermined their efforts to sell their sugar in England. Quentin had to keep Sir Thomas busy for the next few days if his plan to thwart the tyrant was to succeed. He'd been struggling to find a way to get onto the estate. What better than an engagement? Just the idea of Quentin joining the Chapworth family would be enough to drive Sir Thomas mad.

Just say yes, Kitty!

He must indeed have been convincing, for she nodded.

"Very well. I will join you in this engagement of convenience. I only hope it does not prove highly inconvenient for us both."

CHAPTER FOUR

K itty wandered back to the grange, Bollers dutifully at her side.

"Should I wish you happy, miss?" he'd asked when she came out of the folly, making her wonder how much of the conversation he'd overheard.

"Very likely not," she'd told him. Indeed, she was already chiding herself for agreeing to Quentin's outrageous plan. She wanted to help him, even if her role in his ostracism had been small. Seeing him prosper in some way undid the wrong Eugenia had done by betraying him and Kitty. Now she had only to wait until he called later that morning to put his plan into action.

She shook her head as she crossed the lawn. Quentin truly had changed while away from England. He seemed more determined, more in control of himself. He must take his position seriously to want to mend the rift between their families. If she'd had a chance to make peace with the man who'd beaten her, she'd have been more tempted to spit in his eye!

Only one of the gentlemen bowlers glanced up at her as she passed. Mr. Fredericks, one of the fellows in Lucy's train, offered her a friendly smile. The rest ignored her. She was the

26

chaperone, after all. No call to impress her. As it was, they seemed decidedly at loose ends without her fair cousin among them. Kitty went in search of Lucy.

The girl was awake and sitting up in bed—dewy-eyed and sweet-faced, despite the adventures of the night.

"Oh, Kitty," she said, patting the brocade coverlet beside her. "Please, sit and talk to me. I don't know how I shall go on today without Clive."

Her look was more earnest than wretched, as if she were simply seeking an answer to a puzzle.

"I am certain you will survive," Kitty told her, perching on the edge of the tester bed. "I know you felt yourself in love, sweetness, but it was clearly not reciprocated."

Lucy sighed with great feeling. Eugenia had been similarly melodramatic, all to great effect, Kitty now knew. At least Lucy was honest about her emotions.

"You have had any number of suitors," Kitty reminded her. "Did no one else touch your heart?"

Lucy rubbed her hand against the rose-colored fabric. "All of them touched my heart in some way. I never imagined there were so many presentable fellows in the world."

"Well, we have several in attendance at our party," Kitty said, fighting a smile. "Perhaps one of them will rise above the others."

Lucy brightened at that, and Kitty directed the maid to dress Lucy in the blue cambric gown with the full sleeves, the one that brought out the sparkle in her eyes. Kitty's gray lutestring was nearly as fine. Though Uncle preferred her to dress in drab colors as befitting a chaperone, he would not stand for any lady in his household wearing less than the finest materials, seeing as how it would reflect on him.

Still, her cousin might have been gowned in sackcloth, and the gentlemen would pursue her. They flocked to the lovely Lucy, even as they had to her older sister Eugenia. Lucy was far kinder and sweeter. Her chief fault lay in the fact that she was so very biddable. While it had stood her in good stead with her quarrelsome older sisters, all of whom adored her, it did not help her make decisions, about anything.

Once Lucy was dressed and coifed for the morning, they made their way to the library to bid Sir Thomas good morning, as was their custom. The paneled corridors, the elegant staircase, were thoroughly familiar to Kitty. She'd learned the history of the house at an early age. Chapworth Grange had been built in the 1600s, when their shared ancestor had been granted a baronetcy and estate for his services to the Crown. But each generation had attempted to expand its glory. Now the warm stone manor looked out across the Somerset countryside, with a reflecting pond and deep lawn directly at the back, terraced gardens alongside, and a sweeping drive at the front. Her uncle was the king of all he surveyed.

And he knew it.

He leaned back in the leather-bound chair as they entered, brown banyan encasing his widening girth, booted feet upon a cushioned hassock, and *The Times* open on his lap.

"There's my girl," he proclaimed with a nod to Lucy. "Come here, child. Are you enjoying your party?"

"Oh, yes, Father," she said as she went to sit on the chair nearest his. Kitty took her usual place on the settee among the glass-fronted bookcases. She knew she was not the only Chapworth to take comfort in the surrounding sea of knowledge, the tomes crammed close together and dog-eared

28

from generations of use. A shame she could not be certain her uncle had ever availed himself of their wisdom.

Now she could not help studying him to gauge his mood. She'd learned the telltale signs of anger well over the years. His bulbous nose would darken; his blue eyes would turn sharp as glass. And one hand would tighten into a fist. The best thing to do at such times was disappear until he took his temper out on something that felt no pain.

Now his customary bright smile sat on his florid face; his hands rested on the belly that strained the tie on his banyan.

"And what have you done with your newest toy, eh?" Uncle asked Lucy. "I did not see Mr. Bitterstock at the breakfast table with the other gentlemen."

"Well, I . . ." Lucy glanced to Kitty, blue eyes wide in an obvious plea for help.

Kitty straightened her skirts around her on the settee. "Alas, Mr. Bitterstock remembered he had pressing business in London. I fear he will miss the remainder of the party."

"Run off on you, has he?" her uncle said to Lucy. "Shall I set the hounds on him?"

"No, thank you, Father," Lucy said. "Kitty already offered."

Kitty kept her head down. Perhaps that was why her first indication that things were about to get worse was the butler, Ramscy, clearing his throat.

"Mr. Quentin Adair to see you, Sir Thomas."

It took every ounce of will not to react. Kitty studied her hands as his boots made soft thuds on the Axminster carpet. She would have to chide their maid, for her stays felt overly tight. She could not look up as Quentin spoke her cousin's name in greeting, thanked her uncle for receiving him.

29

"So you've crawled back to Somerset," Sir Thomas said.

Kitty cringed at the superior tone.

"I left a prosperous plantation to see about my father's health," Quentin replied, his tone polite and polished.

"Ah, yes." She heard Sir Thomas shift on the chair. "Your father has been droning on about your endeavors in Jamaica, how you turned the plantation around. Made a name for yourself, I take it."

Kitty looked up in time to see Quentin spread his hands. Funny how one glance at him and everyone else vanished. The black cutaway coat was commanding, his boots gleaming, and what she could see of his cravat spotless. Did he instruct his valet to make his hair curl so effortlessly, or was that nature? Her fingers itched to touch the dark strands.

She fisted her hands instead.

"I am what you see," Quentin was telling her uncle. "A man determined to return to the bosom of his family and friends."

Prettily said, but why he thought to find any friends here was beyond her.

Her uncle slapped his hands down on the chair's arms. "Good for you. Unfortunately, we are entertaining at present. I cannot spare Lucy to visit with you."

Quentin offered him a bow. "Understandable. I believe this was her first Season, and I hear she is tremendously popular."

Lucy blushed becomingly and lowered her eyes.

"I came for another reason," Quentin continued. "I have longed to speak with Miss Chapworth."

Uncle frowned as if he could not understand.

Play the game, Kitty reminded herself. She pasted on a smile. "I'd be delighted to speak with you, Mr. Adair."

"Are you ailing?" her uncle demanded, peering at her. "Haven't seen a woman look so green since your aunt cast up her accounts. See here, Kitty, I won't have you ruining the party for my guests."

"I wager it won't be sickness that strikes the other guests around Miss Chapworth," Quentin put in smoothly, with a smile to Kitty, "unless it's love sickness."

"Eh?" Uncle looked at him askance. "Did you spend too much time in the Jamaican sun, boy? You can't be talking about Kitty."

Much more of this and she would speak her mind to her uncle, which was never a good idea. Kitty gathered her skirts and rose.

"Perhaps we should take our conversation elsewhere, Mr. Adair, so as not to disturb my uncle. Will you promenade with me in the garden?"

"Charmed, Miss Chapworth," he said, holding out his arm to her. Then he glanced at her uncle. "If you can spare her delightful company, sir."

Her uncle blinked his protruding eyes. "Well, certainly. Go on, girl."

Lips pressed tight, she placed her hand on Quentin's muscular arm and let him lead her from the room.

"Clamp your jaw any tighter, and you'll likely break a tooth," Quentin said as the carved door shut behind them with a funereal thud.

She made a face at him. "Perhaps I wouldn't have to grit my teeth if your conversation wasn't so sickeningly sweet."

"We are supposed to be besotted, madam," he reminded her as he led her down the corridor to where twin glass-paned doors provided access to the gardens.

"And how exactly did that happen?" she challenged. "We haven't spoken to each other in ten years."

"I've been thinking about that," he said, holding the door open for her. The sunlight caught on her auburn hair, setting flames dancing along the length. There was something determined, purposeful about her. Perhaps it was the way she glided along beside him, gray skirts fluttering about her slippers, as if nothing or no one could break her stride.

"And you concluded?" she prompted as they walked past the reflecting pond where urns displayed a profusion of flowers.

"We wrote to each other," he explained, "sending the letters through my father."

"I did, you know." Her gaze clung to the stone-paved walk rather than her reflection in the pond. "I wrote you a letter of apology. You never responded."

"I never received it," he said, starting down the stone steps to the next terrace, where bright blooms perfumed the air. "I wrote once to Eugenia. She never responded."

"She wouldn't have." She sighed. "She truly isn't the shining star we all thought her, Quentin. She wasn't worthy of you."

Now, there was a switch. All his life, he'd been told his family wasn't as good as the Chapworths in their grange on the hill. He'd been stunned and flattered when he'd come upon the beautiful Eugenia while riding one day to find her more than willing to speak with him. An hour of her charming company, and he'd become her most devoted follower. Weeks of secret meetings and a few fervent kisses had convinced him their love was real, real enough to offer her his mother's pearl ring in token. Now he knew she'd seen him merely as a challenge, a test of her standing, to pull him away from Kitty. What a fool he'd been!

Was he any less foolish now, hoping to stop Sir Thomas from ruining his family? The old fox had hidden his tracks well. It had taken Quentin months to determine why their shipments of sugar languished so long on the Bristol docks, finally going for pennies on the pound. Sir Thomas had worked through intermediaries to bribe the customs officers and port officials. As Kitty said, her uncle still bore a grudge.

All the more reason to convince him to trust Quentin.

"Eugenia no longer haunts my thoughts," he told Kitty as they walked through the avenue of greenery that led to the lower lawn.

"Yet you never married," she said with a glance his way. "Was there no daughter of a plantation owner to tempt you?"

He chuckled. "I was too busy working to pay much attention to society."

"What's it like?" she asked. "Jamaica and the sugar plantation?"

He could give her the usual answer he supplied people asking about his work, that Jamaica was hot and humid and they were well off staying in England. But he sensed she was truly interested.

"When I think of Jamaica," he said, "I think of color—red flowers and dusky green palms, water as blue as a sapphire. I think of people with warm smiles and willing hearts."

Her face puckered. "Slaves."

"No," he said. "I have only freedmen on my plantation, and they earn a share of all profits. We may on occasion have been less prosperous, but our workers want to work."

"And did you not miss your family?" she asked. "England?"

"Only at Christmas." Without really meaning to, he found himself prosing on about life in the Indies, answering her eager questions, sharing stories he had told no one but his father. Something about Kitty made it easy to talk, to share his thoughts. He had forgotten how companionable they had been before he'd stupidly decided to pursue her cousin.

They came to the end of the avenue, and she touched his arm to stop him. Ahead, a young man and woman were strolling, heads together, as they came closer to Quentin and Kitty.

"That is Mr. Danvers and Miss Gaffney," she said, "Lucy's friends from London. Do you wish me to introduce you as we come abreast?"

"No," he said, going down on one knee. "I wish you to accept my proposal of marriage."

CHAPTER FIVE

K itty stared as Quentin took her hand and cradled it in his. His dark eyes gazed up at her, earnest with entreaty.

"Darling Kitty," he said, deep voice ringing, "I have thought of you often over the years of my cruel exile. Never do I wish us to be parted again. Can you find it in your heart to look kindly on my suit?"

He ought to have gone on the stage. Every part of him seemed tensed to hear her answer, as if he had any doubt of it. Even if they had not reached an agreement on this engagement of convenience, what woman of any character would have refused him?

How could she refuse him?

"Miss Chapworth?" Miss Gaffney's incredulous gasp lent steel to Kitty's spine.

She beamed down at Quentin. "Yes, my dear Quentin. Nothing would make me happier than to play the role of your bride."

He sprang to his feet and swept her into his arms. Before she knew what he was about, his lips met hers.

And the world disappeared.

She'd always wondered what it would be like to share a kiss.

It actually sounded rather messy. What if he had eaten onions for dinner or did not follow Mr. Brummel's advice to bathe regularly? And what was she to do about her nose, which, though not overly large, was certainly bigger than the little buttons her cousins had been blessed with.

But the moment Quentin's lips touched hers, none of that mattered. The gentle pressure, the sweet caress, made her bones liquid, and she wrapped her arms about his waist to stay upright as sensation after sensation rolled through her.

"Miss Chapworth." Mr. Danvers's voice seemed to come from a great distance. "It seems congratulations are in order."

Quentin pulled back to eye Kitty, and, for a moment, his smile looked as wobbly as she felt. Then he turned to the side, slipped an arm about her shoulders, and held out his free hand to the other man.

"Gladly accepted, sir, for I am the most fortunate of fellows."

"Mr. Danvers, Miss Gaffney," she said, amazed her brain was capable of coherent thought, "may I present my betrothed, Quentin Adair, late of Jamaica. His family's estate lies to the north of Chapworth Grange."

"I've known Kitty since I was a callow youth," Quentin told them after accepting their good wishes. "Never did I think she would agree to marry me."

"And why not?" the honey-haired Miss Gaffney said with a pretty smile. "You are clearly a gentleman who knows what he wants from life."

Did all women look at him so adoringly? Miss Gaffney's blue eyes positively glowed as she gazed up at him. Was she hard of hearing or simply dense that she did not remember that Quentin was now engaged?

My word. Just because her name was Kitty did not mean she must show her claws.

"Indeed." The dapper Mr. Danvers, brown hair carefully arranged around a pleasant face, was gazing at Quentin more thoughtfully. "I'm certain I've heard your name before. Were you at Eton?"

"Alas, no," Quentin replied. "I learned at the vicar's knee. And I've been spending the last few years managing the family lands in Jamaica, so I doubt our paths crossed." He turned to Kitty. "Let us tell your uncle our good news, my dear. I know he will be delighted."

Somehow, she doubted that.

Mr. Danvers and Miss Gaffney followed them to the house as if intent on seeing the second act of the play they had interrupted. Kitty left them in the entry hall, where Lucy was welcoming the latest arrivals, an older couple named Eglantine with two giggling debutantes who immediately eyed Quentin as he passed. She wanted to shout, "Engaged!"

Which was only slightly better than "Mine!"

Her uncle glanced up as they entered the library. Still in his comfortable banyan rather than a formal coat, he was seated at the desk across the back of the room, his steward standing beside him. Sir Thomas set aside some papers he'd been perusing to frown at Kitty as she approached.

"Something wrong, girl?" he asked.

"No, Uncle," she assured him. "That is . . ." Oh, this would never do. She was supposed to be delighted by her circumstances, deeply in love. She straightened and looked her uncle in the eyes, widening her lips in a smile. "Mr. Adair has asked me to marry him, and I accepted."

"I hope you will forgive me for making off with your greatest treasure, sir," Quentin added.

Kitty nearly cringed. Did Quentin realize Sir Thomas had always referred to Eugenia as his greatest treasure? Surely Quentin hadn't meant to remind her uncle of their painful past.

Her uncle leaned back in his seat and clasped his fingers over his belly. "That depends, my boy. Can you provide for Kitty? Protect her from life's difficulties?"

Now he decided to play the doting relative? She had expected delirious laughter at her announcement.

"I can, sir," Quentin assured him. "Though we've had some trouble with shipping, I believe the plantation will continue to be solvent."

Something flickered behind her uncle's eyes, but he merely nodded. "And you, Katherine? Does this match please you?"

And he cared about her preferences as well? She could not believe the miracle. Still, she glanced at Quentin. His smile warmed his dark eyes, set her stomach to fluttering. His approval truly felt as if it had nothing to do with their ruse.

"Yes, Uncle," she said. "I find it pleases me very much."

Quentin brought her hand to his lips for a kiss, and she nearly swooned.

Her. The woman who'd single-handedly foiled no less than five attempts to elope, four mangled proposals of ill intent, and the worst first kiss in history.

Oh, this man was dangerous.

"In that case," Sir Thomas said, "I'll thank you to go about your chaperone duties with your cousin while I have a few words with your intended."

Quentin saw Kitty pale. Her gaze darted to his again, and her teeth worried her lower lip. And such nice lips she had, too—full, warm, with a responsiveness that had shaken him. In fact, he hadn't expected to react to her kiss. But with her looking as if he'd just be sentenced to the gallows, she could well give away their game, and just when he had the old fox right where he wanted him. He laid a hand on her arm.

"It's all right, Kitty," he told her, keeping his smile in place. "Perhaps you should tell your cousin our good news. I'll join you shortly."

She eyed him a moment longer, as if she very much doubted he knew what he was letting himself in for. Then she leaned closer and murmured, "Don't allow him to bully you." Straightening with a nod to her uncle, she left them alone with the steward, who quickly buried himself in reviewing the papers.

"I know what you're doing, boy," Sir Thomas said.

He had no clue. Quentin kept his smile in place. "Settling down at last, sir."

Sir Thomas barked a laugh. "Oh, you're a cool one, I'll give you that. But you must see that if you were trying to get back at me for our disagreement years ago, you picked the wrong girl. Kitty means nothing to me."

And why? Quentin had asked his father about Kitty at breakfast that morning. His father's face had sagged.

"Tragic, that," his father had said. "I remember her as such a happy girl. And then that terrible accident sapped the life from her, and Sir Thomas's manipulations didn't help."

"Manipulations?" Quentin had pressed.

His father had sighed. "She's served as unpaid chaperone for all his girls, and my valet tells me that any gentleman who shows interest in her is immediately sent packing."

So, Kitty had had suitors, though she might not have realized it. Was her uncle thwarting her plans to find a position elsewhere as well? Quentin wouldn't put it past the fellow.

"If Kitty truly means nothing to you, then that is your loss, Sir Thomas," he said now.

Sir Thomas frowned at him. "You can't make me believe you are serious. Not about Kitty. She's long in the tooth and has a vinegar tongue. Why, if I thought someone would take her off my hands, I'd have sold her years ago." He laughed again, and his steward had the good grace to keep his head down.

Something hot burned Quentin's gut. "Yes, you've had good fortune in getting rid of those who trouble you, even suitors who might have deprived you of a devoted chaperone."

Sir Thomas raised a fat finger. "Now, see here, boy. Don't think you can take such a tone with me."

Quentin straightened to his full height. "And don't think I'll bow to you again. I will not hear Kitty disparaged. She's clever and witty and isn't afraid to stand up for what she believes. A man could do far worse than marry her."

Sir Thomas shook his head. "You're as hot-headed and idealistic as you were ten years ago. Go on, then. Marry Kitty. But don't think that alters my opinion of you. You were a vain upstart then, reaching for things above his station. I thought you'd changed."

"Oh, I have, Sir Thomas," Quentin promised him. "The boy who was sent to Jamaica is not the man who returned. Keep that in mind before you try to cross me."

At last the steward's head came up, even as Sir Thomas's eyes narrowed. Quentin could only curse his impetuous nature. He should have kept silent, pretended to be a lapdog. Yet how could he stand by and see a fine woman pilloried by her uncle's crude opinion?

"Cross you, boy?" Sir Thomas said, his voice silky. "Who said anything about crossing you?"

Quentin spread his hands. "A figure of speech. Forgive me, Sir Thomas. I want only peace between our families. Perhaps my engagement to Kitty will accomplish that."

And keep Sir Thomas oblivious to his true plans.

CHAPTER SIX

"**M**iss Katherine?"

Kitty yanked her ear off the library door to meet their butler's incredulous look. She hadn't been able to hear much anyway, just a word or two when Uncle or Quentin raised his voice. The fact that Sir Thomas had laughed at least twice could only concern her. Her uncle generally laughed when he knew he'd won.

"Yes, Ramsey?" she asked as if it were perfectly normal for her to be found eavesdropping on her uncle. "Was there something you needed?"

It turned out Lucy had somehow managed to misdirect the bags for the newcomers, requiring Kitty to set things to rights. A brief conversation with the butler sufficed.

"And may I say, Miss Katherine," he added as they finished, his usually stern face melting into something kind, "that the entire staff wishes you the best. You will be missed."

She should not be surprised by how fast rumors flew at the grange. "Congratulations may be premature," Kitty warned him.

He mistook her meaning. "Mr. Adair has come home a new man. Even Sir Thomas will see the wisdom of your choice, miss."

She wasn't so sure. Something about her uncle's reaction

didn't sit right. She couldn't bring herself to believe he had any concern for her future, other than to keep her working as he willed. Every part of Sir Thomas's life did him credit—his daughters, his lavish home, his estate and investments on the Exchange. She'd seen him put down dogs that didn't breed true, turn out tenants who couldn't work because of illness or injury. He should at least be thoroughly miffed that, by marrying Quentin, she deprived him of a nursemaid for his cousin and any other needy member of the Chapworth family.

She knew he had no reason for concern. That future still awaited her if she didn't find something better. Quentin had no more intention of making a place for her in his life now than he had ten years ago.

But what if he changed his mind?

The thought sent a shiver through her as she moved about the house, checking on their guests, ensuring everyone was pleasantly occupied and enjoying their time at the grange. She introduced the newcomers to the rest of the group, pointed Miss Gaffney to the latest fashion magazines to giggle over with the other ladies, and made arrangements with the cook for tea, none of which required much thought. In the back of her mind, a future with Quentin bloomed brighter than his father's roses.

What if Quentin came to value her character? What if he fell in love with her?

No, not that. The rosy dream popped to be replaced by the petulant face of Mr. Cadberry, who insisted that the new room she had given him was far too small for his needs. It took only a quiet word with Bollers to have Mr. Cadberry's things moved to a room approximately the same size, but with a commanding view of the west fields and the advantage of having once been used by some minor state official the fellow found admirable.

No, she could not imagine Quentin falling in love with her now. Handsome, wealthy men did not chase after spinsters with no family or fortune to recommend them.

But perhaps they might marry one with sufficient aplomb to do them credit.

She was still mulling over the matter when she glanced in the withdrawing room to find Lucy arranging flowers in a silver epergne.

"Should you not be with your guests, dearest?" Kitty asked, venturing closer to the piano, where her cousin stood poised in the sunlight from the nearby window. The gardener had brought in a bouquet of flowers, which lay on paper before her cousin. "I believe Mr. Cadberry and Mr. Danvers are expecting you at archery shortly."

"I just wanted a moment to myself," Lucy admitted, laying a white rose into the graceful epergne and pausing as if to admire the reflection of the flower in the silver. "I don't know how you do this, Kitty. I have no more than greeted everyone, and I'm exhausted."

Kitty set about sorting the long stems from the short, the buds from the greenery. "I have had more practice than you. And you'll do better in your own establishment, Lucy. You care about how things are done."

"Not as much as you do," Lucy protested. She threaded several ferns around the rose. "Menus, schedules, activities—I don't know how you keep them all straight."

"Perhaps I like a certain organization." Kitty handed her some ruby-colored dahlias to complement the rose. "There is peace to be had in a job well done."

"I suppose so," Lucy said with a smile.

Kitty cleared her throat. "Lucy, there is something you must know. Mr. Adair has asked me to marry him."

"What!" Lucy jerked as a thorn found home. Sucking her finger, she dropped the rose into the vase. "Is that what you want?" she murmured around the digit. "A home of your own? A husband?"

Kitty frowned at her shock. "Most women of our acquaintance strive for no less. Did you think me immune?"

"Well, yes," Lucy confessed, lowering her hand. "You have been the keeper of propriety for as long as I can remember. I thought you liked the role."

The keeper of propriety. Was that the sum total of her accomplishments? Would her family and friends remember her as no more than the spinster aunt who enforced the rules of engagement?

A pox on that!

She eyed her cousin. "It seems I fell into the role, Lucy. But I am finding it does not suit the woman I wish to be."

"And who do you wish to be?" Lucy asked, blinking blue eyes.

A dangerous question. Kitty might wish all she liked. No friendly fairy stood by to grant her desires. And her place in Society gave her little chance of making those dreams reality on her own.

"Someone daring, someone bold," she mused. "Someone suited to marry a man like Quentin Adair."

"But he already offered for you," Lucy said. "Surely he highly esteems you."

"Perhaps," Kitty allowed. "But greater esteem is never to be eschewed." She looked to her cousin, put a hand on her arm.

"No, Lucy, I must be my best self, my truest self, in manner, in conversation, in dress, if I am to win his heart. And for that I need your help."

"Anything," Lucy promised.

Kitty seized her hand. "Come upstairs with me, quickly, before the rest assemble for tea. We have a great deal of work to do if we are to dress this mutton as lamb."

Upstairs, Quentin bent over the billiards table in Sir Thomas's expansive game room. He'd come out of the library to find that Kitty and her cousin had disappeared. A helpful footman had directed him here, where several of the male guests were taking turns at smacking brightly colored balls about the field of green.

He hadn't had much call to play, but the rules were simple enough, and he'd never had trouble excelling at sports. Now he made sure not to win by too much and to put it down to having had excellent teachers. Sir Thomas had enough against him already. No need to fan the flames by annoying the man's guests.

Though he would have felt more comfortable if Sir Thomas had been alongside. At least that way, Quentin could keep a closer eye on him. He had thought the fellow would surely spend time with his guests, but he had yet to leave the sanctuary of his library. Was he merely being a conscientious manager of his holdings, or was he up to something?

"I understand you are lately returned from the West Indies," a narrow-faced gentleman who had been introduced as

Willingham said as Quentin moved the score bead farther along its prescribed path on the wooden rod.

"My family owns a sugar plantation there," Quentin acknowledged, reaching for the white cube and chalking the tip of his cue.

"Frightful place," Mr. Danvers put in, fanning himself with one hand as if he felt the tropical heat even then. "Pestilent, pitiful, and so far from Society."

"I did not miss Society as much as I had feared," Quentin told him, leaning on his cue. "There is much to be said for a slower pace, a quieter life."

"How very prosaic of you," Willingham drawled before bending to take his turn.

A noise sounded in the corridor. Quentin heard Kitty's voice before he saw her.

"And look here, Lucy," she called from the doorway. "I told you we would find the gentlemen in some sporting pursuit. How goes the field, sirs? Have you chased Mr. Adair back across the Atlantic yet?"

The others immediately demurred, dropping their sticks to go assure Miss Chapworth the younger of their devotion. For a moment, Quentin could not catch a glimpse of Kitty.

Then the crowds parted, and he blinked like a man struck by the sun's brilliance.

Gone was the practical gray gown she'd worn earlier. Instead, she had donned a dress he suspected she'd borrowed from her cousin, for it was a pretty pink with ribbons sewn in triple rows along the graceful hem, sleeves, and neck. The small bodice called attention to her womanly curves, the gathered neckline her creamy skin.

Her auburn hair had been curled so that tendrils caressed her cheeks and made Quentin think about doing the same. Her look as she met his gaze around the gabble of gentlemen was amused, but by their attentions or his staring, he couldn't say.

All he knew was that he must be at her side. He shoved his way into the center of the group. "Gentlemen, please. You have no opportunity to stake your claim. Miss Chapworth has already agreed to be my bride."

Mr. Willingham immediately petitioned Lucy, begging her to say it wasn't so while Mr. Danvers looked on with a knowing grin.

"I fear he's correct," Lucy said with a twinkle in her blue eyes. "My cousin Kitty is going to marry Mr. Adair."

Willingham's surprise would have been comical if it hadn't been an insult to Kitty.

And to Quentin.

Murmuring an apology, the butler came forward just then and pulled Kitty aside. Her sunny look clouded as he spoke to her. Now, what was that all about?

As Mr. Danvers and Mr. Willingham questioned Lucy about the arrangements for that afternoon, Kitty returned to Quentin's side. "Forgive me, but I must take care of an urgent matter for my uncle."

He couldn't help perking up. "A business matter?"

"Not really." Her sigh made the ribbons on her bosom flutter in the most enchanting way. Quentin forced his eyes to her face.

"You see," she said, "Sir Thomas hired a hermit to live out on the grounds. It seems he is remiss in his duties, and my uncle is threatening retribution."

He had cause to know how drastic a form that retribution could take. "What duties could a hermit have?"

"In this case, to sit by his shack and look picturesque." She sighed again, and this time he had to adjust his cravat to keep from looking at those ribbons. "Unfortunately, he likes to talk to people, and he's been calling our guests over to chat."

"A loquacious hermit," he marveled. "And this is cause for concern?"

"Concern, indeed," Kitty told him. "My uncle, like me, prefers life to follow a prescribed pattern. When it doesn't, we grow petulant. Besides, Uncle has an ongoing rivalry with Sir Winston Mallery, the magistrate. You remember him?"

Quentin nodded. "Bulldog of a fellow who prefers his hounds to Society. He's offered to buy Father out several times."

"Your lands do lie between the grange and Mallery Manor," she acknowledged. "And Sir Winston's hermit is the model of decorum, according to the ladies of the area. So I'm off to instruct a hermit on the duties of his post."

Quentin shook his head. "You do much to keep Sir Thomas content."

"As much as possible. We've both seen what happens when he is discontent."

Quentin caught her arm as she stepped away. "Has he ever raised a hand to you?"

She lifted a brow. "No one can hear us, Quentin. You don't have to pretend it's any concern of yours."

And yet it did concern him. He couldn't like the idea of anyone undergoing the beating he'd endured. He'd burned the whips of the plantation overseers when he'd reached Jamaica. The thought of anyone striking Kitty made his blood heat, his hands fist. Look how he'd reacted when Sir Thomas had merely disparaged her.

Could it be his feelings for Kitty were deeper than he'd thought when he proposed their engagement of convenience?

CHAPTER SEVEN

The hermit was easily sorted. Promises of treats from the kitchen convinced the elderly fellow to sit and pose for their guests rather than seek their conversation. But when Kitty returned to the house, she discovered that the hermit was not the only celebrity at the party.

She was the most sought after lady present.

Quentin had suggested their engagement of convenience might have just this sort of effect, but she failed to find a reason. It could not be the result of curling her hair or borrowing Lucy's dress. The other young ladies were similarly coiffed and gowned. Nor did she behave any differently. She still settled squabbles and kept things humming along, seeing to the needs of the household and its guests.

Now that she was engaged to be married, however, everyone seemed to see her differently. Instead of observing conversations, she was made part of them. Miss Gaffney asked her opinion on the new style of poke bonnet. Mr. Danvers inquired as to whether she had enjoyed the past Season. Miss Eglantine and her sister followed her about as if intent on observing her least action. It was as if she had been elevated from gentry to royalty.

It was the same way when she and Quentin joined the other couples on a trip to see the village church the next day. The two had agreed that Quentin should join the festivities whenever possible. Yesterday, it had been touring the estate and playing whist, the latter of which he and Kitty had won handily, while Uncle even nodded approval. Today, it was taking in the delights of the village that catered to the various estates in the area. The church there was a fine example of Norman architecture, all square lines and firm stones as if unwavering in its convictions. Everyone seemed most impressed with it.

All the guests had at last arrived, making for a set of five unmarried ladies and six gentlemen. With uneven numbers, a gentleman was forever pursuing a partner. Fortunately, with Mr. and Mrs. Eglantine serving as chaperones for the group, Kitty was spared much of her usual duties to Lucy.

Now Quentin's black boots flashed in the sunlight as he strolled with Kitty through the churchyard, where gravestones marched in an orderly fashion across the grass.

"You will find me a sad trial," Kitty told him. "Here your ruse is succeeding, and all I can wonder is why they suddenly care about my opinions. I am the same person I was last week. I have grown no cleverer, done nothing particularly fascinating."

"Except betroth yourself to the black sheep of the county," he reminded her with a smile.

"Former black sheep," she countered. "And it isn't as if you've done anything particularly interesting since returning either."

Indeed, as if to disprove their expectations of him, he'd

gone out of his way to be congenial. Nothing in word or manner had been the least bit scandalous. She wasn't sure why that fact annoyed her more than her sudden popularity.

"What would you have me do, madam?" he asked with a polite nod to Mr. Danvers, who was once again partnering Miss Gaffney. "Stand on my head on the lawn? Challenge another gentleman to a duel for looking at you with approbation?"

She couldn't help a laugh at the suggestion. "Now that would be interesting. I can just picture it. 'You spoke to my betrothed about banal subjects. I demand satisfaction, sir.'"

He chuckled, earning him a frown from Mr. Cadberry, who seemed to think a churchyard the place for serious contemplation, despite the fact that Miss Alice Eglantine on his arm giggled at every comment he made.

"I'm sure duels have been fought for less reason," Quentin said. "But if their conversation fails to amuse, avoid it."

She sighed. "I could before. Now, I find I must join in. It would be impolite and impolitic to do otherwise. After all, I am supposed to be currying their favor." Especially his. She felt her face heating at the thought and glanced to where the ever-earnest Mr. Fredericks was escorting Lucy along the lane verging on the churchyard. Her cousin's skirts were as purple-blue as the forget-me-nots they passed.

"Once you jilt me, they will all congratulate you on your good fortune to escape leg-shackling yourself to a scapegrace like me." His tone was joking, but she heard the edge to his words.

"More likely they will lament that I let such a matrimonial prize slip through my fingers," she told him. "Spinsters generally do not attract such devoted followers."

"You should." When she glanced at him in surprise, he

drove the point home. "You were an attractive young miss connected to a respectable family, Kitty. You have only grown surer of yourself. Why must you end up on the shelf?"

She could feel her face heating. "That is kind of you to say, Quentin, but . . ."

"Stop," he said. "I am not kind to speak truth, though I begin to think others have been cruel to speak lies. If you wish to marry, Kitty, I'm sure you could find a fellow to accommodate and think himself the most fortunate of men in the bargain."

She was saved a response by the appearance of Lucy, now accompanied by Mr. Willingham. Her cousin had latched onto the lanky Londoner and seemed to have switched her allegiance from the lackluster Mr. Bitterstock, if her besotted smile was any indication.

"I would very much like to know what you are saying to your betrothed to put her in such fine looks, sir," he said to Quentin.

For once, Kitty could think of no answer. At least no answer that would not get her or Quentin in trouble.

Quentin took her hand and brought it to his lips, sending a tremor through her. "And how could a groom fail to compliment such a lovely bride?"

"Oh, well said," Lucy put in, eyes shining.

"Perhaps we should switch partners," Kitty couldn't help teasing. "You gentlemen could walk together, and Mr. Willingham could profit from your vast experience."

"Perhaps he should learn by example." Quentin released Kitty to offer his arm to her cousin. "If you would favor me, Miss Lucy. After all, we are soon to be family."

"Indeed we are." Lucy removed her arm from Mr. Willingham's. With a wink to Kitty, Quentin strolled off with her cousin.

Mr. Willingham stared after them, face darkening.

"You needn't accompany me," Kitty told him. "I wouldn't want to interfere with your moment of pique. A brooding gentleman is all the rage in some circles, I'm told."

He seemed to recall himself and swept her a bow. "Your servant, Miss Chapworth. It would be my pleasure to take a turn with you."

He offered her his arm, and Kitty could not convince herself to refuse it. They set off through the gravestones again. Mr. Danvers had relinquished Miss Gaffney to Mr. Townshend, who was as likely to trip over his feet as to stammer as he toured her about the area. Mr. Cadberry now had the elder Miss Eglantine, who was nodding with all seriousness to his discourse about a general buried here. Mr. Fredericks stood with the younger daughter and her parents by the church steps, but Kitty thought he was only looking for a moment of weakness from Quentin before pouncing in to offer himself as Lucy's partner again.

"I take it you and Mr. Adair have known each other for ages," Mr. Willingham ventured, his gaze on the couple ahead of them. Lucy was leaning closer to Quentin as if drinking in every word. Kitty could not muster jealousy. Lucy might be lovely, but Quentin seemed to prefer his lady to have wit and intelligence. Did that mean she might have a chance?

"Yes," she told Mr. Willingham, knowing she must make some kind of conversation with the fellow. "Mr. Adair and I have known each other since the Wars of the Roses in the fifteenth century. Sadly, he was for York and I was for Lancaster."

He did not pursue her jest. "How happy you were brought back together again. Quite a boon for you, what with Lucy soon to find a groom."

Now Lucy was turning a delicate shade of pink the color of a seashell's heart. Kitty could feel Mr. Willingham's arm tightening under her hand.

"Yes, of course, everyone will expect me to be thankful for his attentions," Kitty said.

Mr. Willingham bent closer. "Mr. Adair seems very good about showing a lady his attentions. I would be more than delighted to show you my attentions as well, dear Kitty. Would you like that?"

Kitty leaned closer to him with a smile. "Not in the slightest. Speak to me in that odious tone again, and I will do you an injury that will be felt by generations of Willinghams, assuming you find a woman willing to marry a fellow so lacking in character. Good day, sir." She pulled her hand off his arm and stalked to the side of the church, where the shadows would hide her face.

Hot tears burned her eyes, and she dashed them away with her fingers. She wasn't even sure why she was crying. It wasn't as if she'd truly believed that someone might be moved to offer for her. But to go from hope to insult in a matter of moments was not to be borne.

She forced herself to take deep breaths of the warm summer air, to focus her gaze out across the village green to the shops and cottages beyond. A horse cantered by, and she recognized the rider as her uncle's steward. Where would he be going in such a hurry?

Quentin rounded the corner of the church to find Kitty staring stonily across the green, fists bunched in her skirts. What had her in such a taking? He'd spent the last few minutes attempting to get more than platitudes and proverbs from her cousin, hoping for some glimpse into Sir Thomas's plans. He'd tried everything else short of spying on the fellow in the last day and a half. Alas, the fair Lucy was as vapid as she was sweet. She could tell him nothing about her father's business dealings. Instead, she had spoken in glowing terms of her fondness for Kitty.

"I thought perhaps I might invite her to live with me," she had confided to Quentin. "But I'm not sure my husband would appreciate my devotion to her. I'm so glad she'll have a home now with you. I do hope you'll live here in England so I may see her."

"I have yet to decide," Quentin had told her. Her plan was well meaning, but she was correct that a husband would likely find three a crowd. And apparently her father had not told her he intended to exile Kitty to Dartmoor once Lucy was wed. He had handed Lucy off to the eager Mr. Fredericks and gone in search of Kitty.

Now Quentin put a hand on Kitty's arm. "Easy," he murmured, bending his head to hers. "I don't know what has upset you, but how would it look to your guests if they saw you take yourself off in high dudgeon?"

Those dark eyes boiled like clouds before a storm. "Frankly, sir, I find I cannot care."

"Frankly, madam, you care too much. If you didn't, you

would never have agreed to my proposal." Grip tightening on her arm, he attempted to steer her deeper into the shadows, away from prying eyes.

"An agreement I regret more with each passing moment," she assured him, digging in her heels. "Unhand me or I shall scream."

He straightened with a shake of his head. "Scream."

She narrowed her eyes at him, opened her mouth, and screamed.

Quentin was so surprised he released his grip on her.

Immediately, they were surrounded—by concerned guests, by worried footmen. Even the coachman who had driven her here abandoned his horses to dash to her aid.

She fluttered her hands before her face. "I thought I saw a mouse. There. On the steps of the church. It might have run across my foot. Why, if dear Quentin hadn't had his hand so firmly fixed to my arm, I could have fallen to my death."

They all assured her of her safety, her bravery under adversity. Two of the footmen began a hunt for the creature. Quentin pitied any animal they might come across. When Lucy suggested Kitty should return to the grange and lie down with a moist handkerchief on her brow, Kitty tearfully agreed. And the minx had the audacity to wink at him as she was led away.

"Tricky thing, that," Mr. Danvers commiserated with a pat to Quentin's shoulder. "Who would have guessed that even the redoubtable Miss Chapworth would be put off her stride by a mouse?"

"Who, indeed?" Quentin replied. He could not help but admire the way she'd turned the tables on him.

But how would Kitty react if Quentin asked her to help him

turn the tables on her uncle? She believed herself beholden to the fellow, after all. Did he dare enlist her aid to stop the man before Sir Thomas ruined his family?

CHAPTER EIGHT

K itty had never liked dampened handkerchiefs. The things were clammy and cold, and some stank to high heaven. But a few moments reclining on a divan with linen soaked in lemon verbena on her brow was a small price to pay for the startled look on Quentin's face when she'd followed through on her threat and screamed. She smiled just thinking of it and the laugh they'd share when next she saw him.

"Thank you, Lucy," she said, removing the cloth and laying it aside as she sat up. "I feel quite restored."

"You are so brave," Lucy said. "I don't know what I would do if a mouse attempted to run over my slippers." She shuddered.

Kitty rose from the divan next to the fire in Lucy's large room. "I'm certain it was the most harrowing experience of my life. Now, then, what do we have planned for your guests this afternoon? I believe it was bowling on the west lawn and then a musicale this evening. What will you be singing?"

Lucy rose as well from the chair a footman had positioned next to the divan. "I thought perhaps I'd accompany you on the pianoforte instead."

"Me?" Kitty caught herself clutching her chest and

abandoned the theatrical gesture. "I haven't been asked to perform in nearly ten years. I doubt anyone expects it of me now."

"Surely Mr. Adair is looking forward to it," Lucy protested.

"If Mr. Adair values music so much, let him take a turn behind the piano." Much as she wanted to return to Quentin, she knew she must speak to Lucy while she had her cousin alone. "Now, dearest, please tell me your heart isn't set on Mr. Willingham."

As if she expected Kitty to argue against him, Lucy lowered her gaze. Kitty could see her lips trembling. "He is very attentive."

"And far too full of himself," Kitty cautioned. "You could do better."

Her cousin raised her gaze, anguish written on every delicate feature. "But who, then, Kitty? Mr. Danvers seems to be taken with Patricia Gaffney, and I cannot but be happy for them both. Mr. Cadberry is too cold. Mr. Townshend is kind, but I cannot convince myself he cares overly much for me. Oh, I don't think I shall ever be as happy as you and Mr. Adair."

Guilt nipped at her. "I would not call us happy, dearest. More contented with what the other is offering. For you, nothing less than a love match will do. We must keep looking until we find the perfect fellow."

Lucy nodded, but still the tension remained on her pretty face. "I do appreciate all your help. But how can we go on as we have once you've wed? You will have your wifely duties. And Mr. Adair may even want you to return to Jamaica with him."

A vision swam up—bright beaches, dusky green trees, blue skies, and warm breezes. Exotic music drumming from the hills, and Quentin leading her into an assembly with pride.

Was it possible? She felt as if the dream was just out of reach, and she didn't know how to grasp hold of it.

"Our plans are not set yet," she told her cousin. "Suffice it to say I will most likely continue playing your chaperone until you have no further need of me."

"Oh, good." Lucy managed a smile at last, face brightening. "I'm so glad, Kitty. You understand me better than anyone. Father always seems so annoyed when I ask questions."

"Annoyance is your father's natural habitat," Kitty replied, turning for the door. "He wouldn't thrive anywhere else."

"Perhaps not," Lucy agreed, following her. "But the last few days he seems to be even angrier than usual. He was talking to Mr. Summers the steward about some business venture. I gather it's a race of some sort."

Kitty frowned as her cousin passed her out the door. It wasn't like her uncle to indulge in horse or yacht racing. In fact, he'd decried the sports as the pastimes of wastrels and profligates.

"What sort of race?" she asked, remembering the steward's uncommon hurry earlier.

"I don't know," Lucy said as they headed for the stairs. "He simply said that he must win at all costs."

Kitty felt as if someone had tossed a rock into her stomach. What sort of venture was this? Had Uncle wagered his estate? It was not held in trust—worse luck. Would she and Lucy soon find themselves with no means of support? Surely the man was smart enough not to take such risks!

Still, she couldn't help keeping an eye out for her uncle as she and Lucy rejoined the festivities. But neither Sir Thomas nor Quentin was anywhere to be seen, and when she asked Ramsey about them, the butler pointed her to the library.

"Mr. Adair has been closeted with Sir Thomas this past hour," he murmured. "And never have I seen the master more earnest. I cannot like it, Miss Katherine."

"Nor can I," Kitty assured him. "Let me know the moment he leaves my uncle's side."

"Certainly, miss."

As it turned out, all the other guests had finished their activities for the afternoon and retired to change for dinner before Ramsey sought her.

"Mr. Adair has returned home to change," he reported.

"And Uncle?" she asked.

"Has gone for a walk."

A walk? Why would her uncle leave the grange this time of the evening, knowing he must shortly preside over dinner? Did his actions have something to do with this race Lucy had mentioned?

Normally, Kitty did her best to avoid meddling in her uncle's affairs. But if Lucy's future was at risk, Kitty could not sit idly by. She needed to know whether her uncle's plan might harm her cousin and how Kitty might mitigate the effects. So, after thanking Ramsey for his trouble and sending him about his duties, she slipped out of the house and stood on the terrace, which had a commanding view across the estate. It was easy enough to spot her uncle, striding toward the folly. Was he another Chapworth who used the little temple for clandestine meetings?

Only one way to find out. She followed him.

Why the folly? Quentin moved silently around the side of Chapworth Grange, intent on Sir Thomas in the distance. He'd spent the afternoon with the fellow, engaging him in a debate about the advisability of selling Rose Cottage to the magistrate. Sir Thomas had been eager to offer better alternatives, quick to argue away any advantage Quentin proposed. Yet the man had stopped short of making him an offer.

"We are at a house party," Sir Thomas had said, leaning back in his chair. "We should see to all the niceties before making any decisions. We can discuss the matter further in a few days."

What else could Quentin do but agree? If he protested the delay, Sir Thomas might think him desperate and make an offer Quentin would only refuse. That refusal might raise questions in Sir Thomas's mind as to why Quentin had brought up the subject in the first place. Besides, he didn't think his father overly eager to sell to Sir Thomas or the magistrate, for all Quentin had urged him to return to Jamaica with him. His discussion with Sir Thomas had merely been a ruse to keep the fellow busy, too busy to confirm any plans for the port.

Yet something about his host's demeanor nagged at him. So, he'd retreated only to the landing, positioning himself to watch the library door. And when Sir Thomas bolted out and took the trouble to lock the door behind him, Quentin had slipped down the stairs and followed.

Now he approached the folly cautiously, looking for the least sign of anything suspicious. Sir Thomas had bypassed the little building and positioned himself in the lane to the village.

Quentin could see Sir Winston strolling closer, his heavy chin coming up as he sighted Sir Thomas. The two so-called pillars of the community stood and conversed, but he could not read their lips or catch a snatch of their conversation.

"Hst!"

He frowned, glancing to the bushes nearest the folly, which seemed to be quivering with agitation.

"Hst!" A spectral hand poked out, beckoning him closer. Glancing at the two men to make sure they were still occupied in each other, he ducked behind the bush.

"What do you suspect him of doing?" Kitty asked.

She'd gathered the sky blue skirts of the dress she'd also likely borrowed from her cousin and crouched on the soft ground. Now her dark eyes begged him for answers she herself must be seeking.

"Perhaps I should ask you that question," Quentin countered, squatting beside her.

"Lucy says it's something to do with horse racing." Her gaze returned to her uncle and the magistrate. "I fear he's lost the estate gambling. It would be just like him not to think of anyone but himself."

She looked thoroughly put out with the fellow, lips tight and hands fisted in her skirts. But if she was right, she had cause for concern, for her cousin and herself. For why would Sir Thomas support a chaperone if he could not support his own daughter?

But why would he work so hard to ruin Quentin's family when his own estate was at risk? That made no sense.

"I'm too tall to get closer without being noticed," he murmured. "What of you? I want to hear what they're saying."

"Too late," she replied, gripping his arm to tug him down beside her. "Here he comes!"

Quentin hunkered low, arms about Kitty's slender frame, the silk of her hair pressed against his cheek. For some reason, she smelled like the lemon verbena his maiden aunt used for rheumatism.

The gravel crunched as Sir Thomas stomped past.

As the sound faded, Kitty released Quentin. "You follow him," she murmured, rising. "I'll talk to the magistrate. We can meet at the folly after the musicale to share what we learn."

She didn't wait for him to agree but slipped out of the bush and strolled down the lane as if out for a constitutional. The magistrate greeted her with a fatherly smile, and the two started back toward the village. She clearly considered Quentin her partner in this investigation. She trusted him to do as she'd ordered.

If only he could know what Sir Thomas was about and how it played into his future, and Kitty's.

CHAPTER NINE

Kitty caught herself tapping her toe under the gray silk skirts of her dinner dress as she sat at the damask-draped dining table. She forced herself to still. She had made the seating arrangements for this meal days ago, long before she'd known Mr. Bitterstock would depart so abruptly or that Quentin would arrive and propose marriage. With everything that had been happening, she'd had no opportunity to change them.

Now she was seated near the middle of the table, and Quentin, looking formidable in his evening black, had taken Mr. Bitterstock's place near the top across from Lucy and next to Uncle. No one seemed particularly pleased with the matter.

Still, she knew how to do her duty. She discussed the changes on the Continent with Mr. Danvers on her left, shared thoughts on the recent thrilling book by the author of *Waverly* with Mr. Fredericks on her right. All the while her ear remained tuned to the conversation higher up the table, and her mind sorted through the few facts she had.

Sir Winston had been reticent to answer her questions when she'd approached him on the lane that afternoon. The elder statesman of the area, with white hair pomaded back from a heavily jowled face, had known her since she was a child.

"If you have questions for your uncle, Miss Chapworth," he'd said, jowls quivering, "you should follow him and ask. He just left."

"But my questions are so general," she'd protested, careful to drop her gaze humbly. "I fear he'll lose patience with me. You know how Sir Thomas can be."

He must know Sir Thomas's reputation in the area, the story of his attack on Quentin years ago. When she glanced up, she found the magistrate stroking his chin thoughtfully. "Very well. What would you like to know?"

Kitty drew in a breath. "I have been so careful about the arrangements for this house party. Did Sir Thomas just invite you to join us? We are already odd numbers at table."

He patted her shoulder. "There, now. I know how these things can weigh on a lady's mind. Have no concern. I will be attending Sir Thomas tomorrow at eleven for billiards, but I have no plans to join you for meals."

Kitty cocked her head. "He met you out here merely to invite you to play billiards?"

"Apparently so," the magistrate said, tugging down on his paisley waistcoat. "We are old friends, after all. Normally, he might have sent a footman, but I imagine they are all busy at present, and he could not rely on Mr. Summers, seeing as how he was headed to Bristol."

So her uncle had sudden business in Bristol. And what would that be?

She clasped her hands before her. "Oh, Bristol! How I love the shops there. So many goods from America and the West Indies. Perhaps I should send someone after Mr. Summers, see if he would have time to pick up sugar and ginger."

Sir Winston chuckled. "I highly doubt you could catch him, my dear. I believe a ship is expected and must be met."

"A ship," Kitty pressed. "Uncle owns shares in a ship?"

Sir Winston's smile faded. "Now, then, this is nothing to concern you. I only know about the matter because my groom spoke to yours. If you have specific questions, you must apply to your uncle."

Only if she wanted to hear lies for answers. But it was clear Sir Winston knew no more of the matter. She'd thanked him and headed for the house, where she'd questioned the head groom, with no more success.

What ship would have her uncle so concerned he'd order his steward to ride hard? He wasn't in manufacturing, and the produce grown on the grange estate went to feed the family and guests. And what did any of this have to do with Quentin?

Now she waited impatiently through dinner, while her uncle seemed content to lob barbed comments at Quentin, all of which he deflected with a laugh or a quip.

She had no opportunity to talk to him after dinner either. Even though her uncle knew she had a musicale planned, he kept the gentlemen overly long at their port so that it was nearly time to retire when they strode into the withdrawing room to join the ladies. Immediately, she caught Quentin's eye, and he detached himself from the others to join her.

"Who's for some music, eh?" Sir Thomas demanded, rubbing his beefy hands together. "I have a rare talent in the family."

Lucy blushed prettily as her guests applauded, urging her to rise.

"We must talk," Quentin murmured beside Kitty. "I

learned nothing of use this afternoon, but I'm certain your uncle is planning skullduggery, and I must ask your help to stop him."

Skullduggery? It must have to do with Uncle's gamble. Kitty nodded to Quentin, a tingle going through her, but before she could answer, Sir Thomas raised his voice again. "Yes, yes, we are fortunate indeed. She is our little secret, you might say. Kitty, come play for our guests."

Her? Kitty stiffened as all gazes swung her way, some surprised, some clearly skeptical.

"You are too kind, Uncle," she said, heart starting to pound against her ribs. "But I must yield the floor to Lucy's greater accomplishments."

Lucy smiled at her, but her father would have none of it.

"Nonsense, girl," he said. "About time you showed them what you're made of. I warrant Mr. Adair would prefer to hear you play."

"Kitty has no need to prove herself to me," Quentin said, gaze on hers. "I am already thoroughly besotted."

For a moment, looking into his eyes, she could almost believe him.

"Well, I for one would very much like to hear Miss Chapworth play," Mr. Willingham said. "I'm certain it will be quite illuminating."

Odious prig. She could see the cunning in his gaze. He wanted her embarrassed. He was still smarting over her set down earlier.

"There you are," Sir Thomas said, spreading his hands. "Stop posturing and play, girl."

Quentin must have realized that further protests were futile, for he took her elbow. "Allow me the honor of turning pages for you."

There was nothing for it. Kitty went to take her place at the pianoforte, Quentin at her back. The others settled on chairs and sofas. Beside their parents, the Eglantine girls watched with wide-eyed anticipation. She remembered gazing as raptly at Eugenia and shuddered at the comparison.

Miss Gaffney and Lucy smiled encouragement, gloved hands folded neatly in their laps. Mr. Danvers and Mr. Fredericks nodded support as well. Mr. Townshend stretched out his feet as if getting comfortable. Mr. Cadberry already has his eyes closed as if expecting to be bored, and Mr. Willingham offered her a vicious grin.

She wished she could play something brilliant, with complicated runs and trills, but she'd never mastered such things. She'd had more pressing engagements, like earning her keep, to allow her to spend the long hours required to achieve anything beyond proficiency.

Quentin bent beside her, his voice a husky whisper in her ear. "Is there something here to your liking?"

Besides you? Dangerous thought. She shifted on the bench, sifting through the sheet music on the stand. Her abrupt movements sent one of the pages sliding to the floor. He bent to retrieve it as someone stifled a laugh.

She felt sweat trickle down her back.

"Easy," Quentin murmured as he returned the music to the stand in front of her. "I have seen you slay impertinent pups with a look. These people are no different."

"If only that were true," she murmured back, as her uncle glared at her.

"Kitty." Her name, said with such fondness, forced her gaze to his. Those dark eyes held compassion and understanding and something far more. "Play something that pleases you. Pretend I am your only audience."

He might not be her only audience, but, she realized as she flexed her fingers over the keys, he was the only one who mattered. With a nod, she drew in a breath and began to play.

Quentin's eyes followed the notes on the sheet music, even as his ears followed the tinkling of the keys. She'd chosen a simple country air, and she played it softly, as if coaxing the instrument to tell the tale. His hand resting on her shoulder, he felt when the tension eased out of her to be replaced by an energy, a passion that sent a jolt up his arm.

Why the reaction? Her playing was no more than passable, yet she brought him along with her as the music danced. When she finished, he found himself smiling. He gave her shoulder a squeeze as the other guests applauded. "Well done."

She smiled up at him, a dimple appearing on the side of her mouth as if marking the spot for his kiss.

Willingham rose and approached the piano, forcing Quentin's gaze away from her.

"That was quite good, Miss Chapworth," the fellow said as if surprised to admit as much. "I wonder if I might make a request."

Kitty turned her smile on him, but Quentin could see it was wary. "Certainly, sir. What would you have me play?"

"A waltz," he said. "If you could manage that, the rest of us might dance."

Her smile did not waver, but her tension returned. So, the pup thought to shackle her to the instrument while the rest of them had fun.

"I fear you'll need to find another accompanist," Quentin said. "If there's dancing to be had, I intend to partner my delightful betrothed."

Willingham's cheek twitched. "Of course, sir. Excuse me." He stalked off.

As conversations started around them, the gentlemen importuning Miss Gaffney and Lucy to play or sing next, and the two Eglantine sisters wiggling in their seats as they awaited their turns, Kitty rose from the bench. "Thank you," she said to Quentin. "But I fear I dance even more poorly than I play."

"Then it will be my pleasure to sit out with you," Quentin said, taking her hand and leading her away from the piano.

Sir Thomas had apparently had enough of music, for he rose. "Who's for a game of whist?"

Though Lucy frowned at the change of plans, the guests began pairing up. Mr. Danvers requisitioned Miss Gaffney and, after a brief but heated debate, Mr. Fredericks ended up with Lucy. The Eglantine girls giggled at Townshend and Willingham, leaving Mr. Cadberry and their parents to join Sir Thomas's set. Perfect. Quentin directed Kitty toward the door and slipped with her down the corridor and out onto the terrace.

The rising moon painted the garden in silver. Taking her hand, he led her past the reflection wavering in the pond and down the stairs to the lawn. A few torches here and there pointed the way to the folly at the edge of the estate.

Another woman might assume he meant to start an

assignation, but she immediately returned to their shared purpose.

"What did you learn by following my uncle?" she asked as they started down the hill.

"Precious little," Quentin admitted. "He returned to the house and retired to his chambers to change for dinner. What did you learn from Sir Winston?"

"Uncle apparently sent Mr. Summers, his steward, to Bristol about a ship," she confided. "He seemed to think it rather urgent."

"Bristol," he pressed. "Not Whitehaven?"

"Whitehaven was never mentioned. Is it important?"

Only to him and his father. Sir Thomas must not discover that they'd rerouted the ship to that port instead, a port where he had no influence to hold them.

"Merely confirming what I heard," Quentin told her.

She lifted her silky gray skirts to climb the steps to the folly. Something rustled in the bushes, but the minx showed not the least concern. So much for being terrified of small creatures.

Nor was she particularly concerned about him as he climbed to her side. In the moonlight slanting past the overhanging roof, he could see her eyeing him. "You are neither deaf nor dim, Quentin. Whitehaven is important. Why?"

She was too clever by half. Kitty had played her part well, but never had he seen her take advantage of her newfound power the way Eugenia had. She remained the dedicated chaperone, the woman of wit and character he was coming to appreciate. She deserved to know all.

He moved deeper into the shadows, unable to shake the feeling that someone was watching from the house even now. "I haven't been entirely truthful about the plantation, Kitty. We are doing better than expected, but for the last few years, every ship carrying our sugar to England has been kept on the quay for months. If I cannot find a way to unload the sugar faster, we may have to sell the estate here and after that the plantation. I could well end up the wastrel your uncle named me years ago."

She laid a hand on his arm. "Never that."

Her faith warmed the cool night. "I have had agents investigating the problem, and I finally discovered the culprit. Sir Thomas has been using his influence at the port of Bristol, going through friends of friends to stop the ships from unloading. You were right. He bears his grudges deeply."

"Bully that he is," she agreed. She cocked her head. "So you did not propose an engagement to make peace for your father. You're trying to stop a war."

He nodded. "Forgive me for not confiding in you sooner. I wasn't sure who to trust."

He thought she might take umbrage, but she merely straightened and shrugged. "Between Eugenia and my uncle, you have little cause to trust those named Chapworth. How can I help you thwart Uncle? We cannot allow him to win."

He loved the fire in her voice, the determination. "You must be careful about taking sides," he warned. "We both have cause to know that Sir Thomas is not an easy man to cross."

"Neither are you," she said. "Look what you made of your life. You should be proud."

"I'll take comfort in my achievements once I know the sugar has been sold," he assured her. "But thank you for your support, Kitty. It means the world."

Her smile brushed him, as soft as spring rain. "As does yours. I can't remember the last time I had a champion."

He reached out to touch her cheek, her skin like satin beneath his fingers. "Your family is blind. They have known you so long, relied on you so often, that they fail to see your worth."

She gazed up at him, lips parted as if she longed to believe that. It was the work of a moment to bend his head and make those lips his own.

And it seemed as if the night danced with a thousand stars, twirling about them. He wrapped his arms around her, drank deep of her kiss, felt her body conform to his. What was it about this woman that made him want to cradle her close, shelter her from all harm, play the champion she named him?

Till death do them part.

Quentin pulled back to stare at her. Dark lashes swept creamy cheeks; her lips were full from his kisses. A tenderness stole over him, and he could only hold her again.

What had he done? Despite the enmity between their families, despite their different approaches to life, how had he fallen in love with Kitty Chapworth?

For how could it not be love? Always before, the attraction, the desire, had been immediate. As quickly as it flared, it had faded. This felt strong and true, years in the making. It would only grow stronger with time.

He'd hurt her ten years ago. She had little cause to trust his feelings.

So how could he convince Kitty to change their engagement of convenience into one of love?

CHAPTER TEN

Oh, but she had to stop this. Each time Quentin touched her, each time his lips caressed hers, her heart dared to hope. She couldn't bear the crushing disappointment of being left behind.

She pushed away from him and smoothed back her hair. "Really, Quentin. There is no one about. You can stop pretending you feel anything for me."

"Wise words," he murmured, running a hand back through his own hair. "Unfortunately, too late to be heeded. I find it difficult to distinguish pretend from reality."

He could not be saying what it seemed. Her heart evidently thought otherwise, for it slammed into her chest as if wishing to force itself back into his embrace.

"The reality is that you are attempting to stop my uncle with my aid," she reminded him.

"And I am grateful for that assistance," he told her. "But surely you can tell my impression of you has changed."

Kitty clenched her fists to keep from reaching out to him. "And why would that be, sir? As you said, I am the same old Kitty—the keeper of propriety."

"Willing to risk all for those you love," he agreed. "Yes,

madam, in that trait you have not changed. But I believe your determined nature is the exact quality I seek in a wife, and I find I wish to expand the number of people you love to include one more." He stepped closer. "Me."

Kitty felt as if her legs would not hold her. But this time, she refused to back away. "There is no need to expand. I have counted you among that number since the day we parted. But then you only saw Eugenia."

He closed the distance between them, feathered his fingers across her cheek. "A callow youth runs after any pretty gem. It takes a man to appreciate a diamond."

She swallowed, gaze searching his. Was that love she saw in the deep brown of his eyes? Or only her most fervent wishes?

"Be sure, Quentin," she told him. "I cannot play this game. My heart will not survive losing you again."

"Then perhaps," he murmured, bending his head once more, "you should leave your heart in my safekeeping. I promise to treasure and protect it always, Kitty."

She wanted to believe him. She needed to believe him. His lips caressed hers once more, a pledge, a vow. Tears heated her cheeks as he drew back.

He licked his lips as if tasting the salt of her tears. "I never meant to make you cry."

"Tears of joy," she assured him. She had to touch him. Reaching out, she took his hand. "Oh, Quentin, can it really be?"

"I might ask you the same. There were times I thought you must despise me. Yet here you are, crying at my kiss." His smile looked watery as he reached out his free hand and wiped away her tears with gentle fingers.

"What do we do now?" she asked.

He chuckled, letting his hand fall. "Now, you go inside before I am tempted to forget I am supposed to be a gentleman. Tomorrow, we will confront your uncle and settle this once and for all."

One step at a time. She nodded, moving back from him. "Very well. I will endeavor to be downstairs by nine. We can face him together then. Good night, Quentin."

He must have been as loath to part as she was, for he pulled her back into his arms and kissed her. When they finally broke away, she thought her feet never touched the ground as she ran back to the house.

Quentin Adair loved her. The thought fueled each step, the very beat of her heart. She could have danced through every room at the grange, leaped up and touched the brass chandelier in the entry. He loved her, and they had a chance for a future together. All she must do was stay strong.

"Bit late to be out on the grounds," her uncle said.

Foot on the stairs to the chamber story, Kitty paused, feeling as if a wintry blast swept down the corridor. Sir Thomas was lounging in the doorway of the library, arms folded across his chest, for all the world as if he had been watching for her. She could not like the glitter in his pale eyes.

"The night was cool and pleasant," she said. "I thought a stroll before retiring might help me sleep."

"I have just the thing for sleeping soundly," he said, pushing off the doorjamb. "Come with me."

"Thank you, Uncle," she tried, taking a step upward. "Perhaps another time."

"Now." He disappeared into the library.

She could hardly refuse. She might raise his suspicions about her and Quentin. She followed her uncle into the library.

The staff had already banked the fire for the night. The hearth gave only a dim orange glow as Sir Thomas headed for his liquor cabinet. Opening the gilded doors of the fine wood box, he drew out a fat-bottomed crystal flask.

"Brandy?" he asked, lifting it in her direction, the amber liquid swirling.

"No, thank you." Something was wrong. A gentleman did not share brandy with a lady. Certainly Uncle had never offered her a drink before. She could not imagine why he was doing so now. She drew in a breath, forced herself to focus. It would not do to give away the game.

Her uncle busied himself pouring a glass.

"I underestimated you," he said as he put the stopper back in the flask. "I always thought that sharp tongue of yours was your only weapon. It seems you know how to use your feminine wiles as well."

She wasn't sure whether to thank him or take umbrage. "This is not a proper discussion for tonight," she said, taking a step back toward the door.

"He's using you, you know," he said. "He thinks because you're family he can hurt me by hurting you."

"What a great miscalculation," Kitty said. "We both know how little you care for me."

He took a sip from his glass with one hand and pointed to her with the other. "There, you see?" he said, lowering the glass. "You are a smart chit. You've done well by my girls, Kitty—a means to an end. But you're right that there's no love between us. Still, you're family, and I cannot allow him to make light of our name. He's the enemy. Make no mistake."

Kitty kept her smile pleasant from years of practice. "I can see you consider him such. But his slight to you was years ago, and of your own making. Eugenia lied to you. Quentin never harmed her. He only dared to think she might return his love."

Her uncle's hand sliced the air. "Effrontery enough. And now his mouse of a father refuses to sell Rose Cottage to me."

Kitty's head came up despite her best intentions. "Is that what this is all about? You want the Adair lands?"

He threw back the rest of his drink and shoved the glass onto the cabinet. "Of course I want the land. You don't think I'd let Sir Winston have it and forever have to listen to his gloating? But Adair won't sell, sentimental fool that he is. So, I've done what I can to force his hand."

At least she could confirm the truth for Quentin. "Do tell."

He smirked. "You'd like that, wouldn't you? Me spilling all my secrets. Suffice it to say the Adair sugar will never leave the Bristol docks until it's accidently tossed into the sea." He took a step toward her. "But I need to know how much he suspects, whether he has plans to circumvent mine."

And he expected her to tell him. The arrogance!

"I'm afraid I cannot help you," she said, turning for the door.

"Oh, you will help me." He was behind her and seizing her arm before she could escape. "You'll be the carrot to lure Adair to his ruin. Be a good girl now, and don't make me strike you."

Good girl? Oh, yes, she'd been that her whole life—dutiful, conscientious, proper. Sometimes she feared that was all she might be. But Quentin saw more in her, and for him she must be more. She reared back her head and connected with her uncle's nose with a satisfying crunch.

He stumbled back with a roar, and she darted for the door, but he was on her in an instant, fist in her hair.

"No, you don't," he warned, dragging her back so hard she saw stars. He shoved her onto the sofa, shouting for the footmen. Kitty sprang to her feet, and he shoved her down again. A moment more, and Taughton and Bollers rushed in.

"Take Miss Katherine upstairs to her room and see that she stays there," Sir Thomas ordered, one hand seeking to stem the blood rushing from his bruised nose. "And no visitors. I'll send for her as I see fit."

"We will stop you," Kitty warned, succeeding in regaining her feet at last.

"You should know by now that I don't take well to threats, girl," Sir Thomas replied.

"That, sir, was no threat," Kitty said. "That was a promise." And she suffered the footmen to lead her out, for now.

ॐ

Quentin couldn't remember the last time he'd slept so well. A note had been waiting for him at home, confirming that the sugar had reached the docks in Whitehaven and merely awaited inspection from the customs officers before being sent to market.

"Excellent news," his father had said when Quentin told him. "You see, there was no need to sell Rose Cottage."

Quentin sat on the edge of the chaise lounge where his father was warming by the fire in his bedchamber. "I'd still like you to consider it. When this matter is settled, I intend to return to Jamaica."

82

His father sighed. "I feared as much. When my valet confided you had offered for Miss Chapworth, I hoped that meant you would stay."

Quentin put a hand on his shoulder. When had his father become so frail? "Forgive me for not telling you about my proposal myself. You see, Kitty and I agreed to pretend an engagement so I could keep a close eye on Sir Thomas. But last night we decided to make it official. I plan to marry her, Father. I love her."

A tear rolled down his father's pale cheek. "So if I'm to see my grandchildren, I must relocate to Jamaica?"

Quentin dropped his hand with a smile. "I fear so."

"Then so be it. We can talk to Sir Winston about the matter. I am persuaded he will take good care of the roses."

So was Quentin. Finally, his life was settling into place. He had no doubt that, with Kitty at his side, they could do amazing things. He could hardly wait to see her again. As a result, he threw on his riding coat, tied his cravat in a loose knot, and galloped his horse over to the grange to arrive before nine.

He thought he would find her in the breakfast room, a sunny space with yellow wall hangings. But though the other guests joined him, making quick work of the ham and eggs and pastries on the sideboard, half past came and went with no sign of Kitty. He was just rising to go in search of her when the older footman entered. Quentin could not forget that he had been one of those to hold him while Sir Thomas had wielded his crop years ago.

"The master would like a private word with you, sir," he told Quentin, gray eyes hard.

"Probably something to do with the wedding," Danvers put in with a smile. Willingham smirked.

Quentin highly doubted Sir Thomas would want any input to their wedding plans. But he chilled as he realized it was possible Kitty's uncle had discovered Quentin's plans. He rose and followed the servant to the library.

Sir Thomas glanced up from the papers on his desk as Quentin entered. The footman left, closing the door behind him. Quentin had the distinct feeling of being caged.

"Your sugar will be at the bottom of the Bristol Harbor by now," Sir Thomas announced.

And he looked entirely too pleased about the matter. Dressed in a blue coat, his smile was nearly as bright as the silver threads on his waistcoat.

But he was wrong. All Quentin had to do was play along. He wandered closer. "How can that be? I've received no word about an accident."

"You will." Sir Thomas chuckled. "Might as well stick your spoon in the wall, boy. I've beaten you."

Not yet. *Please, God, not ever.* "Why go to the trouble?" Quentin asked. "You took your wrath out on me years ago. I've done nothing to provoke you since."

"Your existence provokes me," Sir Thomas sneered. "There is an order to things, boy, and you are always reaching higher. Men like you are never satisfied until they've been shown their place. Your father is the same way. Tiny estate, yet he clings to it, even on his deathbed." Sir Thomas leaned closer. "When word comes about the loss of your profits, he'll have no choice but to sell to me."

"Or Sir Winston," Quentin pointed out. "He's been equally determined to buy us out."

Sir Thomas leaned back. "You'll sell to me. I've seen how

you look at my niece. I thought it was all an act at first, and I couldn't understand. But I believe you actually care about her."

He should deny it. Sir Thomas clearly thought to use his feelings against him. Yet if he denied it, Kitty would surely hear of it. He could not hurt her like that.

"I am in love with her," he told Sir Thomas. "And I will marry her."

Sir Thomas shook his head. "I always thought you were an odd fish, but I must say it's come in handy." His look hardened. "You will stay here, keep silent, do nothing about the sugar. Play the gentleman, or Kitty will suffer."

Quentin stared at him. "You would threaten your own family?"

He waved a hand. "She's lucky I found a purpose for her. Don't think I would lose any sleep by seeing her hurt. I know how to use my riding crop to good purpose, as you will recall."

He meant it. Quentin could see it in his pale eyes, lit from within as if the idea of hurting Kitty excited him. The thought of her enduring the pain and humiliation he'd felt was enough to sicken Quentin. He inclined his head.

"Your point. But I warn you, harm her and my gloves come off."

Sir Thomas smiled, though there was no warmth in it. "No need for concern. Play your part, and you'll soon be reunited with your love. I've invited Sir Winston over at eleven this morning. You will tell him you and your father have decided to sell to me. And then I will thank you to take Kitty out of my sight and never darken my door again."

CHAPTER ELEVEN

K itty paced her room, mind coursing faster than her uncle's prize hunter. She'd managed to snatch a little sleep, but with even her maid denied entrance, she hadn't been able to do more than loosen her stays. Now she couldn't help wondering what fiendish plans her uncle must have for Quentin.

A part of her almost wished Quentin had been using her, if only to see her uncle stopped. But she could not wish away his love. Never that.

There must be something she could do!

She'd already determined she had no way to escape. Her room on the upper story was too high to allow her to jump safely from the window, even if she could have squeezed past the narrow casing. The fireplace was too tight to allow her to shinny up it. Taughton, who had been on duty that night, was immune to her pleas. He feared reprisal, and she could not doubt her uncle would take a dim view of any servant who disobeyed his orders.

So, how could she win free?

A noise in the corridor caught her attention, and she rushed to put her ear to the door. Lucy's voice came through muffled.

"But I must see my cousin. She's the only one who can fasten this chain properly."

Kitty yanked open the door. "Lucy, help me! Your father is holding me prisoner so he can ruin Quentin."

Bollers, who was apparently on duty this morning, joined her cousin in staring at her. Then Lucy's pretty face puckered over her soft muslin gown. "What?"

"Sorry, miss," Bollers said, putting a hand on Kitty's shoulder and attempting to push her back into the room while she dug her slippers into the carpet. "Sir Thomas said no visitors."

"I am not a visitor!" Lucy ducked under his arm and slipped into the room with Kitty. "I am family." She took Kitty's hand and held it tight, and Kitty dared to hope that the two of them might prevail against the burly lad.

But Lucy raised her dainty head. "If Kitty must be punished, then so must I."

"As you wish," Bollers said, and he shut the door in their faces.

"Well!" Lucy said. "I never!"

"Thank the Lord for that." Kitty drew herself away from her cousin and shook her head. "I appreciate your kindness, Lucy, but now we're both imprisoned."

"Not for long," Lucy predicted. "Mr. Willingham and Mr. Fredericks will seek me. We will apply to them for help."

"No offense, dearest," Kitty said, "but I cannot see either of them having the strength of character to stand up to your father."

Lucy's lower lip trembled. "But what did you do, Kitty, to make him so angry as to lock you in?"

"I sided with Quentin over him," Kitty explained. "I'm sorry, Lucy, but your father is a tyrant. He plans to ruin Quentin's sugar plantation so his father will have no choice but to sell Rose Cottage."

Lucy's gaze dropped to the floral pattern of the carpet. "I have heard stories over the years, but I tried to convince myself people told them because they were jealous of Father's good fortune." She glanced up at Kitty. "Your Mr. Adair and his father aren't the first people he's ruined, are they?"

Kitty put a hand on her cousin's arm. "I fear they are the last in a long line. But I never had proof until now."

Lucy raised her chin. "Then we must put a stop to it."

She had never seen the girl so determined. Those blue eyes held a fire, reminding her a bit of her uncle.

"Agreed," Kitty said warily. "But how? We seem to be trapped."

"Leave that to me," Lucy said. "You just determine what we must do once we are free."

Easy enough. She was beginning to think her uncle had a chink in his armor, and she knew how to exploit it. She simply didn't believe that Lucy could set them loose in time.

Downstairs in the elegant withdrawing room, Quentin was also pacing. He knew he should take a seat. Most of the other guests had done so. Though Cadberry and the Eglantine family had yet to come down, Danvers and Miss Gaffney were on the sofa, her blushing prettily at something he had whispered in her ear.

Willingham and Townshend were lounging in armchairs by the marble hearth, sharing a copy of *The Times* and lowering the sheets every few moments as if to make sure nothing else of interest was occurring. Fredericks had positioned himself near the door, as if ready to pounce upon the fair Lucy the moment she appeared.

None of them had as yet remarked on Quentin's agitation. But how could he be still knowing Kitty might be in danger? He'd already circled the house, discounted any direct approach to freeing her short of resorting to violence.

He knew from experience the footmen could be counted on to obey Sir Thomas's orders, even if that meant seeing another harmed. He could laugh in Sir Thomas's face, tell him the sugar was safe in Whitehaven, but who knew whether he'd take his failure out on Kitty?

Willingham must have noticed him at last, for he lowered his portion of the paper with a decided rustle. "Do sit down, Adair. I am assured the other ladies will be here shortly."

"Not soon enough for me," Fredericks said with a nod to Quentin. "I say we go ferret them out."

Townshend lowered his paper as well. "Never met a woman who appreciated having her toilette disrupted. It seems to take them hours."

"Except for your Miss Chapworth, Adair," Willingham put in with a smirk. "She seems to throw on whatever is at hand, even if it's her cousin's."

Normally, Quentin would have turned aside the unkind remark with a quip, but his nerves were stretched to the breaking point.

"Have a care, Willingham," he said. "I am in no mood to hear Kitty slighted."

On the other side of the room, Danvers and Miss Gaffney exchanged glances.

"I most sincerely appreciate a gentleman who champions his lady love," she said with an approving nod.

Champion. Kitty had called him that last night. Yet what kind of champion stood by while the woman he loved was threatened? He had worked for years to throw off the sullen boy he'd been. Were the trappings of Society nothing but chains?

At Miss Gaffney's remark, Willingham held up a hand, most likely to dig his own grave, then paused with a frown. Townshend cocked his head, brow puckering as well.

Now Quentin heard it, too. Rising above the noise of the house was an ethereal voice, singing. The notes fairly leaped upon the air, high and sweet. Surely that wasn't Kitty.

The newspaper slid to the floor as Townshend popped to his feet. "That must be Miss Chapworth."

"The one who finds her wins," Fredericks declared, dashing out the door. Willingham and Townshend were hot on his heels. Knowing there was the slightest chance Lucy was with Kitty, Quentin followed.

It was relatively easy to trace the sound to its source, and to spot the footman standing guard before the door. It was the same young man who had served Kitty the first day she'd met Quentin at the folly. He had not been on staff ten years ago. His stoic expression and muscular height didn't seem to trouble the would-be swains.

"Miss Chapworth, come out!" Townshend called, taking up his stance in front of the door.

"We wait to applaud you," Willingham declared, joining him.

Fredericks alone sided with Quentin. "Something is wrong here," he murmured.

"Agreed," Quentin murmured back. "Be watchful."

Lucy's sweet voice floated through the portal. "I cannot come out. My father has confined me and my cousin to the room. Oh, but I would so highly esteem the man who could brave his wrath and free us."

Kitty was there? Quentin started forward, and Fredericks put a hand on his arm to stop him, shaking his head. Right. Perhaps he should heed his own advice.

Willingham, however, blanched. "Yes, well," he said, backing away from the door. "There is such a thing as honoring one's host."

"Assuredly," Townshend agreed, scuttling away from the footman even faster. "But rest assured we will support you, Miss Chapworth, when you have the opportunity to emerge."

The two turned and hurried back down the corridor.

Fredericks shook his head. "So much for risking all in the name of love. Are you with me, Adair?"

In answer, Quentin took his place before the footman. Fredericks stood beside him, fists raised. "Step aside, my good man," Lucy's suitor ordered, "or I shall be obliged to use these."

The footman stared past them. "I am only doing my duty, sirs."

Fredericks widened his stance. So did the footman.

Quentin thought there might be another way. "A man who honors his master's wishes even when he disagrees with them must not have much of a conscience," he drawled.

Sweat trickled down from under the fellow's powdered wig. "It's a choice of honoring my conscience or seeing me and my wife starve, sir."

Was it as simple as that? "Have you a desire to travel?" Quentin asked as Fredericks lowered his hands to watch him. "As I will be marrying, I must enlarge my staff and could use a footman and maid."

The footman's gaze flickered to his. "How can I trust you to keep your word?"

"If not his word, trust mine," Kitty called through the door. She must have been listening. "I know you have no liking for this, Bollers. Let us go, and I promise Sir Thomas will not trouble you or yours again."

The staff knew who to trust in this house. The footman turned and opened the door. Kitty launched herself at Quentin.

He caught her close, seemed to find breath for the first time in hours.

"I will not have him ruin you," she promised before pulling out of his embrace. "Come with me, all of you, and we will stop my uncle, once and for all."

CHAPTER TWELVE

They found Sir Thomas with Sir Winston in the billiard room. The magistrate looked up with a frown as Kitty, Quentin, Lucy, and Fredericks crowded through the door. Her uncle's nose began to darken.

Before he could speak, Kitty pointed a finger at him. "You, sir, are a sham of a gentleman, and I will not rest until these good people know it."

"Now, then," Sir Winston said, setting down his cue and blinking bleary blue eyes. "This seems a family matter. Perhaps I should withdraw."

Quentin moved to the doorway. "No one is leaving until Miss Chapworth has her say."

"Ramsey!" Sir Thomas barked. "Taughton! Throw this impertinent pup out of my house."

"They cannot aid you," Kitty told him. "Taughton has been locked in his room, and Mr. Ramsey is searching the wine cellar for a bottle of claret I was persuaded you would want for dinner. I will speak."

"But I don't have to listen." He pushed past the magistrate and headed for the door. Quentin blocked his path, red riding coat like a flag of warning.

"By all means, leave," Kitty called after him. "I would rather tell my tale to Sir Winston than to you."

Out of the corner of her eye, she saw her uncle pause.

She stepped closer to the magistrate, who was regarding her with a frown.

"I have served faithfully in this house for nearly ten years," she told him. "Sir Thomas gave me a home and meaningful work, and for that I will always be grateful."

"As you should," the magistrate said, head cocked as if he expected her sweet words to turn sour any moment.

"Twice, however," Kitty continued, "I have seen him go too far. The first time I was young and frightened, and to my shame I could do nothing." She glanced to Quentin, whose look softened.

"Now I cannot be silent." She glanced around at those assembled in the room, whose looks ranged from fascination to concern. "Sir Thomas intends to ruin Mr. Adair and force the sale of his ancestral home. He must be stopped."

Sir Winston raised his feathery white brows.

"Lies!" Sir Thomas thundered, surging forward. "Adair is the one out for trouble. You know his reputation, Mallery. He was nothing but a womanizer and a gamester before he left England, and nothing has changed that I can see. To punish me for some slight, he has turned my niece's head and twisted her heart away from her own family."

The magistrate glanced between Kitty and Sir Thomas. "Yet I cannot ignore her accusation against you, sir. We have both been interested in buying Rose Cottage. Have you proof she is lying?"

Sir Thomas smiled ingratiatingly as he moved closer to Kitty once more. "You have only to look at her, old friend. Plain and penniless and serving as chaperone to my Lucy, she was easy prey for Adair's charms. He insinuated himself into our lives, pretended to care for her. His pretty promises gave her notions above her station, and now she seeks to help him in soiling my good name."

Quentin stepped away from the door. "Pretty promises they might be, but I stand by each one. I love her. Kitty and I will be married, as soon as she wishes."

His conviction rang in his voice, glowed from his face. Warmth flowed through her.

She turned to her uncle. "And I'm afraid I'm craven enough that I should prefer my husband to have some funds to support me. So I cannot allow you to ruin him."

"Mad," Sir Thomas confided to Sir Winston. "The pair of them. I have no idea what she's talking about."

"Then let me refresh your memory, Uncle," Kitty said in the calm voice she'd practiced in his presence for years. "You have been using your influence at the Port of Bristol to see Mr. Adair's sugar languish in the hold. It's taken quite a toll on his profits."

"Business," he said with a smile to the magistrate. "Chit simply doesn't understand how things are done."

The magistrate's frown was now turned on her uncle, and she could see Sir Thomas's stance shift as if he had noticed.

"Yes, well, I am just a chaperone, after all," Kitty acknowledged. "I may have misunderstood. But as chaperone, I've observed many things over my ten years sitting silent in the corner. Remember that I have had a hand in your correspondence, Uncle. It would be a shame if the magistrate had to investigate all the many, many things I may have misunderstood."

Her uncle's gaze met hers, fire dancing in the blue. She refused to quail. This was for Quentin.

For the first time in her memory, her uncle stepped back. "A decided shame. Very well, miss, you win. But I want you out of my house. This minute. And don't bother packing your things. Everything you own I paid for. Be glad I let you keep the clothes on your back."

She would have liked to press the matter, but in truth, it would always be her word against his. And by the frown that remained on the magistrate's face, she had planted a seed that might yet bear fruit and save others from similar heartache.

"But, Father," Lucy protested, "what am I to do without Kitty? She is my chaperone."

"Never fear, dear Lucy," Fredericks said, taking her hand. "I hope to shortly make a chaperone unnecessary."

Lucy's delighted smile was his answer.

"And Kitty's days of playing chaperone are over," Quentin put in. He came forward to take Kitty's hand and smiled down at her before turning to the magistrate.

"Sir Winston, my father's health suffers in England's cold. I am persuaded Jamaica would be better for him. May I have our solicitor call on yours to discuss the sale of our estate?"

Sir Thomas drew himself up as if to protest, but Sir Winston smiled. "I would be delighted, Adair. And if there is any trouble with the arrangements, I may have to start that investigation Miss Chapworth suggested."

Sir Thomas deflated.

Quentin turned to Kitty. "I have no license, and we've no time to read the banns or elope to Gretna."

Kitty shuddered. "I've stopped enough elopements that I cannot wish one for myself."

"Then escape to London with me," he said, grip tightening as if he thought she might still refuse. "I'll purchase a special license, and we can be married before we join my father in boarding the ship for Jamaica."

"Another lie," her uncle sneered. "He'll leave you in the gutter, and good riddance."

"No," Kitty said, gaze holding his. "He won't. Because he loves me, and I love him. We started this engagement for convenience, but we end it with something more."

"All my devotion, all my adoration," Quentin agreed. "All my love and life I offer you, dear Kitty."

Lucy sighed in delight.

And Kitty, who had generally prided herself on a sharp riposte, was once more silent.

But not still. She took Quentin's hand, and they left the grange to start their new life together.

The End

Dear Reader,

Thank you for joining me on Kitty and Quentin's journey. I hope you enjoy all the stories in our *Summer House Party* anthology. If you'd like more information about my other Regency stories, please visit me online at www.reginascott.com, where you can also sign up for a free alert to hear when the next book is out.

Happy reading!

Regina Scott

ABOUT REGINA SCOTT

Regina Scott started writing novels in the third grade. Thankfully for literature as we know it, she didn't actually sell her first novel until she'd learned a bit more about writing. After numerous short stories and articles in magazines and trade journals, and a good kick in the backside from her husband, she got serious about writing. Since then, she's had published more than two dozen clean historical romances for adults and young adults. Her traditional romances have earned praised from reviewers and readers alike. Booklist calls her work "quietly compelling" and "impeccably written." Huntress Reviews says, "Regina Scott delivers," and "I will always buy a book with Regina Scott's name on it."

Regina Scott is the author of the Everard Legacy series (*The Rogue's Reform*, *The Captain's Courtship*, *The Rake's Redemption*, and *The Heiress's Homecoming*), the Master Matchmaker series (*The Courting Campaign*, *The Wife Campaign*, and *The Husband Campaign*), and the Lady Emily Capers (*Secrets and Sensibilities*, *Art and Artifice*, and *Ballrooms and Blackmail*). In November 2014, she launched her Frontier Bachelors series with the publication of *The Bride* Ship.

She makes her home in the Puget Sound area of Washington State with her beloved husband and a hyperactive Irish terrier named Fergus.

Find Regina online at her website: www.reginascott.com
Blog: www.nineteenteen.com
Facebook: www.facebook.com/authorreginascott
Goodreads: www.goodreads.com/reginascott

A PERFECT MATCH

By Donna Hatch

OTHER BOOKS BY DONNA HATCH

The Stranger She Married
The Guise of a Gentleman
A Perfect Secret
The Suspect's Daughter
Queen in Exile
Mistletoe Magic
Constant Hearts
Regency Hearts
Timeless Romance Anthology: Winter Collection
Timeless Regency Collection: Autumn Masquerade

CHAPTER ONE

England, Summer 1818

Inside the family coach, Genevieve Marshall gazed out the window at the abbey, her joyful anticipation of reuniting with her friend fading at the sight of the dark, twisted, almost grotesque structure that would provide the backdrop for the Widtsoes' house party. If the clichéd dead tree, complete with a cawing crow, had framed the view like so many gothic novels Genevieve read, she would not have been surprised.

"I cannot imagine Matilda growing up here," Genevieve murmured.

Indeed, the structure seemed perfect for inspiring melancholy rather than Matilda Widtsoe's irrepressible liveliness.

Mama pushed back the curtain and peered out. Auburn ringlets, the same color as Genevieve's, framed her face and contrasted with her lace cap. "Good heavens, what a cheerless dwelling."

Chuckling, Papa set aside his newspaper to admire the view. "That 'cheerless dwelling' is Bainbridge Abbey, and it has been in existence since the eleventh century."

Genevieve sent him a wry smile. "I don't suppose you can promise a few ghosts, just to add to the ambience, dear Papa?"

"I'll speak to Admiral Widtsoe." Papa's chocolate brown eyes crinkled.

"Tell your ghosts to stay out of our room," Mama said primly. "I'll not have our privacy invaded by their shenanigans."

"I'm sure they can be reasonable," Genevieve quipped. She studied her mother, searching for signs of undue fatigue or distress. One can never be too careful with a weak heart. However, despite a two-day journey, Mama's color remained good at the moment. Still, as soon as they reached the abbey, Genevieve would see to it that her mother rested.

Genevieve resettled into the seat cushions and imagined her reunion with her friend Matilda Widtsoe. It seemed a decade since they'd last conversed, but in fact it had only been a year. Letters were no substitute for face-to-face conversation, although the capitalized and underlined words and the prolific use of exclamation points certainly reflected Matilda's passionate manner of speech. Genevieve couldn't wait to meet the young gentleman who'd captured her friend's heart in London, and who occupied a large portion of Matilda's letters.

The coach bumped over a curving road to the ominous structure and stopped at the main entrance. As Genevieve took Papa's hand and stepped out, she looked up at the dark building.

"See the gargoyles on the parapets?" Papa pointed. "This is truly a well-preserved structure. I'm happy to see they didn't make any additions to try to modernize it."

"Mrs. Widtsoe said they've updated part of it, mostly inside," Mama said. "They even have bathing rooms with shower baths."

A bath sounded delightful after the dirt and grit of the road, but not as delightful as a reunion with Matilda.

As footmen shouldered the family's trunks, Genevieve took her father's free arm and mounted the steps. They'd no sooner been admitted into a cavernous great hall than a squeal of delight and a bundle of ruffles launched itself at Genevieve and hugged her until she let out a squeak herself.

"Oh, Jenny, you're here at last! I have so much to tell you!" Matilda drew back enough to let Genevieve breathe. Though Matilda stood at average height, Genevieve barely reached her chin.

As if remembering her manners, Matilda smiled at Genevieve's parents but continued bobbing as if her excitement refused to be contained. Her honey-colored curls echoed every bounce. "Welcome, Captain Marshall, Mrs. Marshall. We're so happy you're all here. I trust your journey was not too tiring?"

Before Mama and Papa got out more than a few words, Matilda said, "Good, good. Mrs. Pearce will see you settled." She took both of Genevieve's hands into hers, and Matilda's words started tripping all over themselves in her excitement. "Oh, Jenny, I can't wait for you to meet him."

"Why, whoever do you mean?" Genevieve opened her eyes in mock innocence.

Matilda gaped at her as if she thought Genevieve had taken leave of her senses. "The man of my dreams, the love of my life— Christian Amesbury!"

Genevieve smiled. "I know. I'm only quizzing you. Tell me all about him."

"He and his father are attending the house party," Matilda said. "Isn't that wonderful? His father is the Earl of Tarrington, so it's quite an honor that they're coming, but of course that's not why I adore him. Oh, Jenny, he's handsome and stylish and polite, and even a bit mysterious, but I'm sure he'll be more forthcoming here with so many opportunities to converse." With her hands still entwined with Genevieve's, Matilda started hopping up and down with more vigor.

Genevieve laughed weakly in the face of such a force of nature. "Well, I look forward to meeting him. I only hope he's good enough for you, Mattie."

"Wait until you meet him. Oh, just wait!"

"Good heavens, child, show some decorum," came a voice from behind them. Mrs. Widtsoe approached, shaking her head, a resigned smile touching her lips. "Welcome, Captain and Mrs. Marshall, Miss Marshall."

Admiral Widtsoe arrived from another direction, greeting her father heartily and bowing to Genevieve and her mother.

Mrs. Widtsoe asked, "Would you like refreshment first or to rest in your rooms?"

"Tea would be lovely," Mama said. "I do believe I ought to rest soon thereafter."

Genevieve cast an anxious look at Mrs. Widtsoe. Catching her meaning, the perceptive lady suggested, "Shall I send a tea tray to your room so you can rest without delay?"

"Thank you," Mama agreed.

Genevieve disentangled herself from her exuberant friend with a promise to return momentarily. After ensuring her mother got her tea and was resting, with her heart medicine within reach if needed, and good-naturedly enduring Mama's calling her 'little mother,' Genevieve changed out of her carriage dress, freshened up, and followed a maid to the parlor. The longed-for bath would have to wait until after Genevieve enjoyed a coze with Matilda.

In the parlor decorated in shades of rose and pink, Matilda arose from a settee where she'd been perched and cast a glance at her mother, who sat near a window facing the front driveway. "We're going for a walk, Mother."

The lady nodded and gave them a loose wave. Matilda glided, with hardly any bouncing, to Genevieve and took her arm, tugging her outside. The moment they stepped through the French doors onto the terrace, Matilda's flow of words began, as did her bouncing. With her blue eyes shining and her cheeks pink, she painted a lovely picture.

"Oh, Jenny, I have been waiting for this moment for ages! I just know you're going to love Christian. I declare that I will do anything to secure a place in his heart. Wouldn't it be perfect if he chose the house party to propose?"

Genevieve nodded. "Indeed it would."

Matilda pressed a hand dramatically over her heart. "There has never been a more perfect man in all the earth. I am most violently in love with him!"

Genevieve couldn't help tweaking her friend just a bit. "Weren't you violently in love with the Duke of Suttenberg last year?"

Matilda waved away the past. "Oh, well, I admit I did admire him—he's so handsome and, of course, comes from ancient lineage—but we hardly exchanged two words. It was more like admiration from afar than true love."

"And this is true love?"

"Oh, yes! Christian is a bit reticent. If I didn't know better, I'd say he was shy. But that's quite unheard of for such a handsome man of fashion, and an earl's son besides. He's merely thoughtful and doesn't speak unless he has something important to say. Oh, and he's so artistic! I asked him to paint my portrait while he was here, and do you know he agreed? He painted the loveliest portrait of the Duchess of Devonshire. It's simply exquisite! He's developing quite an impressive reputation as an artist of both landscape and portraits. I vow half of the fashionable houses in London are graced with one of his paintings."

"Yes, I believe I saw a landscape of his."

"I wish he had a twin so you could have one of him, too. He has brothers, but none of them are coming. The eldest, the viscount, is off visiting his aunt and uncle somewhere, and the next eldest is at sea—a captain, or a pirate if you believe rumor. And the next one is in London, but he seems to shun society. Oh, but Christian is so handsome. He and his father look a great deal alike, both tall and broad-shouldered and blond. Mama says he looks like Hercules, but I think of him as Adonis."

Such a romantic description. "Your mother approves, I take it?"

"Oh, of course! And Father has already said he'll give permission promptly and not tease Christian when he seeks him out. Can you imagine? Me? Married to such a handsome man, and the son of an earl. Why, all my friends will be so green with envy! All except you, of course. You're a true friend, Jenny."

Genevieve squeezed her hand. "I hope he makes you happy, Mattie. I truly do. So you are on a first-name basis with this Christian?"

"Well, not officially, but he is already Christian to me."

Genevieve made a silent vow to give this paragon a careful study to be sure he wasn't a *roué* who trifled with her friend's heart. After all the losses and heartbreaks her dear friend had suffered, Genevieve would do anything to ensure Matilda's happiness.

Matilda sighed. "I suppose we ought to go back. Mama wishes me to help her greet our guests. The guest list is quite impressive, I assure you. Oh, Jenny, I hope someone comes who is suitable for you. It would be lovely to have a double wedding!"

With a gentle smile, Genevieve said, "I hardly think a week-long house party is adequate time to fall in love with someone and decide to marry."

Earnest blue eyes met hers. "Sometimes love happens instantly and you just *know*." She pressed a hand over her heart. "It was that quick for me."

Genevieve kept her doubts to herself. She sent up a silent prayer that if this so-called perfect Christian Amesbury weren't good enough for Matilda, his flaws would become apparent before their relationship progressed farther.

They turned back to the house as more guests arrived. Carriages lined up, and servants scurried to help settle the arrivals.

Matilda halted before they entered the great hall. She took both of Genevieve's hands. "I'm so glad you're here, Jenny. It's been torture to be in such raptures without anyone to share it with who really understands and listens . . ."

Her words trailed off. Genevieve followed her gaze to a tall, distinguished man with silver streaks brushing his dark hair. He stood amid the chaos of boxes, trunks, and scurrying servants, surveying the scene with barely suppressed disdain. Sophisticated in his stylishly tailored riding clothes and lean form, he fingered his riding crop as if wishing he could control the servants the way he controlled his horse.

Matilda lowered her voice. "That's Lord Wickburgh, a viscount and an acquaintance of my father's."

"He's a very elegant gentleman."

"Yes. Very." For once, Matilda didn't elaborate.

Lord Wickburgh's gaze passed over the great hall. As his focus landed on Genevieve, he looked so hard at her that she turned her gaze downward. His stare contained a chill that settled into her backbone.

Admiral Widtsoe greeted the impressive lord, and soon the viscount ascended the staircase, presumably to his room. Others arrived, and Matilda greeted them with her mother. Genevieve hung back, so as not to be in the way, and offered assistance when possible.

In the midst of the arrivals came a very young man who didn't appear to have reached his majority, with his brown hair in the youthful Cherubin style.

Mrs. Widtsoe clasped his hands. "So happy you are here, Sir Reginald. I hear you got your degree from Oxford?"

"Yes, indeed I have, ma'am. My mother sends her love." He turned warm eyes onto Matilda. "Always a pleasure to see you, Mattie."

Matilda grinned. "Good afternoon, Reggie. I suppose you feel all grown up now, eh?" All at once, Matilda let out a strangled sound of glee, clearly forgetting Sir Reginald. "He's here!" Her urgent whisper drew Genevieve's focus.

There stood a breathtakingly perfect young gentleman. Genevieve had frequented art museums, had seen many sculptures and paintings of mortal men and gods, some so beautiful she could almost fall into a swoon over them. Never in her life had she seen one come to life. Though she'd always had a preference for dark-haired men, probably influenced by her penchant for reading Gothics, this stunning perfection was a study in gold, from the gold of his glorious hair, to the golden tones of his sun-kissed skin, even the gold threads in his waistcoat. His dark blue riding coat brought out the summer-sky blue of his eyes that glanced about and then darted to a man who could only be his father—a thinner, older image of the blond vision. The young gentleman's eyes narrowed in concern as he reached out to touch his father's sleeve.

The older man waved him off and straightened his broad shoulders. A wan smile touched the older gentleman's mouth as he greeted Admiral and Mrs. Widtsoe and Matilda.

Ashamed for staring, Genevieve cast an anxious glance at Matilda. Her friend gazed rapturously at the vision, her hands clasped to her bosom. The young gentleman glanced at her briefly before lowering his gaze, a half smile curving his full, shapely lips that conjured visions of stolen kisses underneath rose bowers.

Genevieve flushed. She was here to meet the gentleman of her friend's dreams, not form dreams of her own. She squared her shoulders and vowed to discover whether his heart were as fair as his face and form, and if he were good enough for her friend.

CHAPTER TWO

Christian Amesbury greeted the Widtsoes while keeping an eye on his father, the Earl of Tarrington. Leaving the healing waters of Bath and traveling to this house party might prove too taxing to the earl's failing strength. However, this had been the first social event his father had expressed a desire to attend since Mama's death, so Christian had encouraged their attendance. Besides fatigue, the earl seemed well enough at present, even showing a keener interest in his surroundings than he had in months. Perhaps the trip would boost his flagging spirits and revive his vitality in a way Bath had failed to do.

Furthermore, Christian had never visited this rugged terrain before, and his artist's eye had already found new subject matter to paint. Not to mention, Admiral Widtsoe had commissioned him to do a painting of the abbey, and his lively daughter had requested a portrait of her. The trip might be good for his father and him.

Standing behind the hosts' daughter stood a young lady who captured Christian's attention. With a fascinating shade of auburn hair, the flawless skin of a doll, and exquisitely delicate features, beautiful seemed too tame a word to describe her. She fixed a pair of rich, brown eyes on him that seemed to peer into his heart. He looked away before he tainted her beauty with his darkness and studied the patterns on the floor.

The earl drew Christian into the conversation as he greeted his long-time friends. "You remember my son, Christian—my right-hand man."

Christian offered a polite smile to the Widtsoes and their daughter, who beamed at him with unabashed adoration. Christian resisted the urge to tug at his collar. She was a pretty enough girl, but she watched him too closely, too hopefully. And she quivered a bit, rather like a poodle one of his mother's friends used to carry about under her arm everywhere she went. Still, as the daughter of their hosts, Miss Widtsoe deserved courtesy. He'd just have to be careful not to raise her expectations.

"Of course we remember your son, my lord," Admiral Widtsoe said. "Welcome, young Mr. Amesbury. We hope you will enjoy yourself here. I hope you don't mind if I whisk your father away from time to time so we can catch up."

Christian murmured a greeting and inclined his head in an abbreviated bow. He'd found bowing a good substitute for speech when he couldn't think of anything to say.

"Lord Tarrington, Mr. Amesbury," the young Miss Widtsoe greeted them, although her eyes rested solely on Christian. Her smile revealed practically her entire set of pearly teeth. "I can't wait to show you around! I'm sure you, as an artist, will find many views of interest to paint here! And it's such a perfect time of year, too, with all the summer blooms!" Though she never raised her voice above normal speaking tones, her enthusiasm turned her statements into exclamations.

Christian bowed in greeting. His gaze strayed to the exquisite young lady behind Miss Widtsoe. His fingers twitched in desire to paint her, to capture that air of purity and serenity he seldom found in adults; normally only children had such undimmed light. A sense of timelessness crept over him. As if aware of his focus, she glanced his way again. Her brown eyes, ringed with an unusually thick fringe of lashes, searched his face as if looking for secrets best left hidden. Oddly unbalanced, Christian focused his gaze upon the admiral.

Miss Widtsoe spoke again, reaching behind her and drawing the auburn-haired beauty next to her. "Genevieve, this is the Earl of Tarrington and his son, Christian Amesbury. My lord, Mr. Amesbury, please allow me to introduce to you my dearest friend in all the world, Miss Genevieve Marshall."

Genevieve. *Jenn-a-veeve*. Christian switched to the French pronunciation, *Zhahn-vee-ev*. A lovely name for a lovely girl. Of course, he could never call her by her given name. She must never be more than Miss Marshall to him.

As they exchanged their customary bows and curtsies, the earl asked, "Are you related to Captain Marshall, Miss Marshall?"

Surprise widened the auburn lady's eyes. "He is my father, my lord."

"A good man," the earl said. "Is he here?"

"Yes, my lord. He and my mother are both in attendance. They are resting after our journey."

"I look forward to renewing our acquaintance."

"As are they, I am sure."

Miss Widtsoe wrapped her arm around Miss Marshall's and smiled so hard Christian wondered if it caused her pain. Miss

Widtsoe stood almost a head taller than her fairy-like friend, and where her figure was full, Miss Marshall's was lithe, graceful, as if she had been created to wear a pair of wings and flit among the flowers.

"I'll show you to your rooms," the hostess said.

As they took their leave of the admiral, Miss Widtsoe curtsied. "I look forward to seeing you all at dinner tonight."

Her sunny smile brought an answering one to his lips. It was hard not to be cheerful amid such liveliness. He bowed to all, his focus resting again on the beautiful Miss Marshall, and turned to follow the hostess.

After getting settled in his rooms and changing out of his traveling clothes, Christian checked on the earl. He found him reclining on a settee, sipping tea.

The earl gazed fondly at Christian. "Well, son, you have already conquered the ladies without speaking a word, I see."

"Really, Father, we aren't at war. No conquering involved."

"This matchmaking business can feel like war of sorts. Take no prisoners, son." The earl wagged his finger.

Christian scoffed. "I'm not here to make matches. Do you require anything?"

"If I do, I'll ring for my valet. No need to fuss over me like a mother hen. I'll rest for a while. Go amuse yourself. For once, speak to a young lady. Or, if you can't think of anything to say, steal a kiss."

The image of the sweet perfection of the auburn-haired Miss Marshall edged into Christian's thoughts and heated his face. He nearly tugged on his collar.

The earl rested his head against the tall settee. "Admiral Widtsoe hopes you'll choose his daughter."

Christian cleared his throat. "Er . . ."

The earl's mouth curved in a ghostly reminder of the ready smiles he once wore when Mama was still alive. "If you aren't ready to settle down, you could sow some oats—not with a gently-bred lady of course—but here in a new place with new possibilities, there are all kinds of willing women—"

"Rest well, sir. I will see you at dinner—or at tea, if you are feeling well." Christian made his escape before the earl could begin ribbing him about his shyness around women or spout stories of how generations of Amesburys deserved their reputations of philanderers and how his father wooed ladies of all classes and moral codes before he found and married Mama. His older brothers, Cole and Jared, seemed to share the earl's views, but Christian never forgot his mother's urging to treat all members of the fair sex with respect, whether a farmer's daughter or a duchess. Besides, wooing would involve speaking. He'd rather face an opponent at fisticuffs or fencing than have to think of something clever to say to a lady.

He stopped by his room long enough to grab a sketchbook and an artist's pencil and went outside. Pausing, he turned slowly to find a good spot. Ah. There. A nearby hill. He took the shortest route out of the gardens to the hill to get a good view of the abbey. After finding a comfortable spot to sit, he eyed the structure. The multileveled tiers faintly reminiscent of Westminster Abbey, but adorned with gargoyles and built out of dark stone, certainly created a forbidding scene.

A replica of the abbey took form underneath his pencil. After adding details, he shaded in long, late afternoon shadows, which only added to the ominous air. Just for fun, he added a gargoyle springing to life and flying off the building. He smiled.

The earl thought his art a great waste of time, especially with the little fanciful turns it often took, but Christian couldn't have given up art any more than he could give up food. If only he could study under masters at the Royal Academy of Art. But he daren't follow that dream with his father so ill. And his family had always expected that he would become a vicar.

Immersed in his work, he gave a little start when he realized two pairs of eyes stared at him. Misses Widtsoe and Marshall stood watching him, with expressions of rapture and solemn contem-plation, respectively.

He sprang to his feet. "Ladies." He realized, belatedly, that he'd dropped his pencil and pad of paper. With his face heating, he retrieved the items and offered a bow.

As they both curtsied, Miss Widtsoe giggled, her wide smile reappearing.

Miss Marshall lifted a tiny gloved hand. "I apologize if we disturbed you, Mr. Amesbury."

He made a loose gesture to his paper. "I've finished this perspective." He would draw the abbey from a different vantage point another time. He tucked the paper under his arm and bowed to take his leave.

"We missed you at tea," Miss Widtsoe said. "People asked about you, but I didn't know what to tell them. Your father said you'd probably wandered off to draw somewhere, and it appears he was right."

"Er, yes." That explained his hunger. He hadn't noticed the passage of time while he'd sketched, but his stomach reminded him of the lapse. If the earl were at tea, he must be feeling well—an encouraging thought.

"Shall I have something brought to you? Cook makes the

most amazing scones, as light as you'd ever taste, and perfect with Devonshire cream! Or do you prefer lemon cake? I love lemon cake, and seedcake, too, but I'm careful not to overindulge lest it affect my figure." She struck a pose designed to attract his attention to her figure, which was very well endowed.

He only allowed himself a glance.

Before he thought of a response, she continued, "I'm happy to order some brought to you. We try not to starve our guests, even those who wander off and miss tea." She grinned, revealing all her teeth again.

Miss Marshall studied him with that quiet, assessing gaze. "We were just about to return to the abbey to dress for dinner. Do you wish to walk with us?"

Unable to think of a gracious way to extract himself, Christian gripped his pad and pencil as he offered an elbow to each of them. Miss Widtsoe clung to him possessively, but Miss Marshall rested her hand on the crook of his arm with a feather touch. The top of her head barely reached his shoulder. Her tiny, fairy-like form instilled a sense of protectiveness in him. She smiled gently at him. He focused forward and headed down the path leading to the outer gardens. She glided without making a sound next to him as they walked. Everything about her was restful.

As Miss Widtsoe walked, she bounced as if barely containing great amounts of energy. It seemed to drain him. "When do you plan to start the painting of the abbey?"

"As soon as I've decided which angle to use." There. He'd spoken without getting tongue-tied.

"And don't forget you promised to do my portrait, too. I

saw the portraits you did of the Duchess of Devonshire and of Mrs. Clemmons, and I love your work! You haven't forgotten you promised to do my portrait, have you?"

He recalled the elegant duchess and those moments when she'd revealed warmth underneath her frosty exterior. Perhaps he'd discover depth to Miss Widtsoe as he painted her. "I haven't forgotten."

Miss Widtsoe opened her mouth to speak but stopped when Miss Marshall asked quietly, "How do you choose which angle to use when painting something like a castle?"

"I sketch it from many different locations first."

"How did you like today's sketches?"

He glanced at the pad in his hand. "I only did one today."

She made a loose gesture to his pad. "Would it be prying to ask to see it?"

"Oh, do show it!" Miss Widtsoe, who'd been uncharacteristically quiet, exclaimed. "I'd love to see it!"

He hesitated, but surrendered the drawing. If she disliked the additional live gargoyle, it made no difference to him.

Both ladies leaned over and studied the drawing. Miss Marshall let out a long breath, her eyes alight. "It's magnificent—so detailed and perfectly proportioned. You have a unique flair. I love the gargoyle coming to life."

Miss Widtsoe shivered. "It looks like something out of a nightmare." As if fearing she had insulted him, she added hastily, "But it's very good! I can't wait to see the final product!"

Christian sifted through possible replies. "I hope your father will be pleased."

"Oh! I'm sure he will, if this is any indication! You're so talented, and it was so kind of you to accept his commission.

I'm sure you have a great many other duties to attend to, but we're *so* glad you're here!"

Christian almost cringed under the praise she heaped upon him.

Then she landed the final blow. "I'm sure it will be simply perfect."

Perfect. How he'd grown to detest that word after the way his brothers had thrown it at him in that mocking, singsong voice. *The perfectly perfect Christian.* Even years later, it still set his teeth on edge. Of course, with Cole so detached after he'd returned home from the sea, and Jared still away, and the always-aloof Grant taking up residence in London, Christian would rather bear that awful nickname if it meant having his brothers home. But no, they'd left for the war and hadn't truly returned. Then Mama died, and Father began to fade away, too. It seemed everyone he loved left eventually, beginning with Jason's tragic death—a death that would forever haunt Christian and doom him to eternal loneliness.

"Are you all right?" Miss Marshall's hushed voice pushed away his ghosts.

He snapped his head up. "Of course."

A pair of assessing eyes peered at him. In a purely defensive measure, he turned his attention to Miss Widtsoe. "What can you tell me of the history of the abbey? Its background might help me with some aspect of the painting."

With her usual exuberance, Miss Widtsoe launched into a history of the abbey, while Christian picked out relevant parts that might prove useful to add mood to his painting. Her narrative filled the time that it took to arrive at the front steps.

"Thank you, Miss Widtsoe. Until dinner." He bowed to

them both, not allowing his gaze to rest too long on either lady, and excused himself.

After pilfering a snack and dressing for dinner, Christian accompanied the earl to the drawing room where the other guests gathered for drinks and conversation.

Wearing an abundance of bows and white silk, Miss Widtsoe beamed from across the room and bobbed slightly on her toes. Miss Marshall stood between Miss Widtsoe and an older lady with the same color hair, clearly her mother. Also in fashionable white, Miss Marshall wore a simple, tasteful gown with clean lines that flattered her slender form. A green ribbon threaded through her auburn curls that were caught up in a more elaborate style than her chignon of this afternoon. She stood straight and still, focusing on every word her exuberant friend uttered, smiling with the sort of indulgent tenderness one often views in a parent when gazing on a favorite, but mischievous, child.

"Did you enjoy yourself this afternoon, son?"

Christian removed his attention from Miss Marshall and focused it on his father. "I did a sketch of the abbey."

The earl shook his head but made no comment. Since his health had declined, he'd grown more resigned, or perhaps apathetic, toward Christian's artistic pursuits, when in the past he vehemently criticized the waste of time. Perhaps the admiral making no secret about his delight over Christian accepting the commission had softened his father's disapproval.

The butler announced dinner, and Christian found himself in the uncomfortable position of escorting Miss Widtsoe to the dining room where he sat between the girl and her friend. Miss Widtsoe continued to send besotted expressions at him. He'd best think of a way of making it clear sooner rather than later that he did not return her regard. But how the deuce does a gentleman extract himself from such an uncomfortable position? If she continued to make public claims on him, he'd be labeled a cad for raising her expectations and failing to come up to scratch. Moreover, his actions might call into question her reputation. Agreeing to paint her portrait was beginning to sound like a bad idea.

He glanced at his father seated to the hostess's right. Mrs. Widtsoe was an elegant, thoughtful woman with lively eyes; perhaps her daughter would follow suit as she matured and make a good wife—for someone else, not him. Christian had resigned himself years ago to living out his life alone.

On his left, Miss Widtsoe chattered, requiring few answers from him. On his right, Miss Marshall glanced at him throughout the meal, as if she viewed him as a puzzle that must be solved. Perhaps she was trying to ascertain if he was good enough for her friend, but he couldn't shake the fear that she wouldn't rest until she exposed all his secrets.

CHAPTER THREE

Sitting at the dinner table between Christian Amesbury and an older gentleman with thick mutton chops sprinkled liberally with gray, Genevieve divided her conversation between the gentlemen. Matilda kept up a stream of diverting chatter, her usual charming wit and cheery disposition amusing everyone within earshot.

The mutton chop gentleman seated to her right launched into a tale of a recent safari. "Capital game there, Africa. Never knew if I'd be the predator or the prey, though." He chuckled.

"What was it like?" she asked out of pure courtesy.

As he rhapsodized about the land, with all its animals, her attention and, unfortunately, her vision, often strayed to the enigmatic Mr. Amesbury sitting at her left. He was a study in polite reserve and impeccable manners. He shifted, and a masculine combination of bergamot and a spice she couldn't identify wafted to her. She inhaled, letting the scent inspire images of strength and gentleness. His hands, those strong but long-fingered, artistic hands, wielded utensils as if performing a graceful ballet.

When Matilda finished relating an amusing story about her and her friends, the conversation stuttered to a halt.

After a moment, Mr. Amesbury asked Matilda in his soft, rich tones, "Do you wish to travel then, Miss Widtsoe?"

Matilda paused. "I . . ." She watched him with searching eyes, as if trying to choose an answer that would please him. "I suppose I would like to, a little, especially if my future husband wishes to do so. But I'd also be content to stay home with my children, when the time comes." She shot an almost panicked expression at Genevieve, looking for reassurance.

Genevieve nodded, smiling lest Matilda become overset about a perceived failure. Matilda's features relaxed, and she returned her focus to Mr. Amesbury to judge his reaction.

He nodded but made no reply.

Genevieve smiled politely at the mutton chop gentleman as he wound down his description. She murmured a suitable comment and turned her focus back to her friend and her intended beau. An uncomfortable silence had fallen between them.

Genevieve rushed to the rescue. "Do you have any desire to travel, Mr. Amesbury?"

He paused and cast a glance down the table at his father. "I doubt my responsibilities would allow me that luxury."

"Oh, I'm sure you can if you really wish to do so." Matilda touched his hand and then withdrew her touch lest it be viewed as inappropriate. "Surely your father can do without you while you travel. A grand tour, perhaps?" Her face clouded. "That would take a goodly amount of time, though, wouldn't it?"

"A grand tour is out of the question," he said, his deep voice filled with regret. "I cannot be away that long."

Quietly, Genevieve asked, "What is it that ties you here?"

He glanced at her, and her breath caught. She'd almost

forgotten how blue his eyes were. His lips parted, again, filling her with visions of kisses.

What was wrong with her? Her self-appointed task was to ensure he was good enough for Matilda, not fantasize about kissing him. What kind of traitorous hussy had she become?

He hesitated. "I don't dare leave with the earl's health so poor."

Interesting that he referred to his father as "the earl." "Because you oversee estate matters for him?" Genevieve asked.

Matilda cocked her head. "But you're the youngest. Doesn't one of your older brothers do that?"

He stiffened. "They are all either out of the country or otherwise indisposed," he said as if he viewed her question as mildly insulting. The comment about him being the youngest, perhaps? Why should that irritate him?

He gentled his voice. "I've been doing it for years. I know how my father wishes matters to be handled."

"So you don't travel lest the entire earldom falls into disrepair?" Genevieve gave him a teasing smile.

He blinked, and his mouth curved, his body and features relaxing. "That, and ensure the earl follows doctor's orders." A wry tone touched his voice.

She nodded. "How well I understand that. Mama doesn't always remember her medicine, and sometimes must be coaxed into taking her walks and her naps. My dear Papa doesn't keep it straight, and the servants are too easily disregarded."

Matilda giggled. "Genevieve's mama calls her 'little mother' because she can be such a hen." She smiled at Genevieve.

For some reason, that interjection rankled. Surely Mattie meant it to be kind, or funny—not condescending. Remembering her other dinner partner, lest she be considered neglectful, Genevieve turned to the mutton chop gentleman, but he'd turned his head to the lady on his other side and launched into a story about a herd of wildebeests that had stampeded.

She returned her focus onto Mr. Amesbury. He offered well thought out answers to Matilda's queries, even posing a few questions of his own. Nothing in his manner gave her cause to disapprove of a match between him and her friend; there was no reason why she should continue to ask him questions to reveal his character. Yet he fascinated her, and she longed to find out more. Still, she held her tongue so as not to intrude on Mattie's dialogue with him.

Unfortunately, her friend continued to rain adoring expressions upon Mr. Amesbury, who grew progressively stiffer and quieter throughout dinner. Was he uncomfortable with Matilda's openness, or did he fail to return her affections?

Oh, dear. If he didn't return her feelings, Mattie would be crushed. True, she'd developed a "grand passion" for any number of other gentlemen, but if this were real love, she would not so easily recover. Perhaps Genevieve could help Mr. Amesbury see Matilda Widtsoe as a fine young lady with desirable qualities.

Dinner ended, and the ladies left the men to their brandy and snuff. As she trailed out the door, last in line, Genevieve paused and glanced over her shoulder. Christian Amesbury had declined snuff and picked up his half-full wineglass from dinner rather than accept port. He shunned common male vices. How refreshing.

Another pair of eyes caught her attention. Lord Wickburgh stared at her, too long and hard to be proper.

Genevieve hurried out, plotting how she could help matters

between Matilda and her chosen love. As she followed the group of ladies to the drawing room, she turned over matchmaking possibilities. Not being privy to planned activities over the next few days, she couldn't very well arrange romantic encounters between Matilda and Mr. Amesbury. Perhaps the next time she had the opportunity to converse, Genevieve would mention Mattie's many accomplishments, and how kind she was and what a good mother she'd make. Would that appeal to a fine gentlemen like Mr. Amesbury?

She reviewed his qualities. Responsible, judging by the way he managed his father's vast estate. Devoted, since he cared so much for his father. Respectful and thoughtful, by the way he spoke after giving careful thought. Artistic, obviously. Cautious, if he had not yet made up his mind about Matilda. And a bit sensitive that he was the youngest, which implied he'd been mercilessly teased by his older brothers, or perhaps snubbed by a lady of his choice who sought a marriage with an heir. If that were so, surely the love of a good woman would heal his wounded heart. Matilda's love, of course.

Perhaps those traits which he possessed were those he desired in a bride. Genevieve would simply have to ensure those sides of Matilda's personality surfaced in his presence. Of course, he was quiet and reserved when compared to Matilda's enthusiasm and zeal for life, but that simply made them complementary and would balance them out well.

On the way to the drawing room, Matilda appeared at her side. "What are you doing?" she said *sotto voce*. "Trying to make me look bad?"

Halting, Genevieve stared. "What?"

Her eyes shining with unshed tears and her lower lip

quivering, Matilda tugged Genevieve's arm to draw her away from the others. "You kept asking him all kinds of questions, as if flaunting it in my face that I had been talking about myself and my friends when I should have asked about him."

If Matilda had struck her, Genevieve would not have been as surprised. "Mattie, how can you say such a thing? I was only trying to help keep the conversation going for your sake. For a moment, you both seemed uncomfortable."

Matilda blinked but still looked uncertain. "Then you meant nothing else by it?"

"Well, I admit I was trying to learn more about him so as to make a better determination of his character. I must satisfy myself that he's good enough for you. A handsome face and ancient family lineage are not enough to ensure a happy marriage, and I want you to be happy."

Pink colored Matilda's pretty, round cheeks and she chewed her lower lip. "Oh."

"Did I do something wrong?" Genevieve touched her arm and peered carefully into Matilda's eyes. Where Christian Amesbury's eyes were the crystal blue of a cloudless winter sky, Matilda's reminded Genevieve of a deep mountain lake.

Matilda let out a half laugh, half sound of distress. "No, Jenny, you've done nothing wrong. Forgive me. I'm afraid I questioned your motives and became a bit jealous. I shouldn't have."

"Jealous? Whatever for? You know I'd never come between you and your happiness."

Matilda's eyes grew shiny again. "Oh, I know, but you're so stunning. Most of the men in the room couldn't keep their eyes off you tonight. I'd forgotten how much they always do that."

"What a lot of poppycock! You're a perfect china doll. You

and Mr. Amesbury would have beautiful children, with blue eyes and golden hair."

Fishing her handkerchief out of her reticule, Matilda dabbed at her nose. "You don't know what it's like going to balls with you, watching everyone stare at you and fawn all over themselves to talk to you."

"Stop exaggerating. You are never at a loss for partners, and you know it. My entire reason for being here is to help you secure the proposal you desire. So, we need to have a plan."

Matilda's face lightened, and she put away her handkerchief. They entered the drawing room painted to appear made of sand-colored bricks, and with murals of white-clad Egyptians wearing black eye paint and posed with their arms bent at the elbows, such as one would expect to see in a pyramid.

Matilda made a dismissive wave at the decorating style. "Father's latest passion is Egypt . . . stuff." She led Genevieve to a settee carved curiously to resemble an Egyptian sarcophagus. "Now, then. What do you suggest?"

They sat with their heads together, discussing ways to feature Matilda's accomplishments and personality to her full advantage. To her credit, Matilda did an admirable job of keeping her voice down despite her energy while Genevieve made every helpful suggestion that came to her.

"What are you two whispering and giggling about?" Mrs. Widtsoe approached.

They straightened. As Matilda blushed, Genevieve said, "We were speculating on what activity you have planned for this evening and what our role should be."

Matilda's mother smiled as if she knew the truth. "When

the men arrive, I thought a game of charades would be in order."

"How delightful," Genevieve said. "Perhaps until then Matilda might favor us with a few pieces on the pianoforte so that the gentlemen might enjoy it as they arrive." She shot a meaningful look at Matilda.

"Oh!" Her friend sprang up, honey curls bobbing. "Yes, of course. You're so clever, Jenny." She went immediately to the pianoforte in the corner, surrounded by black carved Egyptian cats, and began a sonata.

With the setting sun bathing Matilda in golden light, filtered by sheer curtains over the windows, and a dreamy smile, she created a picture of such beauty that Mr. Amesbury would be a fool not to appreciate the sight. Genevieve vowed to dedicate herself to showing Mr. Amesbury all the many ways her friend deserved his consideration and love.

CHAPTER FOUR

When Christian followed the gentlemen from the dining room into the drawing room, he glanced at his father. The earl moved slowly, his shoulders rounded.

Christian spoke softly so as not to be overheard. "Shall I take you to your room, Father?"

"No need. I'm well enough."

"You look tired. We traveled all day; there's no shame in wishing to rest after such—"

"Yes, well, I came to spend time with friends, not hibernate in my room like an old bear."

Christian said nothing further, but he would get more insistent if the earl appeared to be overtaxing himself. Still, the light in his eyes was an improvement over the apathy of most of the past year. Perhaps this house party would revive him.

The sweet chords of piano music beckoned to Christian as someone played with admirable passion and sensitivity. He entered the drawing room decorated to reveal a taste for Egyptian decor. He admired the skill with which the colors had been blended and noted the technique used to paint realistic-looking clay bricks. The Egyptian people, larger than life-size, were a bit stark but a fair imitation of their original inspiration.

Father wore a half smile. "Egypt seems to be all the rage these days."

The last rays of evening sunlight slanted in through the windows and cast a glow on Miss Widtsoe, burnishing her gold curls and making her white gown luminescent. She obviously held a great deal of emotions under questionable restraint. Seeing her in the unusual setting, bathed in sunlight, Christian paused, considering her portrait. He would have her turned sideways on the bench, not playing, but looking as if she had just completed a piece and was about to stand to receive her applause. It would reveal her talent for music and show her figure to full advantage. He'd give her face an angelic glow. Yes, that should please her and her parents.

Off to one side, watching Miss Widtsoe with an expression of almost maternal pride, stood Miss Genevieve Marshall. She exuded an aura of innocence and serenity as well as a restraint that her friend lacked. Or perhaps she were simply more mature—not in age but in sensibility. Her auburn hair lit by sunlight created a dazzling contrast to her peaceful expression. Delicate as a pixie, she belonged in a garden surrounded by flowers and waterfalls. Yes, that's how he'd paint her, but only if he were commissioned to do so—it would be inappropriate to paint her without permission.

"Pretty girls," the earl murmured. "Have you chosen a favorite or do you want them both?"

Christian's face flashed hot. "No."

"No matter. Plenty of options here, including the maids." He winked.

Christian drifted to an empty space near a group of men who were still engrossed in a discussion over the declining health of the king and whether the Prince Regent would become less dissipated once he took the throne.

Nearby, three young ladies whose names he couldn't remember sat discussing something about bonnets with Italian flowers, whatever those were. The piano music blended with snatches of conversation that swelled and ebbed around him like an ocean current. Miss Marshall drifted to the nearby group of girls, joining in the conversation and bringing it around to music.

She glanced over her shoulder at him but returned her gaze to the group. "Doesn't Miss Widtsoe play beautifully?"

The girls all murmured their agreement.

"She sings like an angel as well," she added. "Perhaps someone should play for her so she can entertain us."

"Do you play, Miss Marshall?" asked one of the girls.

"Oh, not well enough to accompany a singer of Miss Widtsoe's talent."

"Mr. Amesbury plays, don't you?" someone said.

His face flushed at being the object of so many pairs of eyes. "Er, yes."

Miss Marshall clasped her hands together. "Oh, that's perfect."

He winced. There was that word. He needed to build up an immunity to that word.

"You could play, and she could sing. You will, won't you? Please?"

The earnest pleading in Miss Marshall's big brown eyes, not to mention her exquisite face, propelled him into action. He stood. "If that is your wish."

She smiled, and he almost took a step back from the sheer

brilliance. A dark corner of his soul seemed cleaner somehow, less dark, from that single blast of pristine joy.

As Miss Widtsoe ended the piece she'd been performing, Miss Marshall said, "Matilda, Mr. Amesbury has agreed to accompany you as you sing. Do say you will."

Miss Widtsoe's eyes widened, and her tooth-revealing smile appeared. "Oh, I'd be happy to. Do you know 'The Soldier's Adieu'?"

He nodded and took a seat at the piano bench. "Key of B-flat work for you?"

"It's within my range." She smiled brightly before turning her attention to humming scales, presumably to warm up her voice.

Christian glanced at Genevieve Marshall, but she'd already taken a seat nearby. She sat as if anticipating her favorite opera rather than an informal and impromptu performance in a room full of people more absorbed in conversation than music.

He played an introduction as Miss Widtsoe glanced over her shoulder at him, adoration clear in her eyes. How the deuce was he to make it clear he didn't return her affections? Accompanying her as she sang certainly wasn't helping his cause. His gaze strayed to Miss Marshall again. She'd set him up, the little matchmaker. He'd have to be wary of her, too. As he reached the vocal beginning, he nodded to Miss Widtsoe. She began to sing and did, indeed, have a lovely voice. He followed her carefully to give her full advantage.

He glanced about the drawing room. More and more eyes turned their way. The Widtsoes beamed in approval—hopefully of their daughter, not at him paired with her. Another young man with brown curls—Sir Reginald, if he remembered correctly—stared at Miss Widtsoe wearing a hopelessly besotted expression. Hmm. Perhaps he could be an ally in Christian's attempt to step out of Miss Widtsoe's favor.

Lord Wickburgh caught his attention. The viscount, whom he'd only met today, stared in fascination as well, but not at Miss Widtsoe. No, his whole being focused on Miss Marshall. Rather than the interest of a prospective suitor, or the adoration of a lover, he watched her like a hunter sizing up prey and calculating the appropriate trap. A chill ran down Christian's spine, and he played a wrong note but covered it up with a triplet that brought the melody back in correctly.

The song came to a close, and Miss Widtsoe trilled beautifully, amid applause. She turned and smiled. "I had no idea you played so beautifully. Do you know any piano duets? Do you know Mozart's 'The Sonata for Two Pianos'? Or 'Fantasy in F Minor' by Schubert?"

Say no. Say no. He glanced at Miss Marshall. A mistake. She smiled as if he'd just handed her a longed-for gift. "I . . . do know them both." He winced. Stupid! Playing duets with Miss Widtsoe would only raise her expectations. But he could not disappoint Miss Marshall. Why he felt that way, he couldn't begin to guess.

"Let's do the Mozart," she suggested.

He scooted over on the bench and made room for Miss Widtsoe. She sat so close that their legs almost touched. His face heated. But he was already committed, for the duet, at least.

Letting her set the pace, he followed her. As the duet progressed at a satisfactory rate, his attention returned to Miss Marshall. Lord Wickburgh bowed to her. Mrs. Widtsoe gestured as if to make introductions. Miss Marshall looked up at the lord, her eyes wide and her smile forced.

Christian missed a note. "Sorry," he murmured to his duet partner.

Lord Wickburgh eyed Miss Marshall as he spoke to her, and he fingered his cane. Miss Marshall's glances became more furtive, her hands fidgeting in clear distress. How could Christian rescue her? He gritted his teeth. It wasn't his place. But he longed to intervene.

They finished the duet, and Christian glanced at his partner. "I believe your friend is in need of company."

Miss Widtsoe blinked, hurt and confusion in her eyes. He nodded his head meaningfully at Miss Marshall and Lord Wickburgh. She followed his direction.

"Oh. Oh!" She leaped to her feet and all but rushed to Miss Marshall's side.

Christian sauntered to the group as if out for a stroll when his muscles raged at him to race to Miss Marshall's rescue. "Good evening," he said to one and all.

Christian took a closer look at the viscount. When they'd first been introduced, Christian had only made a cursory glance at the slender, elegant older gentleman with a taste for fashion and an air of cold superiority worn by most peers. Now, a deeper chill revealed itself. The lord glanced at Christian dismissively, as adults often do to children, and returned his focus on Genevieve. He looked her over from head to toe, but instead of with appreciation for a fine piece of art, or even a leer for a desirable woman, something akin to puzzlement crossed his expression as if unable to determine what he was doing speaking to a girl half his age.

"Suffolk?" he said as if repeating something Miss Marshall had said. "Yes, I have land in Suffolk, among other places. I don't spend a great deal of time there, more's the pity. I divide most of my time between my county seat and London." He smiled coolly. "I assume you've been to London for the Season, bowed to the queen and all that?"

"Er, no, my lord," she said in subdued tones. "I've been to London—once—but not for the Season, and I've never taken my bows to the queen."

Miss Widtsoe moistened her lips and wound her arm through Miss Marshall's. "Miss Marshall and I have only been 'out' a few years, you see, my lord, so even if she had been to London for the Season, it is unlikely her path would have crossed with such a mature lord as yourself."

Christian almost smiled. *Touché.* A clever way to remind the man he was too old for Miss Marshall.

Lord Wickburgh's eyes narrowed. "*Our* paths have crossed, child, you recall."

"Well, yes," returned Miss Widtsoe, practically quailing under his unnerving stare, "but only because you know my father."

Miss Marshall dropped a hasty curtsy. "If you will excuse us, my lord, I believe—"

He brought up his cane, blocking her path. "Stay." He tried to soften his sharp command with a smile. "I beg you."

Christian's hackles rose. "Actually, I was just coming to ask Miss Widtsoe and Miss Marshall their opinion on something. If I may show you both what I have in mind, I'd welcome your input."

He nodded a farewell to Lord Wickburgh and held out an arm to the ladies. They each took an arm, with expressions of gratitude and relief as he led them to a far corner of the room.

"Thank you," Miss Marshall said quietly.

"What did you wish to discuss?" Miss Widtsoe asked. She practically batted her eyelashes at him.

Christian faltered. Surely Miss Widtsoe knew he'd contrived that statement as an excuse to extract Miss Marshall from the gentleman's unwelcome attention. Perhaps she intended to ensure the ruse appeared believable.

He scrambled for something to say. As inspiration hit, he gestured to the pianoforte. "I thought perhaps I could paint you at the piano." He led her to the instrument. "Sit on the bench as if you are playing. Good. Now, act as if you have completed and are turning to receive your applause. Perfect. Hold that pose. Miss Marshall, if you would be so kind." With her arm still on his, he stepped back to give her a look at the setting.

Miss Marshall glanced over her shoulder, probably at Lord Wickburgh. She drew a breath before turning her full attention to her friend at the pianoforte. She took a moment to consider before nodding. "That's lovely. The walls painted in those subdued colors to imitate brick, and the light coming in through the windows, gives her an excellent backdrop. Matilda, you take a look."

The ladies traded places. Miss Marshall sat surrounded by a halo of soft lighting, her mouth curved in an affectionate smile as she watched her friend. The setting sun cast fiery burgundy lights in her hair in an array of colors it would take Christian days to mix and blend to get just right. If he were to paint Genevieve Marshall, he'd move the carved black cats out of the way, drape a sheer curtain behind the piano, and add a few vases of flowers and perhaps potted plants to invite the garden inside, accenting her fairy-like quality.

"I like it," Miss Widtsoe announced. "It would show off my talent for music, and I think the Egyptian influence adds a touch of the exotic, don't you think?" She beamed.

The vision of Miss Marshall filled his senses so completely that he barely managed to nod in acknowledgement.

"How soon can we start?" Miss Widtsoe asked.

He faltered, trying to remember what she wanted to start and scrambled for a reply. "Perhaps tomorrow afternoon, to catch the best light."

"Perfect!"

She enthused about the portrait, but his attention returned to Miss Marshall, whose focus shifted to something behind him. Her peaceful countenance clouded. He glanced back. Lord Wickburgh stared at her. Miss Marshall arose and joined Miss Widtsoe and him.

"Stay close," Christian said softly to Miss Marshall. "He'll get the message." If not, Christian would have to have words with Lord Wickburgh about leaving the lady alone.

She nodded. "Thank you."

Miss Widtsoe glanced between them with a puzzled frown tugging at her brows. "Jenny?"

She offered a brave smile that failed to touch her eyes. "Don't mind me."

Keeping his posture casual and his steps unhurried, Christian led both ladies toward Miss Marshall's parents, who stood conversing with another couple. "I don't believe I've had the opportunity to meet your parents. Would you do me the honor of introducing me?"

"It would be my pleasure." She glanced at him, her smile warming and reaching her eyes.

"Oh, the Marshalls are just wonderful people!" Miss Widtsoe beamed at Christian. "Did you know her father was a sea captain during the war? Why, his ship was instrumental in the victory at Trafalgar. That makes him rather a war hero, doesn't it?"

The Marshalls turned at their approach, and Christian greeted them as Miss Marshall made the introductions to the distinguished gentleman and his diminutive wife, an older but still attraction version of Genevieve. Christian made a casual scan of the room, but Lord Wickburgh stood engaged in conversation with another gentleman and no longer focused on Miss Marshall.

The hostess called to the group and began a game of charades. Throughout the evening, Christian covertly observed Lord Wickburgh, but the older man made no further attempt to approach Miss Marshall. Unfortunately, the more Christian tried to keep his attention off of the beautiful lady, the more he stared.

As the games ended, guests broke off into smaller groups, chatting and laughing. Others retired for the evening, including his father, to Christian's relief. When Genevieve Marshall left with her parents, he relaxed; she'd be safe from Lord Wickburgh in their company. And Christian would be spared the agony of trying not to look at her.

Christian bowed to the host and hostess. "Good night, sir, ma'am."

Miss Widtsoe appeared at her parents' side and gazed up at him. "So soon, Mr. Amesbury?"

"I wish to be well rested for the hunt tomorrow." He bowed and turned to leave, but her voice stopped him.

"Oh, of course. Do you enjoy hunting, then?"

"I do." He added, "Although what I enjoy most about it is a good bruising ride through the countryside."

"My friend Jenny does, as well. I believe I heard you like the steeple chase?"

"Very much. Well, good night." He said the last part to all three of them.

"Good night." She smiled so brightly, so hopefully, that he fled like a frightened lad.

CHAPTER FIVE

E arly the following morning, Genevieve ducked to avoid a low hanging limb and tapped her horse with the riding crop to urge him forward. She didn't dare fall behind the hunting party and give the men a reason to suggest she return home to sit with the ladies sewing while the men had all the fun. She enjoyed sewing on occasion, but riding sidesaddle at breakneck speed over rugged terrain filled her with exhilaration few other activities provided.

The woods thinned, and the group charged down a hillside following the barking, howling dogs. She galloped with the hunting party, laughing for sheer joy as the wind sang in her ears, and her body moved in harmony with the horse's stride. Fresh, woodsy scents filled her lungs, reminding her of rides with her father back home.

Christian Amesbury glanced back at her again. Whether he checked on her so often out of simple chivalric duty since she was the only woman in the group, or out of belief that she couldn't handle herself, she did not know. Each time he did, a warm flush raced down her limbs. The other men gave their full attention to the hunt, except Papa, who occasionally shared a grin with her.

As dogs barked, tack jingled, horses whinnied, and hooves pounded, the party raced along a ravine and then up the other side, winding between trees and scrub. The dogs' barking and howling reached a crescendo, and then all at once, they lost their prey. No amount of sniffing and false starts found the scent. Their quarry vanished. Some of the men voiced their displeasure, but many shrugged and said it was all part of the game.

Lord Wickburgh scowled as if the host had failed in his duty, but Genevieve refused to let him dim her pleasure.

Christian Amesbury wheeled around, grinning and rosy-cheeked from the chill morning air. "Race you back?" he called out to the nearest few riders.

Though not specifically included, his challenge was general enough that Genevieve joined in. They galloped, leaping over fallen trees and stumps, crashing through brush, and dodging rock formations that leaped in their path. As they reached the perimeter of the abbey's gardens, Mr. Amesbury's stallion pulled ahead. His nearest two contenders leaned over their horses' necks and made a valiant effort, but Mr. Amesbury reached the paddock first. Genevieve arrived only seconds behind them.

The men laughed and congratulated each other on a fine run. Genevieve walked her horse around the perimeter to cool him before returning to the stable doors.

"May I assist you in dismounting?" Lord Wickburgh appeared next to her horse. Classically handsome and elegant in his red riding coat, the older man smiled and extended a hand. But a chill in his gaze cooled her joy of the ride.

"Er, my father usually helps me," she said lamely, looking around for Papa.

She found him slapping Mr. Amesbury on the back and laughing with the men who'd encircled the impromptu race's winner. He seemed unaware of her plight.

"It's no inconvenience to me, Miss Marshall," Lord Wickburgh said.

Since there seemed no graceful way to refuse, she accepted his aid. His hands stayed longer than necessary on her waist. She stepped back and held onto her riding crop with both hands to put some distance between them.

His smooth voice reminded her of melted glass in a glassblower's shop. "Your riding habit is beautiful. It suits you."

"Thank you," she said breathlessly, looking down at her hands to avoid his chilling stare.

"And you ride uncommonly well. I was surprised you chose to accompany a hunt—surprised your father allows you to do something so dangerous."

"He and I often enjoy vigorous rides together." She gathered the train of her riding habit and laid it over her left arm. "If you will please excuse me, my lord." She bobbed a quick curtsy and strode toward the house.

Her father caught up to her. "Jolly good morning, eh?"

She hushed her disquiet and found a smile to give him. "Perfect weather for a ride."

"That Amesbury fellow seems to have caught your eye, Jenny."

"Oh, no, he is not for me. Matilda has formed an attachment to him, and I am only trying to take measure of his character."

"Uh-huh." His disbelief rang clear.

"Truly, Papa. I would never encourage the attention of a gentleman that a friend—"

"I know, daughter. I am not questioning your intentions. But he is young, handsome, the son of an earl . . ."

"He is gallant. And gentle. And intelligent." She might have listed at least a dozen more qualities she'd observed in him but stopped, lest her father misunderstand her praise. "I am persuaded that he will be an excellent match for Matilda."

"Yes, he will be an excellent match for any young lady."

An uncomfortable prickling between her shoulder blades had her glancing over her shoulder. Lord Wickburgh stared after her. He nodded before turning away.

"Papa, what do you know of Lord Wickburgh?"

"Very little except that he is a viscount, a man of fashion and considerable wealth and influence. He has buried two wives."

"Oh, poor man. He must be lonely." That must have been it. She'd misunderstood him. What she'd perceived as a cold sort of ruthlessness must have been pain and loneliness.

"I am sure." Her father's face clouded, and he cast a glance up at the window where he shared a bedroom with Mama during the house party. Did he worry that he faced losing Mama?

Genevieve linked her arm with his. "Mama has been ever so much stronger lately. Why, the trip didn't seem to tire her much at all."

"Yes, I believe you are right."

"Don't you worry about her. Between you and me, we will make sure Mama lives a long and healthy life."

Papa kissed her temple, and they strolled into the house. After a quick wash and changing out of her riding habit into a morning gown, Genevieve joined the ladies in the back parlor where they sat gossiping and sewing. Matilda sat at the pianoforte, practicing a particularly difficult piece, a Haydn, if she were correct. Genevieve sat next to her, careful not to jostle her on the bench. She followed along and turned the page at the correct time. Matilda stumbled over a particularly grueling passage.

"E flat," Genevieve murmured.

"I know," Matilda snapped. She stopped. Sighed. "Forgive me, Jenny. I'm trying to get this right so I can play it tonight for Christian. I want him to like me."

Genevieve put her hand on Matilda's back. "I don't think his good opinion of you will change if you fail to learn this new piece by this eve."

"I know, but I just wish . . ." She turned sad eyes upon Genevieve. "I confess, I am starting to doubt that he returns my regard. He's very kind, but doesn't appear to feel a grand passion for me." She returned to her music and worked at the passage until she got it right.

"You are a lovely and accomplished young lady," Genevieve murmured. "And he does seem to admire you on some level. Perhaps when he draws your portrait, you will have better opportunity to become acquainted."

"Do you think he favors blue?"

"I wouldn't know. Why?"

"He wears it a lot. I thought if perhaps I wore blue when he painted my portrait . . ."

"Blue is lovely on you. It brings out your eyes."

Matilda's usual buoyancy returned to her expression. "I have a new sarcenet evening gown of Cambridge blue with a pale blue parted overskirt. Perhaps I should wear that for my sitting?"

"I'm sure it's beautiful on you. And even better if he favors the color."

"What else might I do to win his regard?"

"Well, having not made a match of my own, I can hardly say, but Mama says a lady should always ask a gentleman questions about himself and encourage him to speak, while speaking very little about herself."

"But he doesn't say much when I do that."

"Perhaps you aren't asking the right questions. Have you asked him what his interests are?"

"Oh, yes. He's mad for the steeple chase, and he boxes and fences. Almost a Corinthian, isn't he? And, well, aside from art and music, I don't know much else about his interests."

"Try to word the questions so they can't be answered with a simple yes or no."

A few gentlemen drifted in, including the Earl of Tarrington, but not Mr. Amesbury. The ladies continued chatting while the gentlemen filled in around them.

"Where do you think he is?" Matilda asked.

Genevieve didn't have to ask which "he" Matilda meant. "Out sketching the abbey?"

Matilda let out a breath of glee. "I do believe I wish to go for a bit of a ramble."

"I do, as well." Genevieve returned her smile.

They took up hats and gloves, and changed into half boots for walking. Genevieve grabbed a parasol to protect her skin from the sun's burning rays. After leaving behind the manicured gardens, they climbed nearby hills, looking for a place where Mr. Amesbury might have chosen to draw the abbey. They were both tired and almost willing to admit defeat and return to the house when Matilda let out a gasp.

"Oh! There he is!"

Bareheaded amid a stand of poplars at the top of a hill, Mr. Amesbury sat as still as a painting. The dappled light shone on his golden head and played with the blue of his frock coat.

Matilda made a straight course for him, but Genevieve pulled her back. "We must appear to be out for a stroll, Mattie, not hunting him."

Her friend made a sigh of exasperation but slowed her steps as they followed the rocky, narrow path carved into the side of the hill. "You're right, of course. Did you know we're going to have a ball tonight? After dinner, we'll roll up the carpets and dance. Mama even arranged to have some musicians play for us. Won't that be lovely? And Mama agreed that we can even waltz."

"Oh, dear. I never learned to waltz."

"No? Pity. I learned with a dance master Papa hired this winter. I can't wait to waltz with Christian," Mattie said dreamily.

"Would you show me how?"

"Well, it would be difficult without a partner, but if you know the basic steps, you ought to be able to follow when you do have a partner." She cast a longing glance at Mr. Amesbury. "Shall we do it now?"

"Oh, no, let's not waste a moment of your time with him," Genevieve said. She looked back at where he sat, but he remained motionless, as if he had not yet seen them.

"It will only take a moment to teach you the basics." Mattie stood in front of her so Genevieve could follow her. "It's narrow here, and rocky, so watch your step. Begin with your right foot, taking a step back. One. Then bring your left through and to the left side. Two. Then bring your right foot to your left and switch your weight onto it. Three. That's the first half. Then you begin again, but this time stepping forward with your left."

Genevieve followed, her movements clumsy at first but then catching on. Matilda repeated with Genevieve following.

After several times, Matilda's steps began to rotate slightly. "Then start to turn just a little. One, two, three. One, two, three. Ah!" She let out a sharp cry and went down, pitching sideways over the edge of the hill.

Genevieve's breath strangled. "Mattie!" she gasped. She charged after her friend.

Matilda tumbled a few times before coming to a stop as the hill leveled off. She lay still. Stumbling and sliding in her haste to reach her friend, Genevieve rushed to her.

"Matilda?" She slid to her knees next to her friend's motionless form.

Matilda rolled over. "I'm all right. I think."

Genevieve almost sobbed in relief. She helped raise her to a sitting position. "Does it hurt anywhere?"

Heavy footsteps pounded to them. "Miss Widtsoe? Are you injured?" Christian Amesbury took long, commanding strides to reach them. Concern carved itself into his features, and his whole focus fixed upon Matilda.

With her face red, Matilda hurried to straighten her skirts to cover her legs. "I don't think so." She looked down, but the shimmer of moisture on her eyes gave away her distress.

"Do you wish to rest here a moment before you try to stand?" Genevieve asked.

Biting her lip, Matilda nodded.

Mr. Amesbury crouched next to them. "Are you sure you're unharmed?" he asked gently.

Her eyes brimming with tears, Matilda nodded jerkily, not in pain but in embarrassment. Poor thing. And she'd been trying so hard to impress him, not be clumsy. And it was Genevieve's fault it had happened.

Mr. Amesbury's mouth pressed into a compassionate wince. He turned his attention to Genevieve. "Did you fall, too?"

"No. I ran after her."

Matilda drew a shivering breath and pushed herself to a stand. Genevieve helped her, and Mr. Amesbury held his hands out as if to steady her should she need his strength. Matilda's face tightened as she took a step.

"Is your foot hurt?" Genevieve asked.

"My ankle is a bit sore. I must have twisted it. But I can walk."

Genevieve kept pace with Matilda as she marshaled her way down the hill, forgoing the meandering path up the hill, and taking the shortest distance back to the abbey. With each step, her face twisted in progressively more intense pain.

"Lean on my arm," Mr. Amesbury said.

Her face redder still and tears shining in her eyes, Matilda obliged, but her breath grew more and more labored.

"Perhaps you should rest," Genevieve suggested.

Matilda shook her head and pushed on.

Finally, Mr. Amesbury stopped. "You are aggravating your injury." His handsome face took on an earnest expression. "I'll go for help. Perhaps there is a cart . . ."

"Oh, dear. I'm so embarrassed." Matilda put a hand over her eyes.

"This is the first time I've seen you anything but jubilant." Looking truly concerned, Mr. Amesbury led her to a boulder and seated her upon it. He crouched next to her and took her hand. Very gently, he asked, "How can I help you? What do you wish me to do?"

The very core of Genevieve's being melted at his compassion, his gentleness, his gallantry. Matilda had found the perfect gentleman. And he appeared—finally—to show true concern, perhaps even affection, for Matilda. Perhaps he held her in high esteem all along but was too reserved to show it.

Genevieve should have been ecstatic at this encouraging step in the right direction. Instead, the opposite emotion reared its ugly head. Envy. Envy that such a desirable gentleman looked at Matilda. Envy that no one had ever behaved in such a way toward Genevieve. Envy that Matilda would probably marry Christian soon, and Genevieve would still be alone, left to compare every man she met to him, and who, naturally, would fall woefully short.

Oh, heaven help her, but the only man who'd ever turned her head was the love of Matilda's life. Genevieve was turning into a selfish beast.

CHAPTER SIX

C hristian studied the young woman in front of him. Were her tears a result of humiliation or pain or some other heartbreak he could not discern? Regardless, her distress spurred him to action. The fastest way to get her help would be to carry her, but to walk into the abbey carrying a young lady might throw her virtue into question. And such actions might give her the wrong idea about his feelings for her. He hated to leave them alone, but they had, after all, walked there on their own without escort.

"I'm so sorry about the inconvenience," Miss Widtsoe said softly. "It's fortunate that you came along when you did. I don't know how I'd manage, else."

He gestured to Miss Marshall. "Your devoted friend would have assisted you."

"Yes, I've never had a truer friend!" She was already starting to lapse back into her habit of saying everything with an exclamation point at the end.

"I'll fetch a cart and return as soon as possible." Christian raced to the stable and enlisted the aid of a stable hand, who found a dog cart. They hitched a pony to it, and Christian led the stable hand back to the ladies waiting where he'd left them.

Miss Marshall's eyes glowed as he arrived. He had the urge to square his shoulders and draw himself to his full height. Instead, he turned his attention to the injured lady. As the stable hand got the cart as close as possible, Christian helped Miss Widtsoe into the back of the cart. He handed in Miss Marshall, and squeezed in next to her.

Her nearness sent shivers of awareness through him, and he searched for a safe topic. "What happened that caused your fall?"

"Oh, it was the silliest thing." Miss Widtsoe waved her hands in the air. "Genevieve told me she didn't know how to waltz so I was showing her the basic step, but I forgot I was on such a narrow path and lost my footing."

Christian glanced at Miss Marshall, who winced as if she blamed herself for Miss Widtsoe's fall.

"It was foolish, I know," Miss Widtsoe continued, drawing his thoughts. "But I wanted ever so much for my dear friend to know how to waltz."

He quirked a smile. "Perhaps in the future you ought to restrict dancing lessons to a larger, flatter area."

Genevieve Marshall let out a small gasp. "Oh, no, Mattie! I hope your ankle is strong enough to dance tonight."

"Ohh," Miss Widtsoe practically wailed. "How can I dance on it now?"

Miss Marshall's expression turned earnest. "We'll try every remedy we know. Perhaps if you rest it all day and we wrap it?"

"I suppose." Disappointment clouded Miss Widtsoe's features.

"We'll think of something, Mattie," Miss Marshall promised.

They reached the outer gardens, circled around to the back, skirted a ha-ha separating a field where sheep grazed from the back lawn, and headed to a portico.

Christian glanced at the young lady next to him. Her bonnet hid her face from him. Still, the quality of her breathing sent increasingly wild little fingers of awareness over him. She was not only one of the more beautiful ladies he'd ever seen, there was something about her, a quality of elegance and genuine kindness. His father would say something about still waters running deep.

She was the perfect opposite of Miss Widtsoe. Where one was exuberant, the other was restrained, not because she didn't have strong emotions, but she held them in check, as if she only brought them out for special moments. One chattered freely with almost childlike charm, the other spoke after careful consideration, weighing each word to assure it contained the exact meaning to deliver her thoughts. And though Miss Widtsoe seemed cheerful and sweet, there were moments when he suspected her of being childishly self-absorbed. Yet Genevieve Marshall's unselfishness, the way she cared for others, and sought to show her friend in the best possible light, while remaining quietly on the sidelines, won his respect.

Admirably—and regrettably—the young ladies were loyal friends. If he spurned Miss Widtsoe's affection, he certainly could not pursue her friend. Not that he would, regardless of how tempting.

When they'd gotten the cart as close to the house as possible, Christian offered his arm. As before, the strain of practically hopping on one foot showed in Miss Widtsoe's face before they'd gotten very far. His duty as a gentleman was clear. He almost heaved a sigh.

"Miss Widtsoe, please allow me to carry you the rest of the way home. We'll go in a side entrance so you are spared further embarrassment." With luck, no one would see them.

She chewed her lip and then nodded. Glancing up at him from underneath her lashes, her expression changed from discomfort to coyness. "You're so very chivalrous to offer, sir."

Christian almost groaned. Wonderful. Now she'd misread his offer, too, and would view his carrying her as some sort of romantic gesture. Could it get more twisted?

He slid his arms underneath Miss Widtsoe's legs and behind her back and lifted her. She snuggled against him and placed her arms around his shoulders. There was nothing for it. He started walking, Miss Marshall keeping up with him.

"Go to the side entrance," Miss Widtsoe suggested. "No one should be in the library now, not on such a fine day."

Something shadowed Miss Marshall's eyes. Did she fear for her friend's reputation? Christian had built a reputation for being an upstanding gentleman. Miss Widtsoe's behavior was, to his knowledge, exemplary. Miss Marshall was present. And surely the circumstances necessitated some flexibility. Still, had he made a mistake in carrying the girl inside? But, dash it all, what else was he to do?

Miss Marshall glanced up at him. "Are you getting tired?"

He glanced at her as a wry grin tugged his mouth. "Are you questioning my manliness?"

"Of course she isn't!" Miss Widtsoe interjected. "She's just being the little mother again and taking care of everyone."

In truth, his arms warmed uncomfortably. "I can get to the house, never fear."

Miss Marshall glanced up at him again. Sadness shadowed

her soft eyes. Surely she wasn't so upset about her friend being unable to dance? "I'll make sure the room is empty." She strode ahead.

He tried not to admire the grace of her walk nor the way her dress accentuated her slender curves as the wind flattened the fabric against her.

"Don't you just love Genevieve?" Miss Widtsoe chirped. "She is the dearest thing! I hope she finds a man to marry— someone who deserves her. But if she doesn't, maybe she'll come live with me and help me raise my family. That would be sublime!"

"I'm sure she won't have any trouble finding a gentleman who will want to marry her. Someone worthy of her might be more difficult to find, but she isn't meant to live as a spinster."

"I'm sure you're right!" she gushed.

Had he spoken his thoughts aloud?

"So," Miss Widtsoe said, "you come from a large family. Do you hope to have a lot of children when the time comes?"

"I haven't really thought about it."

"Oh." She paused. "If you could live anywhere, where would it be?"

He paused. "I like Bath."

"Anywhere?" she emphasized.

He thought it over. "Perhaps the seashore. I've always wanted to visit Italy, to paint there, but I'm not certain I'd want to live there. We have some property up in Scotland. Beautiful country. Perhaps there. Why do you ask?"

Miss Marshall opened a side door and vanished inside.

"Oh, just curious. I would love to see those places, too." Miss Widtsoe took another pause. "You excel at art and music.

And you like riding and fencing and boxing. What other interests do you enjoy?"

He wanted to squirm under all her questions. "I like to read."

Her exuberance faded. "Oh. I'm not much of a reader. Jenny reads even more than she sews. It's very tiresome to be in a room with someone who's reading. But I applaud that interest in men. I can certainly keep myself amused if my husband likes to read." She cast an anxious look at him.

Christian only barely managed not to wince at her obviousness. He carried his burden up the stairs to the portico and headed for a set of French doors.

Miss Marshall stepped out and gestured to him. "This way. It's empty."

Christian carried Miss Widtsoe inside, and he set her onto a nearby chair. As he straightened, he glanced at Miss Marshall, but her bonnet shielded her face. She sank down on her knees in front of Miss Widtsoe and began removing the half boot.

He took a step back. "I'll leave you now. I hope your ankle mends quickly, Miss Widtsoe."

She beamed. "I'm sure it will. Thank you so much for helping me. You are a true hero."

At that, Miss Marshall turned her head toward him, a secretive smile curving her beautifully formed lips. He wanted to push back her bonnet and run a hand over her silky head and lower his mouth to hers . . .

He almost groaned out loud. There were so many reasons why that thought was wholly inappropriate.

"It was nothing." He sketched a hasty bow and left.

He did not need a woman in his life right now. He must

care for the earl and manage the estate. His brothers would produce heirs to ensure the continuation of the Amesbury line. Therefore, Christian had no duty to have children. No, he'd spend his life trying to atone for a host of failings and not drag some poor, undeserving lady into his world.

CHAPTER SEVEN

Genevieve and Mrs. Widtsoe applied every kind of remedy upon Matilda's ankle, but by the time she planned to meet Mr. Amesbury for her first sitting, her ankle had swollen enough to discourage the wearing of all but the softest slippers, and the skin had darkened to purple.

Letting her breath out in frustration, Genevieve glanced at Mrs. Widtsoe. "No dancing?"

The dear lady shook her head. "I'm afraid not."

Matilda's face crumpled. Genevieve tried to offer consolation, but Matilda only sobbed. How could Genevieve help her friend? And how could she do it without allowing her jealousy to rule her?

Moments later, a note arrived for Matilda from Mr. Amesbury, asking if she still wished to sit for her portrait today.

"Oh!" Matilda clasped the note to her bosom, her irrepressible spirit restored.

As a maid arranged her hair, Matilda placed cool packets of lavender and chamomile over her face to help reverse signs of tears. "Never mind, Jenny. I will enjoy myself today at the sitting and tonight at the ball, no matter what. And when you aren't dancing, you'll sit with me, won't you?"

Genevieve would have given her a stern look, but Matilda had packets over her eyes. "Need you even ask?"

"Sorry. I'm letting my insecurities show." She removed the compresses from her eyes. "How do I look?"

Wearing an elegant blue evening gown, and with only the sides caught up and the rest of Matilda's thick golden curls tumbling over one shoulder and down her back, her skin creamy as ever, and once more bright-eyed, Matilda looked exquisite. If she didn't turn Christian Amesbury's head, he wasn't a man.

Truthfully, Genevieve said, "You look like an angel."

Matilda rewarded her with a bright smile. "I hope he likes it."

They used a wheeled chair a footman found in the attic to convey her down the corridor, and two footmen carried her, chair and all, down the stairs to the drawing room. Along the way, Genevieve reminded herself that her task was to ensure Mattie and Mr. Amesbury had enough nudging to fall in love. Once Genevieve ensured Matilda's happiness, she'd give a thought to her own future. Perhaps she'd meet a fine gentleman later in the summer during their stay in Bath who would make her forget all about her improper fascination with Matilda's true love.

Mr. Amesbury sat behind an easel, preparing a palette of paints. He wore a large, paint-stained smock over his clothes. Focused on something only an artist would see, he held his lower lip between his teeth.

Mama sat with Mrs. Widtsoe in the corner of the room, chatting quietly as they sewed, their voices creating a soft murmur. After wheeling Matilda to the bench next to the pianoforte, Genevieve helped her out of the wheeled chair and onto the piano bench. Once Matilda got settled, Genevieve arranged the folds of her skirts. Then she turned her attention to Matilda's hair, carefully placing her curls.

She turned to find Mr. Amesbury looking at her. A soft smile curved his full mouth. His intensely focused gaze locked on her face, probing into her eyes. As tangible as a caress, his attention brought a rush of heat to her cheeks and a quiver in her midsection.

Gesturing to Matilda, she said, "Do you think she will do?"

He shifted his gaze to Matilda, blinked, then cocked his head as if remembering he agreed to paint her portrait. "The color suits her complexion and is the perfect hue against the background."

Matilda offered an uncertain smile and glanced hesitantly at Genevieve. Genevieve wanted to yell at him. Didn't he see how much his opinion meant to Matilda?

He seemed to realize his error. "You look very pretty, Miss Widtsoe. Perfect for a painting."

Her signature smile blazed, and all was well again. As Mr. Amesbury called out instructions for Matilda to turn her knees slightly to the side, raise her chin, and angle her head, Genevieve withdrew.

As she approached her mother sitting in the corner of the room with Matilda's, Mama nodded her way. "Jenny, dear, the rest of the guests are just about to begin a game of croquet. Do join them on the east lawn."

"Very well." Better to avoid being in the room with the beautiful Christian Amesbury while he gently wooed her friend. Just as she'd hoped he would. Didn't she?

She grabbed her gloves and her bonnet, tying it firmly

underneath her chin, and hurried to the east lawn. The guests were already pairing up, but a slender young man with brown curls that made him look like a mischievous boy stood off to the side alone, holding his mallet and ball.

As Genevieve approached, she threw out convention and called, "Sir Reginald, isn't it?"

Instantly smiling, he bowed. "Yes, Miss Marshall."

"Are you, by chance, in need of a partner?"

"I certainly am. Your arrival is most timely." He fixed warm brown eyes on her and handed her a mallet and matching ball.

The cheerful young man with the fashionable Cherubin hairstyle proved an enthusiastic and skilled partner. He teased her into smiling, making outrageously flirtatious statements and inquiries about the size of her dowry. One part shocked and two parts charmed, she shook off her melancholy. By the end of the game, she and Sir Reginald were laughing like old friends.

Clouds flirted with the sun as the merry group completed their game, calling dares, wagers, and jeers. The only blight in the afternoon came from Lord Wickburgh, who watched Genevieve too closely. He'd left his cane somewhere, which confirmed that he only carried it as a fashion statement. Fortunately, he remained at a distance, so she soon forgot him and focused on her friendly partner who felt rather like a brother. Without Matilda nearby to absorb all of her attention, Genevieve enjoyed getting to know the other guests.

Sir Reginald nodded his chin toward a group ahead of them near a spreading oak. "Mr. Ashton keeps looking at you. I believe you have captured his interest."

Genevieve glanced in the direction to catch the gaze of an attractive, dark-haired young gentleman she'd met previously but couldn't recall his name until Sir Reginald reminded her. "I can't imagine how. We've hardly spoken."

Sir Reginald grinned. "Speaking isn't requisite to admiring beauty."

"No, I suppose not." The first moment she saw Christian Amesbury, she had admired him without exchanging a word with him. With a sigh at what could never be, she focused on the game. They finished in the middle, not victors, but at least not last place.

Sir Reginald bowed. "It was a pleasure to partner you this afternoon, Miss Marshall."

"The pleasure was mine, sir." She grinned at the guileless young man.

As they put away their mallets and balls, a shadow fell over her. "Miss Marshall."

With a start, she met Lord Wickburgh's gaze. Quickly, she looked down to escape that oddly searching stare and curtsied. "Lord Wickburgh."

"You seemed to enjoy the game." Nothing in his tone sounded improper. Then why did he unnerve her so?

"Yes, I . . . I did, due to the company, I'm sure."

Sir Reginald eyed her curiously and took a few hesitant steps away.

She held a hand out to her partner. "Pray excuse me, my lord. I promised Sir Reginald I'd walk with him after the game."

At her words, the young man squared his shoulders and offered her his arm. She curtsied to the viscount and took Sir Reginald's arm gratefully.

Several paces away, she murmured, "Thank you."

"Is he bothering you?"

"Not precisely, but something about him makes me nervous. Thank you for playing into my ruse."

"Always a pleasure, Miss Marshall." They fell silent as they strolled toward the house. "You and Miss Widtsoe are fast friends, I take it?"

"Oh, yes, for years."

"She has spoken of you often." He let out a sigh. "She's so beautiful. The loveliest creature I've ever seen."

Genevieve smiled. "She does turn heads." At his smitten expression, she debated whether to discourage him. Perhaps it would be kinder to warn him that the way to Matilda's heart was barred. "I am persuaded she will make a match very soon."

His face fell. "With that Amesbury fellow." It wasn't a question.

She held her expression steady. "Perhaps. They have no formal understanding, mind you, but . . ." She let her voice trail off.

Another sigh. "I am less than two years her senior, so I have only just reached my majority—I couldn't court her until then. But I have admired her for years. Then when we danced in London . . ." Another sigh. "Do you think I'm too late?"

She wanted to tell him he was not too late, that he had a chance. The temptation arose to even help him try to wrest Matilda's interest away from Christian Amesbury. But that would be disloyal, and she did not wish to raise Sir Reginald's hopes where hope might not exist if Matilda and Mr. Amesbury made a match.

"I don't know if it's too late," she said. "She has a clear preference for him. Whether he returns her regard is anyone's guess." There. That was honest.

The young gentleman's mouth twisted to one side. "I see." Then he brightened. "I don't mind a little friendly competition. His father might be an earl, but my grandfather was the Duke of Suttenberg—not the present one, of course, he's a second cousin—but his father. And Amesbury is only a few years older than I. Do you think she prefers blond over brown?"

Genevieve almost tousled his curls which made him seem younger than his age. "I can't imagine the color of your hair would deter any sensible young lady."

He grinned. As his gaze fell on something off to the side, he pointed with his chin. "Look. I think the younger set have started a game of Blindman's Bluff. Shall we join them?"

She looked back at Lord Wickburgh, but he had already mounted the steps leading to the abbey, absorbed in conversation with a gentleman his age. She wouldn't have to worry about his disturbing presence if she stayed outside.

And Christian Amesbury remained inside with Matilda, where he should be. They should be together. And she should be happy for them. There was no compelling reason for her to enter the abbey at the moment.

"Yes, I'd love to play Blindman's Bluff." Anything to keep her away from temptation.

During the game, Genevieve laughed at Sir Reginald's jokes until her sides burned and her cheeks ached. Mr. Ashton continued to send her admiring glances, and Sir Reginald grinned conspiringly at her like an old friend.

When she found herself standing next to Sir Reginald, he winked. "I believe you have conquered Ashton."

Genevieve certainly had no desire to conquer anyone, least of all a man who had failed to engage her in conversation. "Nonsense."

"He can't keep his eyes off you."

"Perhaps he likes my hat," she quipped.

"Have you looked in the mirror?"

The blindfolded person staggered toward them, and they ducked to avoid the outstretched hands.

A footman announced tea, which dissolved the game. Guests moved in small groups and couples toward the abbey. With a meaningful glance at Mr. Ashton, Sir Reginald winked at Genevieve and strolled off, whistling. Shaking her head, Genevieve smiled. And people thought women were incorrigible matchmakers.

While Genevieve headed for the abbey, footsteps rustled the grass beside her. "Good afternoon." Mr. Ashton bent his elbow and offered it to her. "May I escort you back?"

"Thank you." She took his arm.

They walked in silence as Genevieve admired the rugged terrain and the way the hills cast long shadows over the land. Wildflowers danced in the breezes, and songbirds trilled as if all the world were a concert hall.

"Lovely weather, isn't it?" he said.

She looked up at him in surprise. Really? The weather? "Er, yes." Perhaps he was merely nervous, having never conversed with her since their brief introduction. "I confess, I have not played Blindman's Bluff in years. I can see I missed out on a lark."

"Yes, unexpectedly fun." He spoke evenly, but without any emotion.

"I don't think I've laughed so hard in a long time."

"A welcome diversion, to be sure."

They walked on in silence as she tried to remember if she'd

seen him smile or laugh during the game. Genevieve tried to come up with something to say to the solemn gentleman next to her. "Have you been here before? To the abbey, I mean."

"Yes, I live nearby. My father is the vicar here."

"I believe I did hear that."

"He is grooming me to take his place."

"That must be a rewarding line of work."

"It will be sufficient." He spoke in monotone, suggesting he didn't find the thought very appealing.

She almost asked him what vocation he would prefer but didn't voice the personal question.

They reached the abbey and continued to the sectioned off part of the drawing room where the guests enjoyed tea. A summer breeze blew through the open terrace doors, bringing in the scent of wildflowers and sunshine. Several of the older set conversed together, creating a low cacophony of conversation.

As they reached the others, Genevieve curtsied to Mr. Ashton. "Thank you for escorting me."

"My pleasure," came the monotone reply.

Matilda sat at the piano, somehow chatting with an animated expression without moving her head. Christian Amesbury drew Genevieve's gaze. In the midst of admiring his fine form and handsome face as he painted Matilda, unaware of Genevieve, a new awareness spread through her, a desire to ease his burdens, to ask him about his hopes and dreams, to ride pell-mell at his side through the woods, even to sit with him and read or sew as he created a work of art. Or simply admire him.

If he and Matilda made a match, those privileges would belong to Matilda. The thought sent a dart of pain into her heart. But that was silly. Really, she hardly knew him. Surely her interest stemmed from a passing fancy.

CHAPTER EIGHT

Christian tuned out Matilda Widtsoe's chatter and focused on the animated expressions of her face, trying to capture the best one for her pose. Though lovely and pleasant, she had a tiring effect on him. Still, on the rare occasion she fell silent, he asked her another question to keep her talking for the sake of the portrait. By the end of the afternoon, he'd created an expression that combined a subdued form of her usual enthusiasm while capturing the liveliness of her eyes. He'd also done rough likenesses of her, the piano, and enough decorations to suggest Egyptian flavor without overwhelming the main subject of the portrait.

Other houseguests streamed in, probably in anticipation of tea. Christian sat back, satisfied with the proportions, and rolled his shoulders to loosen the tension before removing his smock and rolling it up.

When Miss Widtsoe took a breath in her steady stream of chatter, he said, "That will do it for today."

Her mouth remained open as if she had stopped mid-sentence. Recovering, she closed her mouth and smiled. "This bench is getting hard anyway." She stood, visibly keeping her weight on one foot. "Will you help me to a settee, please?"

"Your wheeled chair is here." Reluctant to initiate more physical contact than necessary and give her another reason to mistake his intentions, he brought it to her and held it steady while she turned and settled herself in it, then he pushed her chair to a stop beside the settee.

While he gathered up his painting supplies, she called, "May I see it?"

"It's not finished."

"I know, but—please?"

He stowed all his supplies, tucked the easel under his arm, and brought the canvas to her. "I'll add color tomorrow."

Her expression of expectation fell as she looked at the canvas, but she nodded and said with forced cheer, "I'm sure it will be lovely when you're finished."

She turned the full brightness of her smile on him, but her praise was rather demoralizing, much like when as a child he showed a work of art to adults who patted him on the head and told him his art was nice when really they meant it was the silly scribblings of a beginner.

Genevieve Marshall sank down in an armchair next to Miss Widtsoe and leaned in to see the portrait. "Oh my, the proportions are amazing, and you captured her lively spirit beautifully."

It was all he could do not to puff out his chest in pride. Before replying, he searched for a note of humility. "I'm gratified to receive your approval. I'll finish it before I leave."

"I'm sure it will have no equal." Her admiration seemed genuine, without the coquettishness of so many ladies of the *ton*.

Though tempted to sit and bask in her soothing presence, he bowed. "If you will both excuse me, I need to go put this away."

"A footman can do that for you," Miss Widtsoe said with a flutter of lashes.

"I prefer to do it myself. I have a rather particular way of storing it." He returned to his room to put everything away. After cleaning the paint off his hands and brushes, and checking to be sure he hadn't splattered paint on his face or clothing, he checked on his father.

He found the earl sitting next to the fire, staring into the flames. Dressed in his breeches and shirtsleeves, with a banyan draped over his shoulders and tied loosely at the waist, he made no sign of awareness of Christian's presence. Next to him sat creased letters.

Softly, so as not to startle him, Christian said, "Sir, do you wish to join us downstairs for tea?"

The earl let out a sigh and looked up at Christian, his eyes unfocused. He blinked and seemed to return to himself. "I'll have a tray here."

Christian stepped inside. "Don't you think spending a few moments in the company of others would be better than staying here alone?"

His father's mouth tugged off to the side in a loose smile. "I suppose you are right." As he stood, he summoned his valet, scooped up the letters, and handed Christian his signet ring. "Take care of these, will you, son? I'll finish dressing."

Sitting at the desk in his father's room, Christian read over the contents of the letters, estate business that he easily handled. It was a shame his father took so little interest in his properties or even Parliament, which he used to serve so diligently. Mother's death drained Father of all his *joie de vivre*. But this trip seemed to have done him some good. Surely he would make a full recovery in time. Christian wrote out two replies the way his father would have wanted and sealed the wax with his father's signet ring.

Finished, he stood as the earl returned, groomed and dressed. Christian flanked his father as they entered the drawing room. While his father sauntered to Mr. Widtsoe and Lord Wickburgh, Christian meandered toward a group of young men closer to his own age.

As Christian neared, Mr. Ashton, the vicar's son droned, ". . . a good match. Her dowry and behavior are respectable enough."

Sir Reginald shook his head, making his curls bob. "She's lovely and witty and charming, that's what, and if you don't appreciate her many fine qualities, you don't deserve her."

"Set your sights on her, have you?" Mr. Ashton asked.

Sir Reginald shook his head. "I like her, but my heart belongs to Miss Widtsoe." He placed a hand over his heart.

Ah. So Matilda Widtsoe did indeed have the attention of the young Sir Reginald. Could Christian help facilitate a change of loyalty on the girl's part?

Casting off his curiosity over who they had been discussing earlier, Christian sidled up to the curly top. "Miss Widtsoe is lovely."

Sir Reginald gave a start and a decided straightening of his shoulders. "She is. I've known her for years—watched her grow up, as it were."

Christian almost grinned at the challenge in the young man's eyes and voice. "Childhood friends, were you?"

"Something like that."

Christian nodded. "My parents were, as well. They enjoyed a very happy marriage."

Sir Reginald eyed him as if he didn't quite trust Christian's meaning. "Always a desirable arrangement."

His gaze strayed to the girl under discussion, and Christian followed his line of sight, but didn't get past Genevieve Marshall. She drew him like a moth to flame. If he got closer, would he get burned or find a long-absent warmth?

Before he knew it, he'd approached her and found himself standing in front of her in the center of a group of young ladies. Fortunately, Sir Reginald had accompanied him.

"Good afternoon," Christian said. As all the young ladies nearby responded, he scrambled for something to say, since he had not intended to approach. *You're beautiful and restful, and I want to know you better. Will you go for a long walk with me?* That hardly seemed appropriate. Or worse, *If I kiss you, will you kiss me back or slap me?* He was tempted to try it and risk the consequences.

As his panicked thoughts swirled chaotically, Sir Reginald came to the rescue. "Mr. Amesbury and I were discussing the waltz and that many of the young ladies here might not know how. So, in preparation for tonight's ball, in which waltzing will be encouraged, we have decided to offer our services as practice partners."

Christian glanced at him, brows raised at the wild tale. That was brilliant, actually. He held out his arms, half turning to encompass all the young ladies who held their teacups frozen in front of them, their mouths slightly agape. Using his most charming smile, Christian added, "We realize it's a bit unconventional, but this is a house party, after all—not Almack's

Assembly Rooms." He extended a hand to Genevieve Marshall. "Care to have a practice waltz, Miss Marshall? I'm not dance master, but perhaps I can help."

Smiling, she rose and placed her hand in his. At her touch, an unraveled place inside him sighed and wound itself into the tapestry of his soul. It might be mad, but all his reasons for avoiding the idea of love or marriage no longer mattered. Having this woman—this incredible lady—in his life became a taunting desire.

"May I?" Sir Reginald bowed before another young lady.

As if a challenge had been issued, half the unmarried gentlemen in the room approached young ladies of their choice, bowed, and drew them into dance position. A murmur of one-two-three's filled the room. The older adults' conversation died out, and a few sputtered at the strange, impromptu dance, but no one voiced a true protest. Not that it would have mattered. At that moment, dancing with Genevieve consumed Christian's every desire.

Well, not every desire. Taking her into a secluded room and kissing her senseless would be a preferred activity, but he must woo her with every appearance of honorable intentions.

"Shall I count?" she asked, a teasing half smile curving her delicious lips.

Christian smiled at the gentle observation that they were standing in waltz position but not actually dancing. "I will, if you have no objection."

That delicious curve in her mouth deepened. "None at all."

"The best way to learn is to do. Keep your arms firm and put your hand here." He repositioned her hand to a spot higher on his arm near his shoulder. Did he imagine her quick intake of breath? "This is our frame. Keep some tension in your arms to maintain this distance. As long as we keep our frame steady, you should have no trouble following me."

She nodded, her eyes large and her pupils dilated. That meant she felt some form of desire for him, too. Right? He'd spent enough time on the dance floor that he'd seen expressions of admiration or lust many times. He'd even grown accustomed to women gazing at him in clear desire, and had always found a way to gently refuse—except in the case of Miss Widtsoe, of course, who didn't seem to respond to subtlety. But with Genevieve Marshall, he could not be sure of the meaning behind her expression. He might be in the uncomfortable and unprecedented position of having to work to win her affections. For the first time, he wanted a lady to desire him. He looked forward to the challenge.

"Are you ready?" he asked.

"I hope I don't step on your feet."

He affected a mournful expression. "You do appear to weigh as much as a fallen leaf; if you step on me, I fear I might not survive the encounter."

Her eyes danced and her smile almost blinded him. "I might surprise you."

"You already have, in many ways." Before he made a fool of himself right here and now, he said, "Step back with your right foot. Ready? One." He stepped forward with his left foot, guiding her back. "Two." He guided her to his right. "Three." He closed his steps. "You follow beautifully."

Again that blast of cleansing brilliance. "I love waltzing."

"We're not actually waltzing yet. That was just one half of the box step."

"Silly me." A husky tone entered her voice.

He cleared his throat. "Now we reverse. You step forward with your left as I step back. One. Two. Three. There. That was a complete box set. Let's do it again just as before but without stopping."

While he counted, she followed him as he took her through the box step several more times. Then he added a turning step. She followed like an expert. He taught her several more moves, leading her and counting as he showed her the hesitation, the outside turn, the spin, and the promenade. Each touch of her hand, the brush of her thigh, his hand on her back nearly sent him over the moon. Through it all, her expression remained that of pure rapture.

He smiled down at the fairy-like girl in his arms who radiated such purity and joy. "You can say it now, if you like."

"Say it?" She angled her head off to the side, looking so adorable that he almost kissed her right there.

"That you love to waltz."

"Oh, I do!" she said breathlessly.

"Just wait until we add music."

"I can hardly stand the suspense."

He agreed with the sentiment.

"Gentlemen, I think the young ladies have had enough of waltz instruction for the afternoon," Mrs. Widtsoe's voice cut in. "We wouldn't want to exhaust them before tonight's revelry begins."

Christian raised a brow and asked softly, "Are you exhausted, Miss Marshall?"

"Not a bit. But the point is taken."

"Or perhaps our hostess merely wishes to limit contact for this very scandalous dance."

"Probably that, as well." Her eyes shimmered in mirth.

He had to tell himself to let her go twice before his arms actually obeyed. She gave him a conspiratorial smile, curtsied when he bowed, and turned away.

As he joined the other gentlemen, Sir Reginald said, "Glad to know I don't have to compete with you for the fair Matilda."

"No, indeed," Christian said. "My affections are definitely engaged elsewhere."

Mr. Ashton's gaze flicked in his direction, and his brow narrowed as if he were annoyed. Christian gave him little thought. Tonight, he would leap any hurdles to ensure he waltzed in truth with Genevieve Marshall.

CHAPTER NINE

Genevieve joined Matilda's group of young ladies, positioning herself so she couldn't see Christian Amesbury. It wouldn't do to look at him too long or too frequently. His warmth and texture remained on her hands as a ghostly reminder of where she'd been, and where she desperately wished to return.

Matilda spoke to her audience of young ladies, who either had not joined the dancing lesson or had already returned, with her usual animation but clearly attempting to keep her voice down. ". . . I vow, with him studying me so closely as he painted my portrait, it was all I could do not to blush the entire time! He asked me ever so many questions about myself, my family, and my interests. I expect he will ask to speak to my father any day now!"

She spoke of Christian Amesbury, surely. Which meant either Matilda nursed a grand delusion or Genevieve had misunderstood his intentions as she danced with him.

Though Genevieve had come to the house party fully expecting to meet the man Matilda would marry, the thought no longer gave her the pleasure it once did. But that was a selfish attitude. Matilda's happiness meant the world to Genevieve. Mr.

Amesbury was in Matilda's heart long before Genevieve saw him. Her only choice now lay in whether she would sulk like a child longing for a toy that belonged to another, conspire to betray her dearest friend, or help her friend secure the proposal she desired.

She put out of her mind the desire to suggest that the object of Matilda's affection did not return her regard and she should look elsewhere—like at the delightful Sir Reginald who loved her.

Rallying her good senses, Genevieve touched Matilda's arm. "I am persuaded that having Mr. Amesbury paint your portrait was an exceedingly fine idea—a perfect excuse to spend time with him."

Matilda beamed. "It was, wasn't it?"

Genevieve glanced over her shoulder at Mr. Amesbury, who listened to one of the younger gentlemen with amusement. As the other gentleman came to the end of the story, everyone laughed, including Mr. Amesbury. His whole face lit in mirth. Genevieve barely resisted sighing at the stunning sight. Then she remembered she wasn't supposed to look at him.

To cover up her mistake, she squeezed Matilda's hand. "I am happy you have attracted the attention of such a fine gentleman. He's perfect for you."

"He is perfect, all right," one of the other girls said. They all tittered.

Matilda glanced at Genevieve. Something darkened in her expression. "You certainly seemed to enjoy your little practice waltz with him."

"Er, I—Yes, I did. He was kind to teach me. Your Mr. Amesbury is certainly a fine gentleman."

Matilda resumed her usual sunny expression. After tea, they chatted and gossiped, all the while Genevieve pointedly keeping her attention on the girls, and not on Mr. Amesbury. The act of refraining from looking at him almost caused physical pain. She rubbed her hands against the fabric of her muslin gown to brush off the warm sensation of his touch. But to no effect.

She was a terrible friend!

"Come, Jenny, we should dress for dinner," Mama's quiet urging broke in from behind the settee where Genevieve sat.

Genevieve nodded. "Yes, Mama. Do you need help getting to your room, Mattie?"

"I'll help her," Mrs. Widtsoe said as she reached the circle.

Genevieve followed her mother out of the room and upstairs. They ascended the grand staircase, and Genevieve admired the carved stone and gothic details.

"Are you enjoying yourself?" Mama asked.

"Yes, very much. We played croquet and Blindman's Bluff, and I own that I laughed quite with abandon."

"As did the others, I understand."

"Yes. And I am persuaded the practice waltz will be helpful for tonight's ball."

"I suspect it will. You attracted the attention of some gentlemen."

Genevieve lifted her shoulder in a dismissive shrug. "My partner in croquet was very attentive. And Mr. Ashton escorted me back to the abbey."

"And young Mr. Amesbury taught you to waltz."

Genevieve blushed at the memory of his touch on her hand, her back, and the small brushes as their bodies touched during the waltz. No wonder people viewed the waltz as scandalous.

"Has anyone captured your heart?"

She hesitated a fraction too long in answering. "In so short a time? Of course not."

"Except, perhaps, one who has also captured the heart of your best friend?"

Genevieve sucked in her breath. Though tempted to deny it, Genevieve acknowledged that Mama already knew. She let out her breath. "Is it that obvious?"

"Probably not to others, but I can tell. You try too hard not to look at him, but when you do, you soften like I've never seen you do. You positively glowed when you danced with him."

"It's pointless. Matilda loves him."

"Does he return her regard?"

"She seems to think he does. He's fairly reserved, but he was quick to come to her rescue this morning when she hurt her ankle."

"That is the mark of a gentleman, not necessarily a young man in love."

Genevieve secretly agreed but tried to convince her mother of a truth to which Matilda clung. "He's attentive to her, and they had a lovely chat while he painted her portrait."

"He might merely have been looking for the right expression for her portrait. Or he's simply polite."

"I cannot hope for that, Mama. She loves him. And I want her to be happy."

Mama put her arm around Genevieve and gave her a sideways hug. "I know. Matters of the heart are never easy. You are young yet, and have many prospects."

While Mama retired to the chambers she shared with Papa, Genevieve went to her room and flopped on the bed. What kind of friend was she? Loyalty and honor were qualities her parents had instilled in her as long as she could remember. Her friendship with Matilda transcended any interest in a gentleman.

Only one more day. Genevieve could last one more day. Then the house party would end. She and her parents would leave and spend their summer in Bath helping her mother restore her health. She would never see again Christian Amesbury, except at Matilda's wedding.

Her maid, a middle-aged woman who preferred to be called simply by her last name, Hill, entered. "Do you wish to rest, miss? I could return later."

Genevieve sat up. "No, come in."

The abigail set out the two gowns Genevieve had not yet worn at the house party.

After a glance, Genevieve gestured. "The silk ball gown, please. We're dancing tonight." Poor Matilda. She'd been so excited to waltz.

After a quick sponge bath, Genevieve dressed in a clean shift and stays, and donned a dressing gown. Seated at the dressing table, she stared at her reflection without seeing it. Instead, she plotted how to survive the evening without allowing her discomfiting jealousy to affect her thoughts or behavior. If Matilda were at a loss for company, Genevieve would sit with her. If Mr. Amesbury sat with Mattie, Genevieve would find an excuse to leave them alone. If he were to speak with Genevieve, she'd only talk about Matilda. Matilda would attain her heart's desire, and Genevieve would be happy for her—even if it killed her. Which was silly, really, as she hardly knew Christian Amesbury.

No matter how often she reminded herself of that fact, it never offered comfort.

"Are you unwell, miss?"

"Oh, no—just thinking."

She should tell Hill to do her hair in a very simple chignon—something as plain as possible so as not to compete with Matilda—but she couldn't make the words come out. Besides, her hair was almost finished now, and to ask for a different hairstyle would be unkind to Hill, who'd already combed her hair into soft curls. After the abigail dampened the fine hairs on either side of Genevieve's face and curled them around her finger to make ringlets, she added a green ribbon as the finishing touch.

"Lovely, Hill," Genevieve said. "Thank you."

She stood and lifted her arms so Hill could lower the gown over her head. As the abigail fastened the gown down the back, Genevieve eyed her reflection in the full length mirror. Green ribbon threaded through the sleeves and around the bodice accented tiny green leaves embroidered on the ivory silk, and the ball gown fit beautifully. If only she had been blessed with curves like Matilda, instead of the figure of a fourteen-year-old. Mama called her "elfin," but saw her through the eyes of a mother's love. Removing her focus off her reflection, she tugged on her silk stockings and stepped into her dancing slippers.

Mama tapped on the door and stuck her head in. "Are you ready? Oh!" She clasped her hands together. "You look lovely!"

It was impossible to wallow in self-pity while her mother admired her so enthusiastically.

"You do, too, Mama."

And truly, she did. With auburn hair the color of

Genevieve's, still untouched by gray, and a lovely face, her mother looked far younger than her age. Only the faintest lines around her eyes belied her departure from the first blush of youth.

Putting on the final touch, Genevieve pulled on long gloves and a cashmere shawl before she joined her father, who waited for them in the corridor.

Papa kissed her brow. "What a lucky man I am to escort two such lovely ladies."

In the drawing room, half the guests waited, sipping sherry and conversing. Matilda had yet to make an appearance, but Christian Amesbury and his father had already arrived. Wearing a dark blue frock coat and a gold and white brocade waistcoat, he had an elegant sense of style. Next to him stood the cheerful, curly-haired Sir Reginald and the solemn Mr. Ashton, both sizing up Mr. Amesbury.

Did they view him as competition for Matilda? Did Matilda know she had so many admirers? If she knew, would she be less likely to set her sights on Christian Amesbury?

Genevieve squelched the traitorous thought. Matilda hadn't formed an attachment for him out of a lack of prospects; her preference came as a natural result of his kindness and charm. Being handsome and the son of an earl only added to his allure. For many reasons, he was a desirable match, and Matilda was smart to recognize it.

Genevieve glanced about the room. Noting Matilda's absence, she turned to her mother. "Matilda isn't here yet. Should I have looked in on her?"

"Not necessary, surely. Do join the other girls." Mama gave a gentle nudge.

Genevieve moved to a group of chairs drawn up to make a conversation area.

". . . only my first Season, so Mama says not to become discouraged," one of the young ladies said.

"That's all well and good for you," said another, "but next Season, Mama is launching my younger sister. This house party is my last chance to receive an offer."

Matilda arrived, and all the girls turned their attention to her and her well-being until dinner was announced. After dinner, the guests filed into the drawing room that had been transformed into the ballroom, with flowers and hundreds of candles blazing in the chandeliers and tall wrought iron candelabras. Local musicians played their instruments in that odd discord of pre-performance tuning. While Matilda sat like a queen on her wheeled chair up front where she would command a view of the room, several girls clustered around her. Surely most of her current companions would be asked to dance shortly, which would leave her alone. And if she were alone, Genevieve would keep her company.

The musicians struck up a quadrille. Heading up the set stood Christian Amesbury across from the girl in white muslin who'd expressed a fear of losing her only chance at marriage. Genevieve moved to join Matilda so she would not find herself alone, but before she had taken more than a few steps, a voice stopped her.

"May I have this first set?" Sir Reginald appeared at Genevieve's side, his hand extended and his warm eyes merry.

Genevieve hesitated. "I had planned on keeping Matilda company."

He glanced at Matilda. "Miss Widtsoe is surrounded by

friends at present. Once the set ends, I plan to stay with her, but I must first dance."

She cocked her head to the side. "You surprise me, sir; I would have thought you'd take every chance to be at her side."

He grinned. "I don't wish to make a cake of myself by sitting at her feet like an overeager puppy."

Genevieve gave in to the urge to tease him. "Are you using me to inspire a bit of jealousy in her?"

"Not entirely." With a covert wink, Sir Reginald took her hand and led her to the dance floor. He stood next to Christian Amesbury and grinned impishly at her as two other couples made up their square.

Using every shred of self-control not to look at Mr. Amesbury, she fixed her focus on her partner. As the music started, they took hands for the moment it took to dance past each other to the other dancers in their square, which led her to Mr. Amesbury.

He looked directly into her eyes and smiled, a slow, heart-melting curving of his lips that quite literally dried her mouth. Trying not to fall flat on her face, she danced past him to the next gentleman where they repeated the steps. After she made her way around the square, she arrived back with Sir Reginald, did the required little skip-step, and took hands as they watched Mr. Amesbury and his partner, the girl in white muslin whose smile practically illuminated the room, dance within the square. Genevieve would probably be wearing a similar smile if she were his partner, only hers would be dimmed by guilt.

Under his breath, Sir Reginald said, "You're staring."

Dragging her gaze off Mr. Amesbury, she whispered tersely, "I am not."

His eyes twinkled. She lifted her chin, pointedly looking everywhere but at the dashing figure in blue. Each time she found herself temporarily partnered with Christian Amesbury, he looked into her eyes as if he were trying to memorize her face. Clearly, her imagination had gotten the better of her.

During the course of the set, she managed not to collapse at his feet, and while she danced with the other gentlemen in the square, even kept her eyes off him—most of the time.

Upon completion of the set, Sir Reginald escorted her to her mother and bowed. "A delight, Miss Marshall." He all but sashayed to Matilda's side where he bowed over Matilda's hand and promptly took a seat next to her.

Matilda smiled at Sir Reginald flirtatiously. "Reggie, how kind of you to join me." She frowned briefly in Mr. Amesbury's direction but resumed her smile at Sir Reginald.

Mr. Ashton stepped into Genevieve's line of sight. "If I may have the honor?"

"Of course," she replied.

During the country dance, she again danced a few steps with Mr. Amesbury, whose gaze again darted over her, his lips curving in a way that seemed to beg her to ask what he thought.

"Stand up with me the next set?" he murmured as they circled.

A warm rush ran over her skin. "As you wish."

He smiled, and she stumbled. Must he be so handsome?

The steps took them apart and brought her back to Mr. Ashton. He said nothing and his expression remained solemn as they danced, but in his defense, the vigorous dance provided little opportunity to converse. Dancing always brought her joy, and at the end of the first dance in the set, she stood laughing and trying to catch her breath. Her focus fell on Mr. Amesbury, who watched her with such intensity that her heart fluttered. He inclined his head, smiling in a way that felt almost secretive. Only by sheer willpower did she manage a courteous smile rather than gape at him. He turned his focus onto his partner, his expression smoothing over into polite interest.

"This is the last night of the house party," Mr. Ashton said, stealing Genevieve's attention.

She glanced at him, ashamed she'd had the bad form to stare at another while on the dance floor with a partner. "Yes, it is."

He nodded. "Not much time, then."

"Oh, I think it's been a lovely few days. Of course, it's always a little disappointing when a party ends, but that's better than wishing for its end, don't you agree?"

He gave her a curious look. "I am sure you must be right."

At the conclusion of the set, Mr. Ashton returned her to her mother. Genevieve's gaze roamed the room, and she gave a little start. Lord Wickburgh stared at her. The lord stood still as a statue, gripping his walking stick with white knuckles. He, too, inclined his head in greeting as Mr. Amesbury had, but his gaze left her with an urge to seek protection.

Mr. Amesbury appeared, his smile in place, his hand outstretched to her. "If you would be so kind." Did she imagine a sultry quality in his tone?

She laid her hand in his and walked with him, her feet barely touching the floor.

He stepped closer. "It's the waltz."

"How lovely," she said, breathless. "I hope I remember how to do it. I'm not sure one brief lesson with a real partner is enough."

Oh, dear. Matilda hurt herself teaching Genevieve how to waltz, and now she, instead of Mattie, was waltzing with Mr. Amesbury. Guilt shadowed her joy.

The music began, and as he drew her into waltz position, he smiled down at her. "I am honored to be your first, Miss Marshall."

Her attention focused on his lips. Her first what? Kiss? Her heart pounded at the thought.

He added, "I hope to be a worthy waltz teacher."

Waltz. Of course. How ridiculous she was being! After only a few moments, she moved with him with little thought, following his skillful lead and moving with the music. He did several basic steps, giving her a chance to become acquainted with the rise and fall and with the music's timing. A timelessness, a sensation of everything being so right in the world while she danced in his arms filled her. A missing ingredient to the recipe of happiness had been added to her life.

But she had not known him long enough to know if he were her perfect match. He might be a passing fascination. Perhaps, in a few days or weeks, she would meet some other dashing fellow and forget all about Christian Amesbury. And perhaps she would discover that fairies truly did open flowers and Cupid's arrows were real—it seemed just as likely.

As they sailed across the floor, his smile faded to a solemn expression. "Miss Marshall, as a close friend of Miss Widtsoe's, you are best qualified to advise me."

Oh, no. He would ask her about Matilda's favorite flower, or what kind of wedding ring she would want . . .

"I have somehow raised her expectations."

Genevieve's thoughts stuttered to a halt.

At what must have been confusion in her expression, he rushed on, "I assure you it was purely unintentional. In fact, aside from painting her portrait—well, and helping her when she twisted her ankle—I have made every attempt to appear distant while still being polite. Nonetheless, she seems to think there is some sort of understanding between us."

Everything inside her went still. "Then you have not formed an attachment to her?"

Sincere eyes fixed on her. "None. I never meant to give her that impression. I cannot imagine how she got that idea."

Genevieve didn't know whether to jump for joy that his heart remained unclaimed or weep for what would be a stinging disappointment for Matilda.

She moistened her lips. "I advise you to be direct. Quietly take her aside and tell her."

He winced. "I cannot imagine how I will find the words to deliver such a cutting speech."

"The longer you delay, the worse it will be."

He nodded, his expression clouding. "She might accuse me of raising her expectations."

"That is a concern. Have you spent any time in her company in public?"

"Only a few dances in London. The most time I've spent with her was painting her portrait. And helping her when she injured herself." He winced as if recalling a painful memory. Was he castigating himself for carrying Matilda and giving further fuel for her imagination? Or did he sympathize with her plight?

"That hardly signifies," she said. "Have you ever danced with her more than once at a ball?"

"No." His earnest blue eyes remained focused on her face.

"Sat with her and spoken for any length of time?"

"Never, beyond her sitting for the portrait."

"And I can assume, then, that you never . . . kissed her?"
Her cheeks burned at the personal and impudent question. Or
did they burn because she daydreamed of what it might be like
to kiss him?

His eyes opened wide. "Heavens, no."

"Then it sounds to me that if her expectations have been
raised, they were from her own desires. No one in society would
expect you to make an offer, unless they believe what she's been
saying about you."

A crease formed between his brows. "What has she been
saying?"

"That she believes you return her feelings." She didn't dare
voice Matilda's declaration that she expected a proposal.

He let out a long exhale. "I'd best talk to her before it gets
out of hand."

Genevieve nodded, too conflicted to speak. He could be
hers. But Matilda would be crushed if Genevieve encouraged the
gentleman for whom Matilda had developed a grand passion,
and who had spurned her. And Genevieve would be a disloyal
friend.

"Do you think you are up to some steps beyond the basic,
Miss Marshall?"

"Absolutely."

He led her through all the steps he'd taught her earlier in
the day, as well as several new moves. Following him came as
naturally as if they'd danced together for years.

"You are an excellent student of the waltz."

She smiled. "If I am, it is because you are an excellent teacher."

He opened his mouth and inhaled as if to speak, but pressed his lips together instead.

In a flash of unladylike boldness, she asked, "What were you about to say?"

He shook his head, and his eyes suggested he carried a secret.

Gently, she said, "You've already confided in me regarding Matilda, surely you can tell me what you were thinking just now."

His lips curved. "I never put much credence in the term 'love at first sight.' But I am beginning to understand, at least in part, why people say that."

Her heart quickened. "What are you saying?"

"More than I should, for now. The party ends tomorrow, and we will part company. Do you go back to your home?"

"No, we are continuing on to Bath so that my mother might partake of the restorative waters. She has delicate health."

A golden-brown brow raised. "My father and I are returning to Bath, as well."

"I hope I shall see you there."

"Oh, you can count on that." An unmistakable promise rang in his tone.

The orchestra ended their song on a flourish, and he led her into a little dip.

"Thank you for the waltz," he said as he raised her up. "You were a delightful partner."

"You, as well."

They stood in dance position, not moving, while other

couples left the dance floor. He searched her eyes, his hands warm on her hand, and his mouth parted.

As if remembering himself, he released her and stepped back. With an extended arm and a slight bow, he led her back to her mother. Genevieve watched as he strode to Matilda, bowed, and after a brief conversation in which Sir Reginald appeared alarmed, wheeled Matilda out of the room. At the doorway, he glanced at Genevieve before he exited.

He was about to break her friend's heart, but all Genevieve could think of was the possibility that he might have captured hers.

Did that mean she had made assumptions about him and that a similar heartbreak was in her future?

CHAPTER TEN

Christian pushed Miss Widtsoe's wheeled chair toward the doorway in search of a place to conduct a private conversation without pushing the bounds of propriety. Only his deeply instilled manners kept him from rushing back to Genevieve Marshall's side to claim another dance. Those brief touches had been torturous, leaving him longing for more. He'd always believed his own damaged heart to be insulated from the charms of a lady. But Genevieve Marshall proved him wrong. Was it possible that he might have found that missing color in the palette of his life?

He glanced back to the ballroom. Serene and elegant but with a slightly impish curve to her lips, Genevieve curtsied to Mr. Ashton, who spoke with her. Christian pitied the young man who was obviously smitten with her, but she clearly did not return his preference. Christian hesitated, his confidence slipping. She preferred him. Didn't she? Or was he also to be pitied?

No. She'd given him several warm glances she'd given no one else at the house party.

As he wheeled Miss Widtsoe, he paused at the doorway and looked back. Genevieve glanced at him, that warm look coming into her eyes and her impish smile deepening. Then, as if remembering herself, she demurely lowered her gaze and adjusted the shawl around her shoulders. If only he could get her alone, he'd test that demure exterior to find the woman underneath.

Egad, he was starting to sound like his father.

Returning his mind to the unpleasant business at hand, he pushed Miss Widtsoe out to the main hall where a few others gathered. Good. They would be considered chaperoned out here. He pushed her to a small cluster of chairs in a corner where they were far enough from the others not to be overheard.

She smiled at him expectantly. "You wanted to speak to me?"

He perched on the edge of a chair. "Yes. I . . ." He swallowed. How did one go about this sort of business? He broke out into a cold sweat. "I fear there has been something of a misunderstanding between us."

"Oh?"

"Yes. It appears that—That is to say, it seems as if you . . . feel that there is a certain . . . understanding between us." He swallowed hard and stared at the floor so he wouldn't have to look into her eyes. But that was cowardly. As a gentleman, he owed her eye contact. Witnessing her disappointment would be fitting penance for his carelessness. He took a breath. "If I have done anything to give you the wrong impression, I offer my humblest apologies."

Her expression remained fixed, still hopeful, even.

This was not going well. He rubbed at the trickle of perspiration at his brow and tried again. "You see, I never meant to give you the idea that I have any particular . . . preference for you."

Miss Widtsoe blinked. Then her hopeful expression faded.

He pressed on. "In truth, I have always believed that I would never marry. I help manage my father's estate and watch over his care, and I do not expect that a wife will fit into those duties."

That expectation fell flat as he considered Genevieve Marshall in his life, as did the real reason he'd believed himself unsuitable for a wife. Perhaps happiness was not beyond his reach, all his past mistakes notwithstanding.

Miss Widtsoe's eyes grew bright with tears. "You . . . you don't feel any particular regard for me?"

He faltered. "It was never my intention to court you—merely paint your portrait and one of the abbey. When my father and I return to Bath, I do not expect to see you again—ever." He winced at his own harshness.

Her lashes fluttered, and her mouth quivered. "You don't have a grand passion for me?"

Very gently, he said, "No, Miss Widtsoe. And I beg your forgiveness if I have misrepresented myself to you."

She stared down at her hands twisting in her lap. "I see."

"There is much to recommend you, and half the gentlemen here are trying to catch your eye—Sir Reginald, for example. But you and I would not suit."

She said nothing, just sat with bowed head.

His heart twisted in compassion and regret. He'd taken the light out of her eyes. There appeared to be nothing more to say. He stood. "I am so sorry."

As he turned away, she said, "It's Genevieve, isn't it?"

He paused. "As I said, I'm not certain it is my lot to marry." If he married Genevieve as he hoped, those words would make a liar of him. "But yes, Miss Marshall has intrigued me—against my better sense."

He made himself turn around and look at her. She slumped in her wheeled chair, her hands over her eyes, her shoulders shaking. Returning to the ballroom, he paused behind a potted plant to catch his breath. He felt like he'd just kicked a puppy who'd been licking his hand. He hailed a passing footman and asked him to attend to Miss Widtsoe, whom he'd left alone in a wheeled chair.

Despite his weariness of heart, he moved back into the main area, searching for Genevieve, craving her soothing presence. The musicians packed up their instruments, and guests gathered in clusters. Genevieve stood next to two young ladies whom he had partnered earlier in the evening. Genevieve caught his eye like a red rose in a garden of lilies—so lovely, so vibrant, and yet so serene.

Remembering to don an appropriately *savoir faire* expression, lest he appear a juvenile who'd discovered girls for the first time, he squared his shoulders and sauntered toward Genevieve.

Before he reached her side, Lord Wickburgh sidled up to her and dismissed the other girls with a single glance. Christian checked his steps. As a titled lord, the man commanded greater precedence. As his elder, he deserved Christian's respect and deference, but the man clearly bothered Genevieve. And there was a cold hardness about him that raised Christian's hackles.

Lord Wickburgh bowed to Genevieve. The color left her cheeks, and she lowered her head, clasping her hands in front of her as if trying to form a shield.

"The viscount appears to have selected his new bride." The earl's voice snapped up Christian's head.

Standing next to Christian, the earl gestured with his glass at the scene. "He seems as fascinated with her as you are."

"I'm not . . ." he trailed off. Denying it was pointless. "She is remarkable."

"Her father may have a particular preference for a lord over a youngest son."

The words pricked his hope. Could that be the case? His suit could be refused because he was a younger son? No, he refused to step back. "The Marshalls don't seem like mushrooms."

"They aren't, but most fathers want the best for their daughters, and they often weigh the wrong criteria, even if they aren't social climbers. I made that mistake with your sister."

Christian winced, recalling evidence of Margaret's unhappy marriage the moment she returned from her honeymoon. "I'm not prepared to offer for Miss Marshall, Father."

"You might have to move quickly before Lord Wickburgh does, or her father may choose the higher ranking suitor for his daughter."

Christian paused. Surely, Captain Marshall would take his daughter's preferences into consideration. And she preferred Christian to Lord Wickburgh. Didn't she?

He watched them converse, Lord Wickburgh elegant and worldly, and Miss Marshall, gentle and reserved. Her mouth curved in a small smile to the viscount. Was she changing her opinion about the older man? He offered money, as well as the power and privilege of rank. Christian could only offer her a modest living.

Did he truly want to offer her anything?

He would have to find out. Standing in the shadows, watching another man pay court to her would not help him make up his mind.

For the first time in years, a flicker of hope lit inside him that he might not have to live his life in complete darkness.

He snatched a glass of lemonade from a tray and continued toward her. As he reached her side, he nodded to the viscount, who snapped his mouth shut and glared.

Holding out the glass, Christian smiled broadly at Genevieve. "I brought you a drink."

She smiled, but it was restrained. "Thank you." As she accepted his glass, she cast a glance at Lord Wickburgh. "I wish you the best at your endeavors, my lord." She sipped her drink and turned her body to face Christian.

Though her words had been a clear dismissal, Lord Wickburgh held out an arm. "It is rather stuffy in here. Shall we take a turn about the garden and breathe some fresh air?"

She pressed her lips together and flitted her gaze at Christian. "I'm afraid I have already promised to do that with Mr. Amesbury. If you will excuse us, my lord?"

She reached for Christian, and he readily offered her his arm, glad to assist in her charade and trying not to puff out his chest at her clear preference. Did she only want his company to escape a man who frightened her? Did she play some kind of game?

Lord Wickburgh raised his walking stick and placed the tip of it in front of Christian like a barrier. "Have a care, boy. You'd do well to step aside like a gentleman."

Christian stiffened. If this arrogant bully thought he could cow Christian, he was in for a surprise. "I do not believe the lady wishes for your company."

The lord drew his brows together. "Watch your mouth, boy. I don't care who your father is; I will not tolerate insolence."

Anger simmering in his core, Christian stepped in closer until they were almost nose to nose, noting with satisfaction that he had almost an inch over the older man. "I will not be the gentleman and step aside, unless the lady asks me to do so. Good evening."

He turned his back on the lord, replaced Genevieve's hand on his arm, and led her outside. Moonlight and Chinese lanterns guided them across the terrace and down the steps while Christian drew several breaths to release his anger. Genevieve remained quiet until they reached a fountain deep in the garden. Frogs and night insects sang a chorus, and a warm breeze ruffled Christian's hair around his face.

"Thank you," she said. "I suppose it was cowardly of me to pull you into it and make up a story about our walk in the garden, but something about that man seeps the courage out of me."

Feeling foolish for letting his insecurities cast doubt on her character, he turned to her and put a hand over hers where it rested on his arm. "I am happy to be of service."

"How did your talk go with Matilda?"

He hesitated.

"Forgive me. I do not wish to pry, but she is my friend."

He lifted a shoulder. "I tried to be as tactful as possible, and she seemed to take it well. But she was a bit overset when I left her. I am sorry to have been the cause of sorrow to your friend."

"I adore Matilda, but she fancies herself in love all the time.

She seemed to have developed a true attachment for you, but if you did not return her regard, she had no basis for her claim."

"She really has much to recommend her. I hope she meets someone worthy of her."

"So do I." Genevieve sank down on the marble edge of the raised pond around the fountain.

In the moonlight and amid the garden, her fairy-like quality became even more apparent, as did that magical serenity she carried about her. He drew in a breath, inhaling her scent, letting her peaceful presence soothe him. His focus fixed on her lips.

He sat next to her and took her hand. "Miss Marshall, from the time I was a child, I have never expected to marry. Since my father's decline, I have virtually taken over all his responsibilities for managing the entire estate. I meet with his steward, tour the properties, and everything else required of him—except sit in the House, of course."

"It sounds like a great deal of responsibility."

"It is. And, I always felt rather as if I were . . . well, unworthy of love." Curse it, he did not plan to confess that. "But my oldest brother, Cole, has returned from the war, and I expect he, as the heir, will take my place soon. When he does, I will be free to paint more—although, my family expects me to take the position of county vicar when it becomes available." Upholding family expectations was important, but he'd always hoped to study art with the Royal Academy of Art, perhaps travel to Italy to paint.

"Why do you feel unworthy of love?"

He shied away from the truth, from the horrible challenge that led to his brother Jason's death, and the scattering of his brothers over the fight Christian caused between them and the earl. He breathed through the pain lancing his chest. "I have done things in my past that I deeply regret. Lost people I thought would always be there—some through my own actions."

She slipped her hand into his and squeezed it gently. "Everyone deserves to be loved, to be given a second chance. Even you. Especially you."

Her earnest expression, the tenderness in her eyes touched his heart and loosened knots in his soul tied by years of sorrow. Perhaps she was right. Perhaps he did deserve love. Despite his earlier determination to take things slowly with her, his brain disengaged, and his body sought the sweetness of her lips. He leaned in and kissed Genevieve.

Her slight intake of breath should have stopped him, but her warm and malleable lips moved with his. Whatever was left of his reason vanished, and he kissed her as if nothing beyond this moment ever existed.

CHAPTER ELEVEN

Genevieve's good sense always came through for her when other men tried to kiss her, but it fled the instant Christian leaned in, his desire apparent. Instead of backing away like a proper young lady, she raised her head and met his mouth with hers. Fireworks at the park last summer failed to match the explosions of light and color inside her. Beyond glorious, kissing Christian instilled a sense of absolute belonging—to him, to the life they must share or she would never again experience the wholeness of this single, perfect moment.

This, then, was love. The seedlings of it had planted themselves in her heart the first moment she saw him, and each word, each glance, each touch had nurtured them until they flowered into the love about which poets wrote. She loved Christian, and nothing was ever so wondrous as the rightness of that knowledge.

Though uncommonly gentle, his kiss embodied everything passionate and lovely about human contact. The desire to immerse herself forever in his kiss consumed her down to her core. Enfolded in his arms, her mouth completely at one with his, she sighed in glorious pleasure.

He ended the kiss before she was ready, but he showered kisses on her cheeks and brow. Finally, he just held her. "I wanted to take this slowly with you, Genevieve, but I lost my head."

"I cannot tell you how happy I am that you did." She blushed at the seductive quality in her voice.

He pulled back to look at her. "You aren't going to chastise me for taking advantage?"

She laughed softly. "Considering that I participated quite happily with you, it would be hypocritical."

He grinned at her. "How refreshing that you aren't playing the shocked little miss. I had planned to declare myself and ask your father's permission before kissing you."

Declare himself? Ask her father's permission? He planned to propose!

Shivers raced over her and burst outward. "I suppose we've taken a different path. Are you sorry?"

"Not at all." He kissed her again, and a sense of chaotic, hot desire mingled with that sensation of absolute belonging. His lips moved against hers, equal parts firm and gentle, and all passion. At the moment she ceased to exist except as a creature of need, he let out a husky chuckle. "We'd best go inside."

He was right, of course, but leaving his arms seemed almost too much to bear. Still, the pure, sweet bliss of knowing her heart had found its match strengthened her. "I suppose we must."

His eyes alight with joy equaling her own, he raised her to a stand. He touched her cheek, his lips curving gently. She sighed. There would be other moments—other kisses—with Christian, throughout her life. Hand in hand, they took a circuitous route past two other pairs of lovers enjoying the moonlight.

"Just so you know," he said, his voice low. "I mean to court you properly and publicly in Bath."

"I wouldn't have it any other way." She grinned at him, and his eyes burned from inner fire.

Christian released her hand before they crossed the terrace, leaving behind a lingering warmth. In the drawing room, a few groups clustered together, enjoying their last evening together. Her parents, it seemed, had already retired to their room for the evening. There was no sign of Matilda.

"Good night," he murmured, his glance hungry.

She bade him good night, barely managing not to throw herself into his arms again, and practically skipped into her parents' room.

"Mama, Papa, I have the most . . ." Her voice trailed off at their serious expressions.

"Sit down, Genevieve. We need to talk," her father said grimly.

Dread rang through her like a bell. She shot a frightened glance at her mother, but her color remained good, so her health could not be the reason for their sudden solemnity.

Genevieve sank into a nearby chair. "What is it?"

Her father spoke first. "You have attracted some male attention."

Oh, dear. They must have seen her in the garden with Christian. "Well, yes, but you see, his intentions are honorable—"

Her father interrupted before she could continue, "This very eve, I have received not one but two offers for your hand."

She blinked, hardly processing his words. Christian said that he hadn't spoken to Papa yet. He'd only promised to court her in Bath. Wait—two?

"Mr. Ashton and Lord Wickburgh have both asked for my permission."

The blood drained out of her face. "Lord Wickburgh? And . . . Mr. Ashton! Surely not. We've only conversed a few times. Mr. Ashton is the blandest man I have ever met."

Mama spoke up. "Consider carefully, Jenny. He is the respectable son of a vicar, who can offer you a respectable life."

"And Lord Wickburgh is a viscount—a Peer of the Realm with wealth, status, and power," Papa said.

"I am not interested in marrying either of them. I am in love with Christian Amesbury. And he has made his intentions known to me just tonight."

They exchanged glances. Mama said, "I thought he was courting Miss Widtsoe."

"No, he isn't. She only hoped she had his heart; he never said or did anything to encourage her. He has vowed to court me in Bath."

Mama put a hand over Genevieve's. "I know you've been infatuated with him since the beginning, but I caution you not to be too hasty."

Her father took up the conversation. "A vicar's wife would come naturally to you, and that position will allow you to live in the country as you wish and help many in the parish. On the other hand, a viscount can offer you a life of luxury and position no one else can. With the wealth and position of the wife of a peer, you would have considerable influence."

Genevieve shook her head, unable to even imagine being married to the man who turned her cold with a single look. "Not Lord Wickburgh."

Her father's voice grew stern. "He's a *lord*, Genevieve—so

much more prestigious than a youngest son with little to his name. I urge you to consider one of these other offers."

Mama squeezed Genevieve's hand. "Mr. Amesbury is handsome, I'll give you that, but he is also very young. There is more to marriage than a pleasing face. And consider how he misrepresented himself to your friend. He might be a flirt or a rake who's simply perfected the art of being discreet."

Genevieve gaped. She thought they understood. Rising, she squared her shoulders. "I have made my choice. I will allow no one but Christian Amesbury to court me, and when he asks me to marry him, I will accept him. Besides, he expects to be a vicar as well, when the position at his father's county seat becomes available. Until then, he acts as his father's right hand, and his painting grows more popular every day. I have no fear that he will be an adequate provider. I will, of course, leave the details to you, but please trust that I know my own heart."

Her parents exchanged a long look. Genevieve steeled herself to continue the battle.

Papa's stance relaxed, and he nodded. "Very well, Jenny. I trust you."

Letting out a breath, Mama smiled. "We just wanted to make sure."

So, this was some sort of test of her convictions. "Then you will refuse Mr. Ashton and Lord Wickburgh?"

Papa said, "I will."

Genevieve let out a pent-up breath. "Thank you." She kissed them both good night and left the room. There, on the floor of the corridor, lay her shawl, carefully folded. She picked it up and hugged it. She must have dropped it when she went out into the garden with Christian. She hugged it, reliving their glorious kiss. Humming, she went to bed, where, despite her excitement at the newness of her relationship with Christian Amesbury and her trepidation of facing Matilda on the morrow, she slept like a baby.

In the morning, she went automatically through her morning routine, donning her carriage dress in preparation for the journey. Though every thought of Christian sent little thrills through her, the knowledge Matilda would be heartbroken dimmed her pleasure. She moved with heavy footsteps to Matilda's bedchambers but found them empty. Instead, Genevieve found Matilda in the breakfast room, stirring her plate of eggs. Surprisingly, she alone occupied the room for the moment.

Genevieve sat next to her friend and touched her arm in concern. "How are you, Mattie?"

"You know, don't you? He told you?" Matilda raised her eyes.

Genevieve nodded and said apologetically, "He confided to me his concern that you had misunderstood his intentions. I advised him to clear it up before it was too late."

Matilda dropped her fork. "It was already too late. I thought he loved me."

"Mattie, he—"

Accusing eyes pinned her. "I thought you were my friend. But you stole him from me. The moment he saw you, he forgot all about me. And you . . . you encouraged him."

Genevieve recoiled, but she deserved Matilda's ire. She bit her lip as tears burned her eyes. "I'm so sorry, Mattie. I never meant—"

"You already had everyone else panting after you, but that

wasn't good enough. You had to have him, too—the only man I really loved!"

"It wasn't—"

"Don't ever speak to me!" Mattie stood up and limped out of the room, her sobs trailing behind her.

Genevieve rocked back at the onslaught, cold down to her toes. She pressed a hand over her mouth.

Matilda was right. All the while knowing Matilda's feelings, Genevieve had still encouraged Christian. If she had tried harder to point out Matilda's fine qualities, or if she had removed herself from the house party, perhaps Christian and Matilda would have made a match.

Who was she trying to fool? Her loyalty to Matilda didn't change the fact that Christian had never harbored a preference to Matilda. Her friend had invented the understanding in her head because she'd fallen for Christian's handsome face. But she didn't know him. Her tumultuous moods would never have suited Christian's artistic and poetic side. They couldn't even carry on a conversation, for heaven's sakes. Christian needed someone steady and calm—someone like Genevieve—but that knowledge did not change the fact that Matilda blamed Genevieve. And now she had lost a precious friendship.

Sir Reginald strode past the door toward the great hall. "Matilda," he called.

Other houseguests entered the breakfast room, their chatter filling the silence. Her appetite lost, Genevieve left the breakfast room. She halted at the sight of Sir Reginald and Matilda in the great hall speaking softly. He offered her his arm. Leaning heavily on him and limping, Matilda went with him toward the back of the house. Perhaps his loving heart would console Matilda.

Seeking consolation of her own, she went in search of Christian. She peeked into the drawing room. There, on an easel, sat an exquisite, full-color painting of the abbey, in all its gothic glory. Next to it, sat a portrait of Matilda so lifelike that it might have been looking out a window at her, glowing with beauty, with a lively smile and a twinkle in her eyes. He must have worked all night to complete them.

Where was he? She wandered into the great hall where others bade the hosts good-bye.

Genevieve approached her friend's mother. "Mrs. Widtsoe, have you seen Mr. Amesbury?"

Mrs. Widtsoe stiffened, obviously blaming her for Matilda's failure to capture Christian's proposal. She drew herself up. "He has already left."

"What? When?" Her heart stilled. Surely he hadn't left without saying good-bye.

"A few moments ago."

No. She was not losing him! Without a shred of decorum, she raced outside to the main drive leading to the highway, searching for a coach with the Tarrington coat of arms.

No coach traveled down the path. She was too late. Had she lost him as well as Matilda? Had she misunderstood him last night? Had he changed his mind? A life without her best friend, and worse, a life without the only man she would ever love, stretched out in endless gloom before her, and her heart cried out in despair. Her legs wobbled, and she nearly collapsed on the drive.

No. She would not give up on him. Whatever had happened, she'd find him and make it right. If she didn't catch him here, she'd find a way to see him in Bath and remind him why they belonged together, conventions be hanged.

Male voices reached her. Christian? She followed the voices to the side of the house. There stood Christian, wearing a gray coat and the buckskin breeches gentlemen favored when riding. He hadn't left, not yet. Her heart gave a leap, and she clasped her hands together.

Posture stiff, fists clenched at his sides, Christian faced Lord Wickburgh and spoke with hard, biting words, "I have no intention of stepping aside for you, unless she tells me that is her wish, and I know for a fact that she has no desire to spend time in your company."

"You know nothing, boy," Lord Wickburgh said. "I'm warning you; she is mine and I mean to have her. If you continue to interfere, you will meet an unhappy end."

"Stay away from her, or it is you who will meet an unhappy end."

Genevieve would never have imagined the hardness in Christian's voice. They stood, both determined, neither backing down, glaring hard enough to bore holes through one another.

"Christian, let's go!" the earl's voice called from the front steps.

Wickburgh let out a sneering laugh. "Go to your father, boy."

"Coming, Father," Christian said. To Lord Wickburgh, he said, "We are finished here. And you will not bother Miss Marshall again." He gave Lord Wickburgh one final long look and strode away.

Genevieve stepped back quickly and headed toward the house. It would not do to let Christian know she'd seen the encounter. Her heart pounded. Seeing Christian locked in such a dangerous play with Lord Wickburgh filled her with both

210

dread at his danger, and excitement that he'd been willing to fight for her. She hurried toward the front door, meeting the earl as he stepped off the stairs.

Lord Tarrington nodded as they passed. "Miss Marshall."

"My lord."

"I expect I'll be seeing you in Bath?" He drew on his gloves.

"I hope so, my lord."

He eyed her, and she met his gaze, allowing him to make up his mind about her. His expression softened as if he found something that pleased him. Then he lifted his gaze to a point behind her. She turned. Christian, still grim, strode toward her. As he raised his head, his focus fell on her. His expression became wary.

"Miss Marshall," Christian said as he approached, falling into formal speech, probably for the sake of his father.

"Ah, the coach is here." The earl gestured. "I'll wait for you inside, son."

Christian nodded, not taking his eyes off Genevieve. Why the wariness in him? Perhaps he was still angry over his encounter with Lord Wickburgh.

She gave him a tentative smile. "I saw the paintings. They are exquisite."

His smile was almost pained. "I'm glad you liked them. Mr. Widtsoe seemed pleased."

His palpable tension created a sudden jitteriness. Had his kiss simply been the product of moonlight on the final night of a house party?

Her fears wormed out of her and into her voice. She whispered, "Were you going to leave without saying good-bye?"

He hesitated. "I had not yet decided."

Her breath rushed out of her. "Did it mean nothing to you?"

Eyeing her with such guardedness, he said nothing for a long moment. "It meant something to me. I was sincere. But it seems my suit is not adequate."

"What do you mean?"

"You left your shawl in the garden, and I was returning it. I heard you and your parents; the door was open. They don't want you to settle for a youngest son."

Her breath rushed out of her in relief. He had not used her, or changed his mind, he simply questioned her commitment. Stepping closer, she took his hand and said boldly, "They only wanted to make sure I knew my own mind. And I do."

His eyes, so intense, probed hers until everything softened in his expression. He tugged on her hand, drawing her near. "You don't mind that I'm the youngest?"

"Not if you don't mind that I'm the daughter of a sea captain."

A slow smile stole over his expression. "I should not have doubted you."

"No." She smiled to soften her words and intertwined her fingers with his.

The same light that shone from his eyes last night returned. "It's probably too soon to say this, since I haven't formally courted you, but I love you. And I want to spend the rest of forever with you."

Surely her heart would explode with the love filling it past capacity. She'd never dreamed the power of those words. "Forever may not be long enough."

Hope and happiness filled those beautiful eyes. "I can't offer you a title or coffers of money."

She couldn't resist being just a little bit saucy. "I would prefer not to starve, but if you can promise me food on the table and love in our home, I will be content—happy, even. Delirious."

Someone cleared her throat, drawing Genevieve's attention off Christian. Matilda stood, clasping her hands in front of her nervously. "I just came to say good-bye." She glanced back at Sir Reginald waiting by the front door before fixing her gaze on Christian. "Mr. Amesbury, I apologize for placing you in difficulty. I misunderstood—through no fault of yours. And I thank you for the lovely portrait. I've never seen its equal."

"It was my pleasure," he said graciously.

Matilda turned her gaze to Genevieve. Her face crumpled, and tears filled her eyes. "Forgive me, Jenny!" She rushed forward, her arms outstretched.

Genevieve met her and caught her into an embrace. "There is nothing to forgive. I am grieved to have caused you pain."

Matilda shook her head. "You were only following your heart, as you should. You two are a perfect match. Good-bye for now. I hope to see you soon . . . in a church?"

Genevieve smiled up at Christian.

He met her with an adoring gaze. "That is the idea—as soon as possible."

Matilda hugged Genevieve again. "Until then, good-bye." She headed toward the house as Sir Reginald trotted down the front steps to her. They walked together down a path around the side of the house.

With a sultry gleam in his eye, Christian pulled Genevieve

into his arms. "I love you, Genevieve." He cupped her cheek and kissed her so expertly, so thoroughly, that her knees wobbled.

"Oh my," she said when she could speak. "I think we'd best have the banns read as soon as possible."

He lifted a brow. "Are you asking me to marry you?"

"I believe I am."

He grinned. "Perfect."

Christian and Genevieve's story continues in *A Perfect Secret*, available at online retailers everywhere.

About Donna Hatch

Donna Hatch is the award-winning author of the best-selling Rogue Hearts Series. She discovered her writing passion at the tender age of eight and has been listening to those voices ever since. A sought-after workshop presenter, she juggles her day job, freelance editing, multiple volunteer positions, not to mention her six children (seven, counting her husband), and still manages to make time to write. Yes, writing IS an obsession. A native of Arizona, she and her husband of over twenty years are living proof that there really is a happily ever after.

For sneak peeks, specials, deleted scenes, and more information, visit Donna's website: www.donnahatch.com

THE
PAUPERS' HOUSE
PARTY

By Sarah M. Eden

OTHER BOOKS BY
SARAH M. EDEN

Hope Springs Series
Longing for Home
Hope Springs
Love Remains
My Dearest Love

**The Lancaster Family
Series**
Seeking Persephone
Courting Miss Lancaster
Romancing Daphne

Regency Romances
The Kiss of a Stranger
Glimmer of Hope
An Unlikely Match
For Elise
All Regency Collection
British Isles Collection

**Timeless Romance
Anthologies**
Winter Collection
Spring Vacation Collection
European Collection
Summer Wedding
Collection
Love Letter Collection

**The Jonquil Brothers
Series**
Friends and Foes
Drops of Gold
As You Are
A Fine Gentleman

Historical Westerns
The Sheriffs of Savage Wells
Old West Collection
Mail Order Bride
Collection

CHAPTER ONE

Somerset, England 1811

Edward Downy considered house parties a particularly inhumane method of torture. He enjoyed company, conversation, a bit of sport, and a fortnight or so of finer meals than his meager means supplied, but he'd not yet attended one of these gatherings in which the guests did not, at some point, descend into a comparison, however subtle, of one another's estates, incomes, and positions in Society. Edward would inherit his father's estate in all its charming inability to prove profitable, an income which seldom fell on the preferable side of zero, and a place in Society that had slipped with each generation.

House parties were not for the poverty-stricken nor faint of heart.

Yet when an invitation arrived at Downy House requesting the presence of Edward and his younger brother, Tom, at a three weeks' long gathering hosted by Mr. and Mrs. Warrick in Somerset, Edward found himself unhappily obliged to accept. The brothers had been granted their usual two weeks in London, an indulgence which he knew full well placed a financial burden on his parents. To be relieved of the need to feed them both for nearly a month seemed the least he could offer in acknowledgement of their kindness.

THE PAUPER'S HOUSE PARTY

So Edward packed his finest clothes and least-worn pocket handkerchiefs as well as a small stack of his favorite books, and resigned himself to being quite ceaselessly tortured.

Tom was not so low-spirited. He never was. One might be excused for thinking him dim-witted or naïve. Tom was neither; he simply didn't bother to dwell on the harsh aspects of reality and found enjoyment in whatever he could. Edward had always envied him that a little. He, himself, was too often overly aware of the hopelessness of the family's situation.

"Do you suppose any beautiful ladies will be included in the numbers?" Tom asked, peering out the window as the carriage rolled up the long, pebbled drive. An afternoon rain had made the journey impossible to complete on horseback—more was the pity.

"Beautiful ladies are always included in the numbers," Edward said. He couldn't rightly say whether or not that was a point in favor of these parties. Though his prospects were too dismal to make him a good match in any lady's eye—let alone her parents'—a light flirtation now and then, a dance or two at a ball, couldn't help but lift his spirits. He could enjoy the game, as it were, even knowing he would never be the victor.

"I, for one, am fully prepared to spend this fortnight breaking a heart or two," Tom declared.

"Careful, brother. One of those hearts you injure might be your own."

Tom gave him a look of dry rebuke. "Younger sons know better than to let their hearts grow attached to anyone or anything. I am in no danger, I assure you."

"And I assure you," Edward countered, "that impoverished eldest sons learn the same harsh lesson very quickly."

"Quite the pair, we two." Tom returned his attention to the fast-approaching house. "I hate to say it, but I suspect we are here merely to round out the numbers."

"Why else are the poor but genteel included in such things?"

It stood to reason, really, that he'd lost his taste for house parties. He was *always* invited as an afterthought, as assurance to the hostess that her table would be evenly set. The only difference between him and the chairs themselves was that he breathed and had a pulse. One generally wished to be valued for more than that.

Edward assumed his best manners as they were ushered into the house and directly to the drawing room. An oddity, that. Guests were always afforded time in their assigned bedchamber to recover from their journey. A quick glance around the room told him that he and Tom were not the only ones to be treated to the same unusual reception.

"Downy," a familiar voice greeted him.

Turning, Edward discovered a good friend, John Isley, with whom he'd shared the dubious honor of occupying the bottom-most rung of social distinction amongst their peer group at Eton. Finances had not improved much for either of them over the years.

"I didn't realize you were acquainted with the Warricks," Isley said.

"Vaguely. Mother required a quick skimming of Debrett's before she could entirely place them. Her creative ability was put firmly to the test in making any sort of connection between our families."

Isley chuckled. "My mother didn't even try. 'They're kin to

the Earl of Garrismond,' she said. And that was the end of any arguing."

"Wasn't Harold Barton connected to Garrismond in some roundabout way?" Edward asked, a faint recollection from their school days surfacing at the reference to the earl.

"Indeed, which made me even more loath to meet more of His Lordship's family."

Edward slapped his friend on the shoulder. "I thought I was to be the only penniless wretch foisted upon the gathering, excepting Tom, of course."

"That is the truly odd thing." Isley made a quick, subtle motion toward the rest of the crowd. "I've watched the new arrivals this past hour and noticed something unexpected. Eye their cuffs and neckcloths and the elbows of the men's jackets. Then take a gander at the ladies' gloves and hems."

Edward made a quick assessment and knew immediately what his friend had noticed. "Frayed, threadbare, mended."

"Precisely. I've not seen a single guest who does not show the signs of impending insolvency." He held his hands up, revealing his own frayed cuffs. "I know the symptoms well."

Edward mimicked the gesture. "As do I."

Tom arrived on the scene in precisely that moment. He held his hands up the same way they were. "Is this some social custom I've not heard of yet?"

Edward eyed the thin elbows of his brother's jacket, then met Isley's gaze. "All the symptoms."

Isley laughed silently.

"Perhaps we've all been gathered here to contain the epidemic." Edward looked over the crowd once more. His gaze, however, remained overly long on one particular guest.

She wore a simple traveling dress. Her dark hair was pulled up in an uncomplicated style that might easily have been created without the help of a maid. Her posture and manner was that of a person accustomed to going unnoticed, though there was nothing truly timid in it. She ought not to have drawn his attention at all, being surrounded by ladies and gentlemen of identical circumstances, but he couldn't immediately look away.

Whilst most of the gathering stood about in harried conversation, clearly frantic to make some sense of having been herded so unceremoniously into the drawing room, she kept her own company, her patience not appearing the least strained. She was calm in the face of chaos, tranquil despite the crush. She seemed entirely content to simply wait. Her serenity pulled at him, spoke to his own preference for stillness and peace. It was such a rare thing in Society, which thrived on a constant whirl of business, of coming and going, of proving one's worth by how many people and things required one's attention.

Isley interrupted his thoughts with a whispered, but pointed, comment. "I don't know whether you've spied a particularly tempting decanter of port hidden somewhere across the room or a particularly pretty face, but either way I would appreciate being enlightened."

"Simply attempting to sort out this guest list." Why he felt such reluctance to point out the young lady to his good friend, Edward couldn't rightly say. She was a stranger, after all. He didn't even know her name. To feel a protective instinct for an utter stranger made little sense—it was entirely possible she didn't need him shielding her from others' attention—yet he couldn't deny that he felt precisely that.

"Sort no more, my friend," Isley said. "I believe our hosts have made an appearance at last."

A couple, both likely on the far side of their seventies, glided into the room, bedecked in enough lace and jewels to meet the financial needs of the entirety of southwest England, perhaps beyond. What an immediate contrast they made to their guests.

A hush fell immediately over the assembly. All eyes were on the Warricks, who stood but a single step inside the doorway.

"Welcome, one and all." Mr. Warrick grandly motioned to the crowd, his eyes seeming to take them all in individually. "We are so pleased you could join us for what we have decided is to be our last house party."

A few obligatory sounds of regret filled the otherwise silent room. Everyone other than the Warricks looked as confused as Edward felt.

"We have grown old, as you no doubt can see," Mr. Warrick continued. "Our constitutions are not at all what they once were, and hosting gatherings, traveling to and from, has grown too wearying."

Mrs. Warrick nodded almost regally.

"We have quite carefully chosen those we wished to take part in these farewell festivities." Mr. Warrick treated them all to a magnanimous smile. "And here you all are."

"At last," Mrs. Warrick added.

Something about the display struck Edward as rather orchestrated, as though the speech and postures and expressions of regret had been thoroughly rehearsed to maximize their impact.

"We hardly know them," Tom whispered. "Why would they specifically invite strangers to their *fête d'adieu?*"

"I haven't the slightest idea," Edward whispered back.

"We hope you will all make yourselves at home," Mr. Warrick continued. "Enjoy one another's company and this, no doubt, welcome respite from the weight of your various circumstances."

The first hints of unease began niggling at the back of Edward's mind.

"The servants have been instructed not to accept any tokens of acknowledgement from the guests at this house party, so do not feel as though that is necessary."

They were being told not to leave the expected coins for the servants? Edward had never heard those instructions at any house party.

"We simply want all of you to enjoy yourselves," Mr. Warrick explained. "Ours has been a very prosperous existence, and we wish to do some good with it while we still can."

The Warricks had brought together the destitute, the struggling, and the futureless in order to bestow their graciousness upon them all at once. Edward and Tom were not, then, to serve as extra bodies at this party. They had been brought to Somerset to reside at the Society equivalent of the alms house.

"Now, before you are all shown to your rooms, we have one bit of information to pass along," Mr. Warrick said. "As we never had children of our own and this estate is not subject to an entailment, we are in a position to choose our own heir. At the end of this party, we will do exactly that, from amongst you."

The silence upon the Warrick's arrival had been one of curiosity. The silence that followed that pronouncement was one of complete and utter shock.

"We mean to come to know you, to learn more of who you

are and from whence you come. We will learn all we can, and then will decide who among you is most suited for, most in need of, most . . . deserving of the fortune we are offering." Mr. Warrick emphasized the word *deserving* in an almost sinister voice, as if warning them that they had best do nothing that might bring down upon them the disapproval of their hosts.

"Take time to settle in," Mrs. Warrick said, smiling at all of them. "We will see you at dinner, which will be served at precisely six o'clock. Precisely."

They flitted from the room, jewelry clanking and lace fluttering in their wake.

Isley muttered a word generally not spoken in drawing rooms. Tom stood, mouth slightly agape, staring at the spot the Warricks had occupied only a moment ago. Edward's heart alternately skipped in anticipation and dropped to his toes with dread. The Warrick estate was large, profitable, and, as it turned out, waiting to be claimed.

This Paupers' House Party had, in an instant, turned into a Battle Royal.

CHAPTER TWO

Agatha Holmwood would have walked directly to nearby Yeovil, climbed on to the first northward traveling mail coach, and returned home. She would have, if the choice had been hers. But, no matter that she was nearing twenty-one and not a dunderhead by anyone's estimation, she was female and, therefore, hadn't the slightest control over her comings and goings.

Thus, rather than take a jaunt to Yeovil and have a gander at their famous gloves before hying herself home, Agatha instead stood in the bedchamber assigned to her father, watching him pace and awaiting his decision.

"Estimates place the Warrick estate's value considerably higher than that of Birchall." Father compared every family's estate, income, and standing to that of Birchall, the finest home in their neighborhood.

Birchall, of course, didn't come near the stateliness of Chatsworth or Lyme Park or Attingham, but it was the jewel of the western-most corner of the northwestern-most tip of Shropshire, a distinction which meant a great deal to at least a dozen people. How could Agatha fail to recognize the importance of the Birchall measuring standard?

"Do the estimates include the silver, Father? Because I would point out we have not yet seen that." She lowered her voice and whispered somberly, "It might be plate."

Father was quick to correct that idea. "Plate? In a house of this size?" No one in her family had ever understood or shared her sense of humor.

Agatha made a vague sound of acknowledgement, knowing that was most likely to convince her father to continue on with whatever he meant to tell her.

Father clasped his hands behind his back as he made yet another circuit of the room. "I've been speaking with some of the others, and consensus seems to be that the Warricks are looking for an heir who is young, your generation and not mine."

Agatha nodded solemnly. "One does not wish for an heir with a foot in the grave."

"A foot in the grave?" Father's eyes pulled wide, and his gaze fell on her once more. "How old do you think I am, young lady?"

"Why, you must be very nearly forty." She emphasized the final word with just the right amount of horrified amazement. She knew perfectly well her father was fast approaching fifty, but teasing her family members, even if they didn't understand her jests, was far too diverting a pastime to give up.

Father shook his head and pressed forward with the topic at hand. He would wear a path in the rug with all his pacing. "Everyone is convinced the Warricks will choose a young person as heir, but there is no consensus as to whether they will prefer a male or a female."

Agatha managed not to roll her eyes. How was this part of

the Warricks' puzzle even up for debate? In matters of inheritance, finance, opportunities—in *all* matters, really—a male was always preferred. It was the way of the world.

"There is only one thing to be done, Father. We will return home and allow the young gentlemen to their sport."

"Sport?" Father eyed her with confusion once more. "I hadn't heard there was to be sport today. The season isn't right for birds or foxes."

"But the season is ideal for sniffing out an inheritance," Agatha responded.

"I had hoped you would feel that way." Not only had he missed the note of sarcasm in her tone, an eagerness entered his eyes that left her immediately wary. "With this bequest, you would have a dowry that could fetch you a very well-heeled husband from the highest ranks of Society."

"Or a fortune hunter," she countered.

"Nonsense. We could afford to be fastidious, Agatha. This estate and the income from it would win you a husband who would open doors for the rest of the family." Father's eyes took on an almost desperate glow. "Your sisters could marry. Our home and lands could be put to rights. Your brother would at last have some expectation of an income. You could save us all."

"So long as you haven't allowed your hopes to reach inadvisable heights," Agatha said dryly.

"I am glad we agree. Come sit." Father pointed to the window seat.

She obeyed. He, however, didn't stop his pacing for even a moment. She might have to win this inheritance simply so they wouldn't have to pay to repair the flooring.

"We do not know yet which of the Warricks will have the

most say over the final decision." Father spoke matter-of-factly. Clearly, her participation in the contest the Warricks were hosting was a foregone conclusion in his mind. "Generally, one would assume the husband would have the most influence on financial matters, but I have known enough marriages in which that was not the case to make me wary of simply accepting that assumption. We, therefore, need to decide which of the two *you* are most likely to influence."

"Which of them is most likely to be won over by a plum pudding? I make a delicious plum pudding."

Father waved that suggestion aside. "They have a fine cook, I'm certain. And all the pudding they could wish for."

"Pie, then?"

"I think we can safely rule out food-based strategies, Agatha." Father spoke with tried patience. His fingers tapped against each other behind his back. His brow pulled low. "They are looking for an heir, someone to care for the estate after they've passed on in the way they would wish for it to be looked after. They want someone who feels like family."

"In that case," she assumed her most ponderous tone, "my best approach would be to disagree with them about trivial things, consider it a disproportionately personal slight, and then rehash the argument at inopportune moments."

Once again she was on the receiving end of one of Father's confused glances. "I want her to think of you as her daughter."

"How is that different from what I just said?" She really needed to stop jesting or Father's face would be permanently twisted with bewilderment. "Father, I can appreciate that this inheritance would be a most welcome windfall for the Holmwood family, but can you not see how ridiculous this is? A house full of impoverished people setting themselves against one another in the hope of being handsomely paid for their viciousness? It's rather unseemly."

"Who is to say this undertaking will be vicious? I am certain the participants will be civil."

For a man who had lived fifty years in the world, Father understood so little of it. "I, for one, am looking forward to the farewell musicale when we all join in songs of friendship and mutual approbation, followed by long, drawn-out embraces and promises to exchange letters."

"Don't say things like that around the Warricks." Father spoke in utter earnest. "They'll think you're a bit touched in the head."

"I am convinced they are a bit touched in the head, so this might help our 'seem like family' strategy."

Father sighed, the sound one of frustration rather than true weariness. "There is some comfort in knowing you tend to be quiet and demure around strangers. And you are pretty when you smile. That should help."

"Thank you, Father." She chose to see compliments in his vaguely uncomplimentary comments. It made life simpler.

"Please, for the sake of your family, attempt to make an impression—a *favorable* impression—on the Warricks. This could change our family's entire future for generations."

He was right, of course. Surely there was a way to participate in the "festivities" without completely sacrificing her dignity, especially when a certain fair-haired young gentleman was about.

She'd noticed him the moment he'd walked into the drawing room that afternoon. He'd carried himself with a calm confidence, had immediately greeted another attendee with the warm smile of friendship. He'd come with another gentleman, one she'd guess was his brother—there'd been a noticeable resemblance.

He'd not been there more than a quarter-hour before his gaze had settled on her. She'd done her best to simply breathe whilst under his scrutiny. In that moment, she'd been keenly aware of her outdated traveling dress and twice-mended gloves, and she'd silently decried the poor manners of their hosts to not allow new arrivals even a moment in which to freshen their appearance and smooth their hair. She'd been an utter fright.

Agatha didn't know whether to go down to dinner looking as ghastly as she admittedly still did, simply to prove to Mr. Golden-haired Adonis that she didn't worry overly much about strangers' opinions on her appearance, or to put extra effort into rectifying her horrific demeanor to prove that he ought not to have judged her based on a moment's glance. Of course, that meant admitting she'd judged him as well.

What he didn't know couldn't hurt . . . her.

"I will make certain I say at least three complimentary things about you to him over port tonight," Father said.

An uncomfortable mixture of hope and panic immediately set in. "You are acquainted with him?" At the very least, she might learn the gentleman's name.

"Vaguely," he said. "He belongs to the club my grandfather belonged to and my father had intended to join before realizing the true state of his finances. Still, Mr. Warrick and I have exchanged the occasional generic greeting."

Mr. Warrick. Good heavens, of course he was speaking of Mr. Warrick.

"While I do my best to speak, however briefly, with Mr. Warrick tonight, you need to make an impression on Mrs. Warrick."

"I could recite the monarchs in reverse order," Agatha suggested. "That cannot fail to make an impression."

"No. No puddings or pies. No backwards kings and queens. No oddities, Agatha. Smile. Be demure. Find something about her to genuinely compliment. And please take this seriously." Father sat beside her on the window seat. "A profitable estate and your family's future is at stake—their entire future."

What was a bit of groveling when one's entire family was in such desperate need? It wasn't as though she'd had to beg, plead, borrow, and generally humble herself for whatever bit of charity her neighbors were willing to bestow.

Some young ladies were adept at pianoforte. Others sang like angels. Some could paint beautiful watercolors. Agatha had a knack for setting aside every last shred of her dignity and humiliating herself for her family's sake.

I need a new talent.

CHAPTER THREE

The late Admiral Horatio Nelson would, no doubt, have been impressed to watch the expertise with which the attendees maneuvered and positioned themselves during that night's after-dinner port. A veritable regatta of cravats and faded frock coats encircled their host, tossing out an endless stream of flattering words, about both him and themselves. Had the Warricks realized upon concocting this scheme of theirs that they would be subjected to three weeks of ceaseless attentions?

"This could be a very long house party," Edward muttered to his brother. He and Tom were the only gentlemen not swarming their host. "I doubt *this* will stop even once while we're here."

"That is why I'm taking your approach," Tom said.

"My *what?*"

"All the guests tossing compliments at Mr. Warrick's head will simply blur together in his memory. But you and I, we will stand out because we aren't following suit."

Edward turned more fully to face Tom. "You are joining the competition?"

"It is a fortune," Tom said, lowering his voice. "Certainly you don't think I'm going to pass up a chance at a fortune."

Tom couldn't be serious. "But this entire thing is demeaning. The Warricks have set this up like a dog fight, and we, dear brother, are the dogs."

"I am the younger son of an impoverished family. I am well acquainted with 'demeaning.' What I'd like to be well acquainted with is a comfortable income."

This was unexpected. "You would lower yourself to compete for this inheritance?"

Tom set his glass of port on the tabletop. He kept his voice low. "You may have resigned yourself to living out your life alone, hoping to economize enough to keep the Downy estate solvent. I, however, do not even have that. As humiliating as the prospect is, this dog fight is my only chance."

Edward had never heard Tom speak so matter-of-factly about their situation. For all intents and purposes, his brother had never seemed anything but casually unconcerned about important matters. Indeed, most people assumed Tom hadn't a fully formed thought rattling around in his head.

"I wish I had more to offer you, Tom. Caroline's marriage pulled the estate out of debt, but nothing short of a good investment of money will make it profitable."

Tom sighed even as he shrugged. "If Warrick chooses me, we can use some of the income from this estate to bolster the Downy estate, then we'll both have something of an income."

It was a generous offer and, Edward knew, a genuine one. "If by some odd twist of fate, Warrick chooses me"—Edward still didn't mean to actively participate in the competition, but stranger things had happened—"this estate will go to you, with only enough held back to bring the Downy estate back into profit."

Tom nodded sharply. "I will gladly accept that offer."

Edward only hoped desperation didn't push Tom to do something truly humiliating. Though the income would be a godsend, a man didn't recover easily from sacrificing his pride.

"Gentlemen. Gentlemen," Mr. Warrick's hardy voice called out. "We'd best join the ladies in the drawing room. They'll be expecting us."

He emerged from the crowd, looking well pleased with himself. Edward watched him pass, unsure if he was more amazed at how much the man was enjoying the collective fawning or discouraged to see yet another member of Society who felt his wealth entitled him to such groveling.

Mr. Warrick's gaze settled on Edward, lingering there for a drawn-out moment. Edward hadn't the heart to smile or nod or otherwise acknowledge the singling out that most of the others in the room would likely have drooled over. He found the entire charade nauseating. Mr. Warrick's brow pulled, and his gaze shifted to Tom, who, to his credit, kept himself to a quick dip of his head and nothing more.

As the rest of the gentlemen followed in Warrick's wake, Isley crossed instead to the table. "What are the two of you playing at?" he asked, eyeing them both in turn.

"Not Warrick's little game," Edward answered. "He's making fools of the lot of us."

Isley made a sound of dismissal. "I'll play the fool for three weeks if it'll earn me an estate this size. I made a few discreet inquiries. Warrick likely has at least £5000 a year, quite possibly more."

The sound of Tom's thick swallow told Edward as nothing else could that his brother only grew more desperate at hearing that number. He, himself, wasn't entirely immune to it. In a good year, the Downy estate might bring £100. In a *very* good year.

"Only one person will be named heir," Edward reminded them all. "Everyone else will leave just as penniless as they arrived, but with less dignity. That is a steep price." He, for one, didn't like the idea of contributing to the abasement of two dozen people.

"Appease your conscience if you can," Isley said. "In the meantime, I will be joining Mr. and Mrs. Warrick in the drawing room and hoping to make a good showing for myself. Father did not leave Mother a widow's jointure, and she is living with her sister. This estate has a dower house. She wouldn't be a poor relation." A touch of desperation showed in Isley's face, not unlike what Edward had seen in Tom's expression a moment ago.

This was what he hated most about the Warrick's pitting their guests against one another. Though he didn't know everyone's story, Edward didn't doubt they were all in straits as dire as Isley's and Tom's and his. Hopes were being raised, most of which would be cruelly dashed in three weeks' time.

They joined the party in the drawing room. The Warricks were flanked on all sides by guests eager to assist, praise, and otherwise make themselves a favorite. Even if Edward were interested in participating, there'd be little point trying. Tom seemed to feel the same way; he found a seat and watched the display with barely concealed amusement. Either he was a terribly good actor, or he too had realized the futility of trying to make an impression while so many were already eagerly attempting to do so.

Edward kept to the edges of the room, making a circuit in search of a comfortable chair. His progress was hampered when he reached a window alcove with voices coming from within. He could not pass forward without his presence being made known, but a couple had taken up residence a few steps behind him and he couldn't easily backtrack, either.

"Did Mrs. Warrick seem impressed with you?" a man's voice asked.

"She found it odd that I offered to stir her tea," was the response.

"Stir her—? You—?" Clearly her answer had been unexpected.

"You told me to make myself useful to her, Father. That seemed a useful thing to do."

Had the Warrick's involved a simpleton in their schemes? That was truly despicable.

"I was unable to get a word in with Mr. Warrick," the poor girl's father said. "I will try again when fewer of the guests are about. You do the same with Mrs. Warrick."

"Perhaps I might offer to cut her food for her at breakfast in the morning."

"No, Agatha." Unmistakable frustration filled his words. "Do not do anything which involves personally manipulating her food or drink. Promise you won't. Promise."

"I promise, Father," she said cheerfully.

"I will go attempt to ascertain the other guests' strategies. Try not to make a spectacle of yourself."

"Yes, Father."

A man likely Edward's own father's age stepped from the alcove and directly toward the center of the room. So intent was he upon his goal that he did not notice Edward so nearby. He did not spare his ill-used daughter so much as a single backward glance.

The situation was none of Edward's concern. Indeed, he did not even know the ambitious gentleman or his daughter. Yet, he couldn't simply walk away, leaving the unfortunate young lady to her misery.

He stepped around the corner and into the alcove. It wasn't so secluded as to make his presence there inappropriate. He recognized her: the serene, dark-haired beauty he'd spied in the crowd earlier that day. Had her calmness come not from being at ease in chaotic situations but rather from being slow-witted?

She spotted him there. "Adonis," she said with the exact tone of one recognizing another person.

"No," he said, kindly. "I am Edward. Edward Downy."

A tiny hint of color touched her cheeks. She must have realized how inappropriate it was for him to introduce himself. But what option did he have, really?

"I would do this properly," he said, "but anyone who might make the introduction is otherwise occupied."

"'Otherwise occupied'? I am assuming by that you mean 'on the hunt for a fortune.'" Her gaze shifted from him to the gathering beyond the alcove. "It appears to be an exhausting undertaking. I fully expect breakfast to be a very hardy meal in the morning."

On the surface, her ramblings seemed nonsensical, but Edward wasn't convinced. He sensed, though it was subtle, more than a hint of dryness.

"What of you?" she asked. "Why are you not across the room commending Mr. Warrick on his management of his estate or complimenting Mrs. Warrick on her choice of laces? Do you not realize how crucial first impressions are? Second impressions are comparatively worthless. And *third* impressions . . . those aren't even worth mentioning."

Edward bit back a smile. He suspected his companion was far from the featherhead he had at first assumed her to be. Her wit was simply subtle, dry, understated.

"This is the point at which either of my parents would tell me in desperate whispers not to say such nonsensical things in front of other people." She offered a conspiratorial smile. "They are convinced that someday someone will mistake me for a bedlamite and insist I be locked away, and wouldn't that be a terrible thing." She shrugged. "I suppose there is a certain madness to continually antagonizing one's parents with humor they cannot seem to recognize, let alone appreciate. Although, it is also rather imbecilic to speak nonstop to a gentleman with whom one is not the least bit acquainted." Her expression turned apologetic. "I would tell you that I don't usually talk this much, but honesty compels me to admit that I do."

"And honesty compels me to admit that I am enjoying this admittedly one-sided conversation." He truly was. His as-yet-unnamed companion was decidedly diverting. "Although I would very much appreciate knowing what it is I am to call you."

"Ah, yes. That is where we began this tangent, isn't it? The utter lack of unoccupied guests to make a proper introduction." She squared her shoulders and faced him fully. "I am Agatha Holmwood. And I likely needn't tell you that I have no dowry, no pin money, and no prospects."

"And I likely needn't tell you that I am to inherit a worthless estate that is one poor harvest away from severe indebtedness, a younger brother who will forever be a drain on my future nonexistent income, and have been politely shunned by every matchmaking mother in London."

She nodded solemnly. "London Society can sense poverty the way foxes can sense the approach of the hounds. Terrifies them."

"Except for the Warricks." Edward motioned to their gleeful hosts. "They're encouraging the hounds."

"They are *taunting* them," Miss Holmwood corrected.

At last, someone who viewed the display the same way he did. "Making the destitute compete for something their entire families are desperate for? I was beginning to suspect I was the only one here who found that off-putting."

"My father certainly doesn't. He is convinced this is the answer to all of our problems and means to throw the both of us headlong into this humiliating farce."

"Would you take a turn with me, Miss Holmwood?" Edward wished to continue their conversation but did not care to push the bounds of propriety by remaining even as isolated as they were.

She nodded her agreement, and they walked, side-by-side, out of the alcove and along the outer edge of the drawing room.

"You disapprove of this competition," Edward said. "Is that why you are sabotaging your father's efforts?"

"I am not interfering with *his* efforts," she answered. "I am simply not making any efforts of my own."

He gave a quick dip of his head to one of the guests as they walked past. Then, to Miss Holmwood, he said, "Did you actually offer to stir Miss Warrick's tea?"

She laughed lightly. "No, but I could not resist seeing the shock on my father's face. I really am the worst sort of daughter."

But the best sort of conversational companion. "It seems you and I are the only guests who do not intend to participate. We may find ourselves spending a great many evenings conversing whilst the other guests undertake their scraping and bowing."

"Fortunately for us, talking is one of my particular specialties."

"What are your other particular specialties?" he asked.

They had nearly completed their first circuit of the room. Few people were anywhere other than very close to where the Warricks held court, so Edward and Miss Holmwood had made their turn unimpeded.

"I have a tremendous talent for begging," Miss Holmwood answered unabashedly. "I have, in my day, convinced the collier, the merchant, several dressmakers, and a rather disgruntled creditor of my father's to grant us a bit more time before paying our debts to them. And I once managed to leave the grand estate of Birchall in our neighborhood with a charity basket and a promise to send their brick mason to inspect our crumbling chimneys."

She had begged charity of a fellow member of the upper classes? That was an exercise in humility most ladies of her station would never need endure.

"Yet this"—he indicated the Warricks—"feels different, doesn't it?"

"Yes. Our receiving the basket and mason did not take a basket and mason away from someone else."

242

She hit upon exactly what he'd been trying to put into words. His distaste for the Paupers' House Party went beyond simply disliking the humiliation of it all. The Warricks were turning people who might otherwise be empathetic toward one another into competitors. They were taking away hoped-for futures and would-be friendships.

They were using people's desperation as a source of entertainment. He couldn't change what the Warricks had set in motion, but he vowed not to contribute to the humiliation of the other guests. And though he'd only known her a matter of minutes, he felt particularly determined to keep that promise where Agatha Holmwood was concerned.

CHAPTER FOUR

There was, indeed, no rest for the weary. At breakfast the next morning—morning, of course, falling somewhere between ten and eleven o'clock—the guests were told to report to the back garden for a picnic at noon. Agatha sighed once before finishing her bowl of porridge. She had intended to take advantage of the rare opportunity to partake in richer foods than she enjoyed at home, but Mrs. Warrick had chosen for herself a traditional breakfast of eggs, mushrooms, sausages, and liver pudding, so the large crowd at the morning meal had predictably made the same choice. Porridge, however boring and commonplace, had been a faster option.

Connoisseurs would have scoffed, but Agatha had always preferred efficiency in her meals. That likely came as a result of being the one who prepared those meals.

Father ran her to ground just as the large floor clock in the front entryway chimed the hour. "Agatha. What in heaven's name are you doing in here? You are going to be late to the picnic."

"Is there a picnic today?"

"Surely you—" Father narrowed his gaze. "You knew there was a picnic."

She smiled and nodded. "I did. I was about to step outside when you arrived."

"About to? It is noon. Everyone is already gathered in the garden."

"Already?" She pulled her eyes wide. "What are we doing in here? We should hurry."

For the briefest of moments, Father looked as though he meant to point out that he'd made the same insistent suggestion first. But in the end, he opted to simply take her arm in his and move swiftly to the terrace doors.

"You simply must find an opportunity to speak with Mrs. Warrick," he said as he moved at an impressive clip toward the garden. "Be personable and sweet. Inquire after her health."

Agatha nodded. "I will make certain to express my concern that she looks so pale and sickly."

Absolute horror seized Father's features. "Good heavens, Agatha. Do not say that. Please."

"But you just said—"

"Could you not say something more along the lines of 'How has your day been?' or 'What a pleasure to see you again'?"

She made a show of pondering the suggestion.

"Oh, Agatha." He sighed. "Why is it you sometimes are the most sensible girl in all the world and at other times seem entirely witless?"

She really ought not to tease him as she did. "I will endeavor to be the sensible version of myself when conversing with Mrs. Warrick."

"Can you be?" He truly seemed to doubt it.

"Mr. Downy can assure you of the intelligence of my conversation. We spent most of last evening in a very sensible discussion." She couldn't resist another quip. "Why, I hadn't even a moment in which to offer Mrs. Warrick my food-cutting skills."

"Which Mr. Downy?"

She hadn't realized there was more than one. "Mr. Edward Downy."

"The eldest," Father said to himself, his eyes darting over the crowd. "Ah. Is that he, standing just to the side of the gazebo?"

She didn't bother to hide her smile upon spying Mr. Downy there. His company had been thoroughly enjoyable the evening before, and she had secretly hoped to see him again today. "That is he."

Father tugged her in that direction. "Perhaps he would be willing to keep you company again while *I* converse with the Warricks."

This was an unforeseen boon. She might be granted more of Mr. Downy's time simply because her attempts to avoid the expected flattering of her hostess made her father prefer leaving her in a gentleman's company to sitting her beside the ladies.

"Mr. Downy." Father didn't pause long enough to even offer a bow of greeting. "Would you be so good as to keep my daughter company during the picnic?"

Mr. Downy stood in obvious surprised confusion. He didn't manage a single word, a single sputter, before Father thanked him and rushed off toward the horde surrounding the Warricks.

If only sinking into the ground were an option. "I suppose I should be grateful." She masked her embarrassment with an overly cheerful tone. "Most troublesome puppies are tied in bags and tossed into rivers, rather than handed over to the nearest gentleman."

"*Are* you a troublesome puppy?" Humor twinkled in the back of his blue eyes.

"Well, I did just heavily imply that only your intervention last night prevented me from saying embarrassing things to Mrs. Warrick, which is likely why my father so eagerly handed me over just now." She didn't know whether to apologize or laugh. "I suggested I might ask her this afternoon why it is she looks so pale and sickly."

He laughed warmly. "Troublesome, perhaps, but effective."

"I notice you've managed to neatly avoid the necessity of fawning over our hosts."

He nodded. "One of the perks of being a gentleman who has reached his majority. I have nearly complete sovereignty over my decisions."

She made a noise of pondering. "What would that be like, I wonder? A woman, no matter how old, never has anything approaching sovereignty over her own life."

"I wish that weren't so true." His response was a sincere one. Everything in his mannerisms, in his tone, told her he did regret the lot women were given in the world. "My sister lived so much of her life defeated by her lack of choices. I didn't realize it until recently."

"Is she still feeling defeated?"

"I am happy to say that she is not. She found the courage to claim full ownership of the choices she did have and, in so doing, seized her own happiness." The fondness in his tone told Agatha all she needed to know about his relationship with his sister. She liked him all the more for it.

Agatha eyed the spread of food. "Do you suppose many of the guests are at all hungry yet? Most of us ate our breakfast not an hour ago."

"I predict that if the Warricks so much as mention the existence of food nearby, the guests will happily eat themselves ill." That was truer than it should have been.

The crowd parted quite without warning, and Mr. Warrick emerged. He crossed toward the spot where Agatha and Mr. Downy stood. For the briefest of moments, she thought he meant to come speak with them. Mr. Downy's sudden reticence told her he had the same suspicion.

But Mr. Warrick ascended the stairs of the gazebo instead and stood on its floor, placing himself a bit higher than his guests. After a quick clearing of his throat, he addressed them all.

"Thank you all for attending this picnic. As you, I am sure, have noticed, a variety of lawn games have been set up for your enjoyment. We have always"—he slowed on the word *always*, giving it both a hint of emphasis and warning—"enjoyed lawn games here at the Warrick estate."

The response was immediate. The guests scrambled toward the various games, eager to prove that they, too, enjoyed such diversions. The predictability of their reaction might have been entertaining if it hadn't come as the direct result of desperation. They weren't bowing to the Warricks' every whim out of a vain desire to be favored or fashionable. Entire futures depended upon those whims.

"This is to be the first challenge, it seems," Mr. Downy said. "An afternoon of not-so-friendly lawn competitions."

"I only hope they have not included lawn darts in their

assortment. That is a game best undertaken by those who are not attempting to eliminate one another."

"Indeed."

A gentleman near Mr. Downy's age rushed past, but slowed long enough to call over, "Best move faster than that, old man. You'll be out of an inheritance by dinnertime."

"That taunting came courtesy of my old school chum," Mr. Downy explained. "He means to throw himself wholeheartedly into this competition."

Agatha eyed the rush of eager participants. "He does not appear to be the only one."

Another young gentleman hurried over to them, an eager-eyed young lady following closely beside him.

"Edward, here you are." The gentleman bore a striking resemblance to Mr. Downy. Too striking to be a coincidence. This, Agatha would guess, was the other Mr. Downy her father had vaguely referenced. "We need two more for quoits."

"In the time you are taking to ask me to join you, someone else has likely claimed it," Mr. Downy said.

But the new arrival shook his head. "We absconded with the equipment."

His companion held out her hands, revealing several rope loops and a long, pointed stick.

Agatha pretended to be shocked. "Good heavens. We are surrounded by thieves."

The newly arrived Mr. Downy—if she didn't miss her guess—wasn't the least deterred by her jest. "Desperate times, miss."

"At least let me know what name I ought to give the squire when he arrives to collect the criminals."

He turned to Mr. Downy. "I like her."

"She is Miss Agatha Holmwood," Mr. Downy said. "Miss Holmwood, this scamp is my brother, Mr. Thomas Downy."

Mr. Thomas motioned to his partner in crime. "Henrietta Sumner." Apparently, they wouldn't be bothering with the formalities. "Will you join us for quoits? Henrietta heard Mrs. Warrick say that quoits is a particular favorite of hers."

"You know how I feel about this, Tom." Mr. Downy held his brother's gaze.

Agatha, however, watched Henrietta. Beneath her angelic, serene exterior was something very like panic and the first threat of tears. If Agatha didn't miss her mark, Henrietta was rather desperate to catch their hostess's eye.

"Mr. Downy." Agatha shook her head when both gentlemen turned toward her. The last strands of formality would have to be abandoned altogether. "Edward," she clarified. "We may not care to play the Warricks' game, but that doesn't mean we cannot enjoy *this* one."

He looked intrigued.

"Your brother and Miss Sumner risked life and limb to pillage the quoits set. The least we can do is round out their numbers so they can enjoy the spoils of their piracy."

Edward's subtle smile grew to a grin.

"I like her," Tom repeated. "Come on, then." While he eagerly began his departure without waiting on his brother, Tom made absolutely certain Henrietta was with him.

"How long have they been courting?" Agatha asked as they followed Tom and Henrietta's path.

"They met yesterday." Edward slowly, almost painstakingly, raised an eyebrow. "Are you scandalized?" A single corner of his mouth twitched upward.

"I am not certain I can spend any further time with you, Edward Downy. Your family seems to be a bad influence."

He leaned a bit closer and said, his voice a little lowered, "Next thing you know, I will be convincing you to tell our hostess she looks poorly and then offer to stir her tea."

"When I say things like that, my family looks at me as if I'm entirely mad. I cannot tell you how nice it is to meet someone who recognizes that I'm not only *not* serious about these things, but that it is actually a little funny."

He smiled broadly and motioned her toward the spot where his brother was setting up their game of quoits.

"Are your quoits skills equally funny?"

She grinned. "Oh, they're hilarious."

"In other words, you aren't likely to be selected by Mrs. Warrick based on your upcoming performance."

She shrugged. "Unless she means to select an heir out of pity."

"Shh!" He looked around, an air of furtive worry on his face. "If anyone overhears, this house party will become an unending exercise in competitive sympathy."

"I'd much rather engage in competitive ring tossing." They had reached Tom and Henrietta. "Who goes first?"

Though Tom and Henrietta were clearly quite anxious to make a good showing, the game proceeded with a great deal of laughter and happy jesting. Edward was as lighthearted as she'd come to expect, enjoying the game without the least worry what their hosts or the other guests might think. Her dry humor was met, not with confusion and scolds, but with smiles and chuckles and humor of his own.

For the first time in memory, she didn't feel quite so alone and misunderstood. She'd never truly been unhappy, but in his company she was something more than that. She felt more herself than she had in years, perhaps ever.

Henrietta tossed her rope ring, and it slipped perfectly onto the stake.

"Excellent," Tom declared. "I do believe you are going to win this round handily."

Henrietta beamed at him. "The game does seem to be turning in my favor."

His gaze was every bit as besotted as hers. These two might not have known one another long, but their feelings were unmistakable.

"It was, indeed, a well-executed toss." Mrs. Warrick arrived on the scene. "You have a knack for quoits, Miss Sumner."

Henrietta colored up on the instant, and her tongue immediately tied itself in knots. She managed little beyond a nod and an incoherent muttering of what sounded vaguely like thankful agreement.

Tom came to the rescue. "She has won most of the rounds."

Mrs. Warrick looked impressed. If she really did mean to choose a successor based on that person's ability to play a child's lawn game, then this house party was even more of a farce than Agatha had believed.

"What of the Downy brothers?" their hostess asked. "Have you two made a good showing for yourselves?"

Edward answered on behalf of both of them. "Tom has won the few rounds Miss Sumner has not. I, on the other hand, have shown myself to be every bit as inept at this particular game as ever I was."

Mrs. Warrick turned her gaze on Agatha. She looked her up and down, her gaze resting on Agatha's head. "I will assume based on your rope ring's current location—on the top of your head—that this is not a game you are particularly skilled at, either."

"Oh, but I am," Agatha insisted. "I found my aim is not particularly good when I am attempting to toss the ring onto that stake over there, but I am quite adept at getting the ring onto my own head. I am remarkably skilled at my version of quoits. I successfully ring my target every time."

Mrs. Warrick's white brows pulled in even as her wrinkled lips turned downward. "You are an odd sort of young lady, Miss Holmwood."

"Thank you very much," she answered with a bright smile.

Mrs. Warrick eyed her with the same confused expression Agatha's father so often wore. Edward, on the other hand, was clearly holding back a grin.

Their hostess managed to blink off her bewilderment and addressed Henrietta once more. "I will not further interrupt your game. Once again, well done. It is a joy to see another lady on this estate do well at this game. It has been too many years."

With that, she flounced away, leaving behind a wide-eyed Henrietta, a hopeful Tom, a clearly amused Edward, and a silently annoyed Agatha.

"Do you think she meant that?" Henrietta quietly asked. "Was she truly impressed do you suppose?"

"I believe so," Tom eagerly answered. "She will remember you, I am certain of that."

Henrietta took a shaky breath. "I shouldn't allow myself to hope this much, but being chosen would be an answer to prayers." She looked at each of them in turn, embarrassment heating her cheeks. "My father is not very good at managing his money or estate. We've been forced to greatly retrench these past years. We are living in the dower house on our family estate because we need the rent that comes from letting the main house. There is no money for dowries or trips to Bath, let alone London. This is the only Social event I have ever or likely will ever be invited to, and if something doesn't improve our situation—something like this bequest—things will only grow worse. I don't know what else to do."

Emotion broke the poor young lady's words. Tom took her hands in his. "You are doing the best you can," he insisted. "That is all you can expect of yourself."

Henrietta nodded, even as a lone tear escaped the corner of her eye. Tom offered her a handkerchief.

Agatha met Edward's eye. In his look of commiseration, she saw the same sad frustration she felt. Everyone at this party needed what the Warricks were so callously dangling in front of them.

This game their hosts were playing with everyone's futures was truly cruel.

CHAPTER FIVE

Edward needed to stop eavesdropping on Agatha's conversations with her father, but fate seemed determined to continually place him in that uncomfortable position. He'd wandered toward the back of the house the next afternoon with every intention of taking a turn about the back gardens, only to find himself just outside a small parlor where Mr. Holmwood was pointedly lecturing his daughter.

"I realize you are not necessarily clever," her father said, "but I do not for a moment believe you are this thick-headed."

Edward kept himself from charging in and defending her against such unfounded criticism.

"There is no explanation for your continued bungling of your encounters with the Warricks other than deliberate sabotage," Mr. Holmwood said. "I can come to no other conclusion."

"What you term 'sabotage' is simply me refusing to pretend I am something other than what I am. If the Warricks choose me, Father, they will have to choose *me*, even with all my quirks and oddities."

That was the Agatha he had come to know. In a Society that valued appearances to the point of insisting on false fronts and fabrications, she refused to be anything other than her true and authentic self. That required a level of bravery few could claim.

"We endure your eccentricities because we are your family," Mr. Holmwood said, "but this is not a leisurely summer spent at home away from people. This is a chance at a fortune, not merely for you, but for your entire family. This could save us all, and you are refusing to even try."

"I will not pretend to be something I am not."

"'Something you are not?' You mean, 'selfless'?"

Edward felt the sting of that rebuke all the way in the corridor.

"How have I been selfish, Father?" It was clearly a question meant to point out his error in judgment, but Mr. Holmwood answered bluntly.

"You have placed your pride above your family's well-being. You have turned your nose up at this opportunity in order to prove that you are above the others here—the others who, I would point out, are doing their utmost to save those they love from ruin." His words were sharp and reproving. "But that, it seems, does not matter to you."

"How can you say that? I have set aside my dignity time and again begging for the things this family needs." She spoke not out of wounded pride but, judging from the pain in her voice, as a result of wounded feelings. "The needs of this family have always trumped my self-respect."

"I am not speaking of charity baskets or an extra week to pay the coal merchant. This is a solution to our troubles, not a bandage."

"That our family is bleeding financially is not my fault," Agatha insisted, "nor is it my responsibility to fix it."

"You are right. The responsibility is mine, and I wish there were another means of making it right. There are no other options, no other chances for reversing the situation I, and this family, inherited."

"Father—"

"I have arranged for you to take tea with Mrs. Warrick this afternoon. I expect you to do what is right by your family."

"You wish me to assume a mask, to pretend I am something other than what I am?" A hint of defiance had entered her tone, and yet Edward could not mistake the hurt underlying it.

"I expect you to think of your family and their precarious situation. I expect you to act in a way that shows you consider yourself part of this family and appreciate all we have done for you." There was something of a threat in his words, though Edward couldn't immediately identify it.

"Of course I consider myself part of our family."

"Then act like you do, Agatha. If you aren't willing to sacrifice for us, then I don't know that we can continue sacrificing for you."

There was the detail Edward hadn't been able to put his thumb on. Whether or not the threat was an idle one, he couldn't say, but Agatha's father had essentially warned her that if she did not participate in the Warricks' game of chance, if she didn't abandon her self-respect and grovel as expected, her family would turn their backs on her.

Mr. Holmwood said nothing more. He left the room with determined stride, walking in the opposite direction of where Edward stood. He hadn't been seen there, listening. But he had most certainly heard, and his heart ached for Agatha.

He peered inside, unsure what he could or ought to do. The sight of his usually indomitable Agatha standing with her head hung low made the decision for him. He stepped inside and directly to her.

"You'll think me the worst sort of busybody, but I overheard."

She looked up at him, worry and uncertainty in her eyes. "What did you overhear?"

"Most everything," he admitted.

She shook her head. "I mean, what did—I know what I think my father meant, but I'm not certain. What did *you* hear? What did *you* understand from what he said?"

Ah. He set his hand on her back and guided her to the window seat. He sat beside her, disliking the worry that marred her features. "I do not know your father well," he reminded her, "so I cannot guarantee that I am accurately interpreting his words."

She nodded her understanding.

"On the surface, at least, it sounded as though he is demanding your active participation in the Warricks' competition on threat of being cut off."

She sighed, her shoulders dropping. "That is what I heard as well." She threaded her fingers, her gaze unfocused ahead.

"Would he follow through, do you suppose?" Edward couldn't help being worried for her. The world was a cruel one for a lady alone, without family or finances.

"I don't know. He has mentioned the family's sacrifice in keeping on a daughter with so few prospects, but always as a means of inflicting guilt, not as a threat."

"He dangles that sword over your head?" What kind of father does that to his own daughter?

Agatha stood and paced away. "What if—What if he truly does decide to stop 'sacrificing' for me? What if he truly does cut me off?"

"I can't imagine he would." He hoped not at least.

"I've never seen him so angry. He is usually cheerful—a bit frazzled at times, perhaps, but generally hopeful. He is determined to be the victor in this."

"Determined enough to punish his own daughter?" Edward asked.

She turned back to face him. Her eyes had lost their sparkle. Not a hint of a smile tugged at her mouth. "I think he might be." Her hands clutched one another. "What do I do? Even with my best effort, there is little chance of being selected as the Warricks' heir, but if I don't convince my father that I am tossing myself wholeheartedly into the fray, I might not have a home to return to. Simply failing to be selected might be seen as enough of a failure in his eyes to justify tossing me into the hedgerow."

Edward rose and crossed to her, setting his hands on her arms. "He seems a more reasonable man than that. His threat, I am certain, was meant only to spur you into action. Surely he won't act upon it."

Her eyes belied his bravado. Good heavens, she believed her father capable of so ill-using her. She truly believed it.

"Oh, Agatha," he whispered, agonizing for her.

He wrapped his arms around her. She clutched the front of his waistcoat and rested her head against his chest.

"What will I do if I lose my home?" she asked from within his embrace. "I have nowhere to go."

In that heartrending moment, he missed the lighthearted Agatha he'd come to know the past few days. He missed her smile, missed her humor. More than that, he hated the reason her laughter had disappeared so entirely. His own sister had nearly been forced to sacrifice her happiness for the family's financial well-being. He'd intervened then, insisting on a compromise, and he'd somehow been successful. But he hadn't the right to interfere this time.

"Will throwing yourself into the fray be less miserable for you if I do the same?" he offered. "We can both feel ridiculous together."

"I can't ask you to do that," she said. "I know how adamantly you oppose it."

"You aren't asking," he pointed out. "I am offering, willingly."

"But not happily," she countered.

He pulled her in ever closer and lowered his voice. "Seeing you hurting makes this important to me, Agatha. If participating in the Warricks' competition will relieve even a bit of your misery, then I will do so *happily*."

"Careful there, Edward. I will begin to believe you think rather highly of me." The first hints of her usual teasing tone trickled into her words.

Relief flooded over him at the sound. "I do rather like you, even if you are particularly bad at quoits."

He felt her silent laughter in the moment before she pulled back. His arms slipped away from her. She offered a tremulous smile.

"Thank you," she said. "I feel better. Not great, mind you, but better."

He hoped his smile was encouraging. "We'll convince your father that you are important to your family and they are important to you. We'll find a way."

She gave a small nod. "I hope so." She took a deep breath. "Now, if you'll excuse me, I need to prepare myself to take tea with 'her majesty, the high and mighty Mrs. Warrick' and take some time in my bedchamber emptying my vocabulary of anything she might find odd or unflattering."

"Things like 'her majesty, the high and mighty Mrs. Warrick'?" he suggested.

Agatha's shoulders dropped. "This could be a very unsuccessful endeavor, Edward."

"I will offer you silent words of encouragement all afternoon," he promised.

"You might see fit to include a silent prayer or two as well. I suspect nothing short of divine intervention is going to make this anything but a disaster."

She gave him a quick wave at the door before hurrying out. He remained behind, fighting his own frustration. Here was a witty, companionable, lovely lady who, for the sake of a potential fortune, was being forced to play the part of an uninteresting shell of the person she was. How often would her father require this of her if the Warricks' scheme didn't fall in his favor? How long before pretending became so frequent that she could no longer find the strength or the will to be the person she was?

Exhaustion did that to a person. Misery did as well. And hopelessness.

But what could be done? He knew perfectly well that nothing could be done, and his heart hurt at the harsh reality of her situation.

He stepped from the room as well, his thoughts so entirely preoccupied that he didn't notice Isley stepping around the corner. They nearly collided.

261

"Isley." Edward pulled himself into the present once more. "How has the house party been for you thus far?" He'd not seen much of his friend over the past days.

"Considering none of us can seem to catch the Warricks' attention as easily as you and Tom did during the lawn games?" Accusation sat heavy in Isley's tone.

"What is it you suspect us of?" Edward asked.

Isley held his hands up in a dramatic show of innocence. "I am merely pointing out a fact. You two seem to have emerged victorious, or at least not *un*victorious. Curious, that, since you told me on the first day of this party that you didn't mean to even try."

Such bitterness from a gentleman whom Edward considered a friend. Was this what such competitions did? Ruined friendships? Strained family relationships?

"If it sets your mind at ease, the entirety of Mrs. Warrick's commentary on my lawn game skills was to denounce and bemoan them."

Isley did not seem satisfied. "Are you entering the competition?" he demanded.

"I suppose," Edward admitted. "But only in the barest of senses. I mean to stay and I don't mean to refuse every activity set out for us."

Isley pushed out a breath that sounded something like a growl. "I thought you were my friend," he muttered as he walked away.

And I thought you were mine.

CHAPTER SIX

Agatha sat beside Mrs. Warrick at another interminable early afternoon tea. The past week of teas had seen little conversation beyond inconsequential topics and an unending stream of compliments directed at one—and *only* one—member of the party. Another week of this nonsense, and Agatha would lose her mind.

"You seemed quite a disappointment at first," Mrs. Warrick said between watercress sandwiches. "But I like what I've seen this last week." She pointed at Agatha with her teaspoon. "You are showing promise."

"At last." Agatha didn't catch herself before making the dry response. She pasted on a smile and corrected her tone to an appropriately grateful one. "You are so kind to say so."

"Yes," Mrs. Warrick said sweetly. "Yes, I am."

Good heavens, Agatha couldn't keep up this charade much longer. But her father kept a close eye on her, asking the other ladies about their teas and watching her every move when the entire party was together.

She found she couldn't be entirely angry with him—not really. He seemed more panicked than greedy. The fear she saw in his eyes spoke of desperation, and she knew perfectly well what that level of anxiety did to a person. It overrode reason and, too often, compassion. The look on his face the past few days reminded her that his threat to toss her out of the family might not be an idle one.

Mrs. Warrick set her teacup down and squared her shoulders, looking over them all. Agatha had come to know that look and posture well: their hostess had an announcement.

"You will all be pleased to know that Mr. Warrick and I have planned an activity for this afternoon."

The expected oohs and ahhs and expressions of eager anticipation filled the gap Mrs. Warrick always inserted between her declarations and the more detailed explanations that followed. Agatha offered a smile; it was the closest to fawning she could force herself to come.

Mrs. Warrick folded her hands on her lap, her smile one of pointed magnanimousness. "Mr. Warrick and I first made one another's acquaintance at a house party whilst participating in a gathering game. Each team was given a list of items, each list being identical, and a time limit was set. During the time allotted, the teams were charged with gathering as many items as they could. The team who returned with the most items was declared the winner and received a prize."

Even Agatha had to admit that the game sounded quite diverting, depending, of course, on what the items were and with whom a person was partnered.

"We mean to recreate that long-ago hunt," Mrs. Warrick said. "Each of you has been paired with one of the gentlemen. Those of you who are married were, of course, matched with your husbands."

The necessary smiles and light laughs were offered in acknowledgement of Mrs. Warrick's bit of humor.

"The gentlemen have already been informed," she continued. "They have also been given the names of their partners and have been instructed to come seek you out." A knock on the door brought a conspiratorial grin to Mrs. Warrick's face. "I suppose that might be the gentlemen now."

It was, indeed. A well-timed, likely rehearsed bit of pageantry. The gentlemen sought out their assigned partners, some with sincere pleasure, others with forced expressions of delight on the part of both participants.

Agatha's gaze sought out and quickly found Edward, entering at the back of the group of gentlemen, his brother at his side. Tom said something. Edward grinned. A feeling akin to relief washed over her at the sight. He was a happy person, and modest, and kind. The perfect antidote to the subtle pompousness she had endured nearly every waking moment of the past seven days.

She held her breath, wondering with whom Edward had been paired. There was no denying she deeply hoped she had been selected for that role, but she braced herself for disappointment.

"Do not fret," Mrs. Warrick said. "We have partnered you with a young gentleman who has caught our attention as much as you have these past days. You will, we are quite certain, make a perfect team."

Oh, dear.

But it was, indeed, Edward who approached her. Without a word, he held up a piece of paper with *Miss Agatha Holmwood* scrawled across it.

Mrs. Warrick's brows pulled low, her mouth turned down in confusion. "There must be an error. Mr. *Thomas* Downy was meant to have—"

"Begging your pardon, ma'am," Edward said, his tone pleasant and patient, "but this is the paper I have been given, and it would be terribly ungentlemanly of me to be anything but utterly charmed with my good fortune."

Mrs. Warrick's almost frantic gaze slid over the crowd, settling on, if Agatha didn't miss her mark, Thomas Downy. "Miss Sumner? No, she was meant to have been your partner."

Edward offered a commiserating look. "He did not seem at all displeased with the arrangement, just as I am not the least bit disappointed. All will be well, Mrs. Warrick. I assure you."

"But—"

"Miss Holmwood, I hope you will forgive my eagerness," Edward said, eyeing her with an expression that was just a bit *too* serious. "I very much wish to emerge victorious in today's challenge and, as such, feel a certain earnestness to begin quickly."

"Indeed. We had best not waste a single moment."

He held his hand out to her, and she set hers inside it. A warmth she'd not felt before trickled through her at that simple touch. It was more than the relief at being free of Mrs. Warrick's demanding company for an afternoon, more than the pleasure of being paid a bit of attention by a handsome gentleman. It was Edward. Edward, himself. He had found a place in her heart and had claimed it as his own. His presence filled that place once more, filled it with hope and reassurance and tenderness of feeling.

He led her away from their slightly agape hostess and directly to the corridor.

She lowered her voice and asked, "Was my name the one you were truly given?"

"My paper originally read *Miss Henrietta Sumner*, which I am absolutely certain was due to a grave error on someone's part." He threaded her arm through his. "Tom was the victim of a similar mistake. We, however, sorted it out nicely."

She felt herself relax for the first time in a week. "I've hardly seen you these past days. Mrs. Warrick has begun to suspect that I am not as undesirable a person as she first believed, and, as a result, I can't ever seem to be free of her company."

"Well, in the week since I decided to begin making an effort, I have seen increasingly less of our host. It seems he is not impressed." Though Edward spoke somberly, a laugh hovered just below the surface.

"What a blow to your pride, Edward." She patted his arm.

"Yes. I'm utterly devastated." He led her through the terrace doors and down the stairs to the garden. "Now. Let us find a place to sit where we can look over our list."

"You intend to participate in this hunt?"

His gaze met hers, and, though he didn't look any less merry than usual, his expression was undeniably sincere. "Your father will demand an accounting of you. I will not be the reason you are scolded again. Or worse."

She knew her attempt at a smile fell a bit short. "He grows more frantic with each passing day. I believe there is little hope of avoiding the 'or worse' outcome."

He took her hand in his and raised it to his lips, pressing a tender kiss to the back of her hand. "We will do our best today and pray that his good sense wins out in the end."

They sat on a bench situated beneath the boughs of a

greenwood tree on a small path of the garden. He pulled a folded sheet of paper from his coat pocket and opened it. Agatha leaned her head against his shoulder and simply breathed. With him, she felt less burdened, less worried.

"The list is not terribly long, but it is decidedly odd."

"Fitting," Agatha said.

He chuckled quietly. "We are charged with gathering, amongst other equally confusing items, 'the first arrival of morning' and 'that which runs but does not walk, has a mouth but does not talk.'"

"So long as this challenge is straightforward," she said dryly.

"And we have until five o'clock this evening to bring these simple and, no doubt, easily obtained items to the drawing room."

"What shall we do with all the extra time we will certainly have?"

He shifted the list into one hand and took hold of hers with the other. It was the most natural position in the world to sit with their hands clasped, her head resting against him.

"'The first arrival of morning.' What do you suppose that means?" he asked.

"If one is wealthy enough, the first arrival of morning might be the chambermaid stoking the fire." She had heard that those with a substantial income never had to awaken in a cold room.

"I, for one, cannot countenance the idea of pulling one of the overworked servants away from her duties for the sake of this game, can you?"

"Not at all." She sat up more fully. "Perhaps we could come back to that riddle."

At that exact moment, Tom and Henrietta hurried past.

They stopped long enough for Tom to toss a challenge to his brother. "We've solved one of the riddles. You'd best hurry if you're to catch us."

"Or you could tell us the answer," Edward suggested with a grin.

Tom only laughed. The happy couple continued on their way.

"They seem well suited," Agatha said, watching them disappear through the gate at the far end of the garden.

"Extremely well suited. I have spent some time the past couple of days getting to know Miss Sumner better, and I cannot imagine someone who would make my brother happier than she would. And I firmly believe he would do the same for her."

"Then why do you sound so downtrodden when you speak of them?" She could not mistake the sadness in his tone.

"What future do they have? He is the younger son of a penniless family. She is the dowerless daughter of a bankrupt spendthrift."

"I hadn't thought of that." She held more tightly to Edward's hand, thinking of more than Tom and Henrietta's predicament. She and Edward were in a similar situation. Though it was likely presumptuous of her to think along these lines, she knew herself to be well and truly attached to him, her tender feelings going beyond mere friendship. But he was as penniless as his brother. And while her family's circumstances were not the result of irresponsibility on the part of her father, the end result was the same.

"The river." Edward spoke the two words as if he'd experienced a life-altering epiphany.

"The river?"

He turned to her with wide eyes. "The second item on the list. 'Runs but doesn't walk, mouth but doesn't talk.' It's a river."

He was right, of course. "How are we supposed to bring a river into the drawing room?"

He shrugged. "Perhaps there is something down there we are supposed to fetch?" He stood, his hand still in hers. "The least we can do is check."

"Together. We can check *together*."

Once more he kissed her hand. "I wouldn't wish to spend the afternoon any other way."

It seemed he was as fond of her as she was of him. But did he realize what a risk that was? "My family is destitute."

"I know. Otherwise you wouldn't be at this party." He tucked her hand into the crook of his arm.

She walked at his side. "My family is impoverished. Yours is penniless. It is rather like . . . like . . ."

"Tom and Henrietta," he finished for her.

She realized in that moment how presumptuous her warning had been. He was fond of her, yes, but she had assumed he felt enough to need a reminder of their respective futures.

His arm slid free of hers and slipped across her back, pulling her against his side as they continued their ambling walk toward the back of the property. "I have every intention of enjoying the remainder of this party without letting myself think about pennilessness or spendthrifts or destitution."

"That significantly limits our potential topics of conversation, leaving us with only the discomfort of various fabrics and listing the kingdom's rivers in alphabetical order."

"The Aire. The Avon. The Bann." Edward counted off the rivers on his fingers. "The Clyde."

She raised up on her toes and pressed a kiss to his cheek.

He turned a smoldering smile on her. "If I list four more rivers, will you kiss me again?"

"Anything can happen during a house party search game."

He laughed. "*That* is very useful information."

Tender feeling. Fondness. The words she'd been using to describe her feelings for him were proving inadequate. She missed him when he wasn't there, looked for him when even the slightest chance existed of him arriving. A weight lifted off her shoulders and her heart when they were together.

Agatha Holmwood had done the unthinkable: she'd allowed herself to fall in love.

For twenty-one years, she'd been careful not to grow attached to a gentleman. There was so little chance of a happy ending, that she'd avoided even the beginnings of love.

"It seems we weren't the only ones who realized the second clue referred to the river." Edward motioned to the smattering of couples along the river. "But I don't believe anyone yet knows what to do about it."

She couldn't bring herself to join in the banter. "We'll simply pluck a leaf from one of trees along the bank."

Agatha wrapped her arms around her middle and turned away. With a moment's effort, she might manage to settle her thoughts and calm her heart enough to keep a level head.

"Agatha?" He'd followed close on her heels. "What's the matter, dear?"

Dear. She couldn't be certain he meant anything by the word other than an offhand casual endearment. She was even less sure which she would prefer.

"I've had a rather miserable week, Edward." It was true, though perhaps not the entire explanation for her depressed spirits.

He stepped around her, facing her once more. He set his hands on her arms. "One more miserable week, Agatha, and you need never see Mrs. Warrick again."

"One week." She could even smile. "I can survive another week."

His arms slipped around her, and he clasped his hands behind her back. "You might even manage to enjoy the next week."

"I might, at that."

"We didn't pluck a leaf from the riverbank," he said, his expression one of theatrical concern. "We might lose this challenge."

"I think we still have time." Her smile only grew as she stood there in his arms. Things weren't likely to end well between them, but, as he'd said, she could enjoy the next week. She intended to.

One corner of his mouth twitched upward. "I don't think you are dedicated enough to winning this search."

"And *I* think this afternoon has been . . . nearly perfect."

He took the tiniest step closer to her. "How would one go about removing the word *nearly* from that sentence?" His low voice rumbled in the sliver of space between them.

She knew exactly what would make the moment perfect. "I don't believe it's on your treasure list."

He arched a single golden eyebrow. "'A mouth, but not talking.' That's on my list."

She forced back her growing grin. "Are you telling me I talk too much?"

He leaned in, a mere breath away, and whispered, "That is not at all what I am saying."

His lips brushed over hers, the touch feather light. Her heart answered loudly, pounding and racing and dancing about. His hands spread against her back, pulling her flush with him. He kissed her again, more earnestly, more fervently.

She slid her arms around his neck and lost herself in the warmth of his affection. She had imagined such a moment, but had never truly believed it possible. A girl with no dowry, no family connections, lived her life knowing she was destined to be alone.

But this moment, this glorious moment, pushed all thoughts of loneliness from her mind, replacing the worry with hope.

CHAPTER SEVEN

The Warricks proved oddly specific in their required items. A scone, which apparently was the first arrival of morning. A cup of water from the river. An unburned candle. A badly burned twig. And a cabbage.

No one arrived with even a single correct item. Tom and Henrietta were noticeably disappointed, but took it in stride, spending a great deal of time smiling at one another, utterly content in one another's company. Isley and most of the other guests looked fit to be tied, speaking curtly with one another and quickly losing their friendly edge.

Edward, however, considered himself the victor. Three days passed without that kiss leaving his thoughts. It had been the impulse of a moment, a passing fancy. But everything had changed.

He'd told himself again and again that he felt nothing but fondness for her. Until he'd held her in his arms, until he'd kissed her, he'd managed to believe it. But he had to admit that she wasn't merely a friend. He loved her.

He, who had nothing to offer, no means of providing for the two of them, was in love with a lady who had even less to her name than he did and even less hope of changing her circumstances. He'd bemoaned Tom's impossible love, but he, himself, was in no better a position than his brother.

A nudge from that brother brought him back into the present. His woolgathering had distracted him so much he'd not noticed their hosts had risen and were addressing the assembly.

"As I am certain you have all realized, only a few days remain of this house party." Mr. Warrick gave them all a pitying, commiserating look. "Mrs. Warrick and I are not yet firmly decided on who amongst you will be named the beneficiaries of our estate. As such, this evening we will be undertaking a more pointed attempt to make that decision."

The entire room was silent, hanging on every word he spoke. For the first time, Edward felt tempted to really make a push for himself. He had, as he'd promised Agatha, participated in the many activities the Warricks had thus far used to sort them all, but he hadn't made any eager attempts to capture their interest or approval.

She sat in the seat beside the one Mrs. Warrick had vacated. How her father had arranged it, Edward couldn't say, but Agatha hadn't left her hostess's side in more than a week. Mrs. Warrick seemed pleased with the arrangement, taking full advantage of a young lady who was more or less required to do or fetch or say anything Mrs. Warrick required. Agatha barely concealed her misery.

"Our final request from all of you, and then we promise you can spend the rest of this house party quietly, filling your days with whatever suits or fancy, is this—" Mr. Warrick paused, letting his gaze slowly take them all in.

Edward leaned forward, wondering if there was any chance of winning their approval this late in the effort.

"We will invite each of you, one at a time, to join us in the small sitting room at the east of the house, where we mean to ask you a few questions."

That was surprisingly reasonable. Indeed, if they had taken this approach from the beginning, the entire affair would not have been so distasteful. He met Tom's eye, and they exchanged looks of shocked approval. Tom, Edward knew perfectly well, was quite personable and easy to talk with. This latest would-be heir challenge ought to be a relatively easy one.

"We will begin," Mr. Warrick said, eyeing a piece of parchment in his hand, "with Miss Henrietta Sumner."

At the sound of her name, Henrietta, who sat on Tom's other side, lost every drop of color in her face. Tom offered her a reassuring smile, and she seemed to rally a little. Across the room, where many of the ladies had gathered to fawn over their hostess, Mrs. Sumner rose and motioned her daughter anxiously toward the door to the drawing room.

The Sumner ladies left, every eye in the room watching them. The Warricks departed close on their heels. Not a single word was said. Edward wasn't certain anyone was even breathing. Tonight was to be their final opportunity at escaping the nightmare of their own poverty. It would not be the lighthearted gathering most house parties were.

The moment the door closed behind their hosts, the room erupted. The guests turned to each other, frantically discussing this new development. Futures hinged on that night's events. Dreams and lives and hopes were at stake.

Edward quickly checked on Mr. Holmwood. Finding him

distracted in earnest conversation with Isley, of all people, Edward slipped across the room into the empty chair next to Agatha.

She spoke first. "What do you suppose the Warricks mean to ask everyone?"

"No doubt something invasive and demeaning." Edward wished he could believe something better of them, but the past three weeks had taught him otherwise. "How are you? I cannot help but notice you don't look happy."

"I'm tired. My father spent most of the morning lecturing me. Apparently, I'm not living up to expectations."

Edward slipped his hand in hers. It was still too bold, considering they were not alone, but he couldn't help himself. He cared about her. He cared deeply. And he couldn't bear to see her unhappy. "He does not appreciate you as he ought."

She smiled a tiny bit. "At the very least, I ought to be given tremendous credit for spending so many endless hours with Mrs. Warrick."

"You are down to only three days," he reminded her.

"I know. Counting down has been the one thing that has saved my sanity." Her expression turned contemplative. "Do you suppose the heir they choose will be forced to live with them the remainder of their lives?"

Edward hadn't thought of that terrible possibility. "That seems a steep price to pay for a mere fortune."

With relief, he watched some of the burden leave her eyes. She was tired, that much was clear. But underneath the exhaustion and the worry, she was still the happy, witty, lighthearted lady he had come to cherish.

"Does your father seem less determined to toss you from

the family home?" Edward asked. He had hoped Mr. Holmwood would come to his senses, but far too much worry had lingered in the older gentleman's eyes for Edward's mind to be at all at ease.

"I cannot say with any certainty," Agatha said. "If tonight really is the last challenge the Warricks mean to give us, I suppose I will know before morning what my father's intentions are."

He held her hand and squeezed her fingers, hoping the show of support was understood. Her tiny smile was not the least bit confident. If only the Downys had any prospects. If only he were in a position to actually help.

She slipped her hand from his, though he knew it was not out of displeasure. They were in a crowded drawing room, and there was no understanding between them. He remained at her side as, one by one, the guests were called out to speak with Mr. and Mrs. Warrick. No one who had already been summoned had returned. It seemed the topic of discussion was meant to be kept secret.

When but a small handful remained, the footman who had been charged with announcing the next chosen for their tête-à-tête with the Warricks entered once more, cleared his throat, and said, "Mr. Edward Downy."

"The best of luck to you," Agatha whispered.

Edward gave a quick nod with what he hoped was an expression of calmness. He followed the footman's rigid back down the corridor to the sitting room. He entered to find Mr. and Mrs. Warrick sitting in matching armchairs, facing him. They put him in mind of the king and queen holding court and accepting petitions from the peasants. How fitting.

"Mr. Downy." Mr. Warrick motioned him inside. "We spoke with your brother only a few minutes ago."

"Yes, I know." Did they think he hadn't noticed his brother's departure?

"He seems a good sort of gentleman," Mrs. Warrick observed. "But he is the younger son, is he not?"

"It is the oddest thing," Edward responded, not bothering to hide his dry tone, "but I have often noticed that even a younger son can be a good sort of gentleman."

Mrs. Warrick responded with nothing beyond the slightest tightening of her lips. "Shall we begin?"

"I would prefer that we did." Edward had contemplated the possibility of making one final attempt at winning the fortune they offered, but he simply couldn't force himself to participate in their farce.

Mrs. Warrick folded her hands on her lap and watched him with a beatific look. Edward wasn't fooled. He'd come to realize that both halves of this couple were equally shrewd.

"We will ask you what we have asked everyone else," Mr. Warrick said. "Why, Edward Downy, should we choose you, and not any of the other guests, as our heir?"

For a moment, he couldn't respond. They were asking him to plead his case? Not only that, but to argue against the others? "You must know my situation already, otherwise I would not have been invited."

"We know what is generally known," Mr. Warrick said. "We wish for more. Why are you in particular the best choice? Do you need this more than anyone else? Are you more deserving?"

279

He shook his head in astonishment. This was every bit as bad as he had feared. Edward squared his shoulders. "No."

"No?" Mrs. Warrick broke from her usual pattern and spoke over her husband.

He simply inclined his head. "No," he repeated. "I will not lay bare my family's struggles for your entertainment."

"This is not a matter of entertainment," Mr. Warrick insisted.

"That is precisely what this is." Edward didn't shrink from their disapproving cases. "Your charity comes with quite a price. You want it known far and wide how generous you are. You wish to be the savior in someone's sad story. Setting a house full of the desperate and destitute against one another makes that story all the more intriguing."

At the end of his speech, the smile disappeared from Mrs. Warrick's face. Censure filled the lines of her face, even as her gaze narrowed in reproof. "We are doing good. We are helping people."

"Your 'help' comes at too steep a cost, and I, for one, refuse to continue paying it." He offered an abbreviated bow. "I thank you for your hospitality, such as it was, but it is time and past that I returned home, where the resident family may not have much by way of material possessions, but we have our dignity and our decency, and I value that more highly than any estate."

Mr. and Mrs. Warrick turned their heads in each other's directions and exchanged knowing looks.

"He doesn't have his brother's diplomacy," Mr. Warrick said, "but they clearly share similar sentiments."

"Tom objected as well?" He was both relieved and concerned to hear it.

"He did not refuse to explain why an inheritance would be helpful in his situation," Mr. Warrick said, "but he did quite vehemently decline to speak about anyone other than himself."

"Our parents will be pleased to hear that."

Mrs. Warrick's gaze narrowed on him. "Do you feel, then, that your brother deserves this bequest more than the others who have spoken harshly of the other guests?"

Edward would not be pulled into this trap. He offered no reply, but simply stood, silent and waiting. The Warricks slowly but surely transformed back into the picture of benevolence they'd assumed the past weeks.

"It seems, Mr. Downy, that there is little left for any of us to say." Mr. Warrick spoke calmly and clearly. "We do not require that you leave—we are not so inhospitable—but if you feel you must go, we will not stop you."

"I understand." One more brief bow and he left, pulling the door closed behind him.

Agatha had clearly been chosen as the next to face the interrogators. She and her father stood in the corridor. Mr. Holmwood took only the slightest notice of Edward. Agatha, however, watched his every step and, when he passed, moved away from her father to keep pace with him.

"Edward? What happened? Why are you so upset?"

He swallowed down his first response, to simply spew out every bit of frustration and disillusionment he'd felt over the past weeks. But she looked nervous enough already. "They irritate me."

"I know." Her gaze searched his face. "There is something more. I can see that there is."

"I have been invited to leave."

"No. There are three days yet. Edward?" She clasped his forearm, her expression one of near panic.

"Agatha." Mr. Holmwood spoke insistently.

"One moment, Father." She didn't look away from Edward. "You are leaving?"

He set his hand on hers where it rested on his arm. "I intend to pack, take my leave of my brother, and begin my journey home by five o'clock this evening."

"That is so soon."

"Agatha," Mr. Holmwood repeated more pointedly.

"Will I be permitted to say good-bye before you go?"

He took her hand and raised it to his lips. "I will wait until five, but then I must be on my way."

"Five o'clock." She raised up on her toes and kissed his cheek.

"Agatha Elizabeth Holmwood." Her father barked out her name.

She obeyed the summons, but with repeated backward glances. "Five o'clock," she mouthed in the moment before her father pulled her into the sitting room.

But five o'clock came and went. Then a quarter past five. Edward delayed until five thirty.

She never came.

CHAPTER EIGHT

"Son?"

Edward didn't look up from his ledger at the sound of his father's voice. Work had kept his mind occupied over the five days he'd been home. Balancing accounts and formulating plans for keeping the estate solvent prevented his thoughts from wandering down unwelcome paths.

"You have not eaten this morning, Edward."

"I am not hungry." He checked two numbers on separate pages, needing to be certain the amount they'd spent on beef hadn't changed significantly. "Have we considered sending to Carlsdown for our beef? It might cost less there."

Father sat on the corner of the desk. "What happened in Somerset?"

There was the pitying tone he was working very hard to avoid hearing. "Nothing of significance." He scrawled a note to himself to check the price of sugar in Carlsdown as well.

"I may not be the brightest of men—bless your brother, he resembles me a little too much in that regard—but I am not so easily deceived." Father pushed the ledger away from Edward.

"You are changed since you returned. Your usual responsibility has changed to something far closer to earnest distraction."

"I was simply brought to a greater awareness of our situation. I mean to do what I can to keep this estate solvent."

"And I appreciate it." Father plucked the quill from Edward's hands. "But you are not eating or speaking or smiling, and that is unlike you. I worry because of the change I see, but also because your brother is not yet returned. He is more easily unsettled than you are. If something terrible occurred at this house party, he is likely terribly overset."

Edward could accept that change of topic. Tom's concerns were easier to discuss than his own heartache. "I left early. Tom will, no doubt, return shortly." Edward made no guarantees as to his brother's state of mind.

"I do not remember the Warricks well," Father said, "but I recall them being a touch toplofty at times."

Edward managed a minute smile. "That has not changed."

"They wore on your nerves, did they?"

Edward pushed out his pent-up breath. He could admit to this much. "They were equal parts arrogant and belittling. It was often infuriating."

"It is difficult always being the poorest at a gathering." Father spoke as one who knew from exhaustive experience.

"Ah, but I wasn't this time." He received a look of intrigued surprise. "I suppose I *might* have been, but it was difficult to tell."

Father snatched a nearby chair and pulled it up next to the desk, clearly settling in for a diverting tale. Edward didn't mind sharing this part of the house party with him.

"The Warricks limited their guest list to younger sons of

penniless families, dowerless young ladies, and older sons waiting to inherit impoverished estates."

"Did they give a reason for their selection process?" Father asked.

"Oh, yes. As it turns out, the Warrick estate is not subject to entailment. The Warricks do not have any children of their own, and, apparently, they don't particularly care for their relatives. Though if you ask me, the feeling is likely mutual."

"Was it a charity house party, then?" Father asked.

Edward nodded. "It was more than that, though. They were on the hunt for an heir."

Understanding began to dawn on Father's expression. "They wish to bestow their estate upon someone who needs it."

"Not merely needs it," Edward corrected. "Upon someone who would be eternally grateful and willing to adequately grovel at their feet on the meager hope of being considered."

"I see." Father folded his hands in front of him. "They are enamored of the idea of being a benefactor."

"And their beneficiaries, being poor, therefore decidedly beneath them, would supply them with three weeks of opportunities to congratulate themselves on their giving nature, as well as provide endless entertainment."

"Sounds rather unbearable."

Edward let his shoulders drop. "It was."

"I am surprised you stayed as long as you did," Father said. "I likely wouldn't have lasted through the first day."

A small measure of Edward's unease alleviated at his father's declarations. "Heaven knows, this family could use the money the Warrick estate would bring. I wondered at times if you would be disappointed to know your son and heir wasn't making much of an effort."

"I may not have much to offer my children in terms of material goods," Father said, "but I hope I taught you to value your dignity."

Edward had made certain to comport himself with decency and uprightness. Why, then, did reflections on the past three weeks leave him so uneasy?

"What did your brother think?"

"I don't know that he particularly approved of the Warricks' methods, but he did try hard to catch their notice."

Father nodded. "Life is difficult for younger sons."

Never before had Edward been so grateful for an understanding father. He had not condemned Edward for refusing to compete, neither had he condemned Tom for being desperate enough to take part.

"You will be proud to know that Tom conducted himself well, even when many of the other guests resorted to bickering and backbiting."

Father offered a small smile. "I would not expect anything less."

"Unfortunately, his adherence to basic decency will likely cost him the inheritance. They weren't terribly happy at his outright unwillingness to speak ill of the other guests. Doing so was one of their final requirements."

Father looked appropriately shocked. "To inherit the estate, guests had to be unkind to each other?"

"Essentially. That was the point I could no longer bear it in silence. I told them precisely what I thought of their scheme. They, in return, asked me to leave."

"And here you are."

"Here I am."

Father watched him a moment longer. "I am glad to know what transpired." He rose. "Perhaps in a few more days, you will be willing to tell me what else is weighing on you."

"What else?"

Father chuckled lightly. "I've known you your entire life, Edward Downy. You cannot fool me so easily."

With that, Father left. For once, Edward did not push back the thoughts that flooded his mind. What else was weighing on him? Agatha.

Was she home? Was she happy? Had her father's schemes succeeded? Had she participated in the final challenge? He wondered about that. He *worried* about that. Her participation was not her own choice, but he wanted to believe that she would not have allowed herself to be bullied into true unkindness. And yet failure to do so might cost her whole future, her family.

He wanted to hold her again. He wanted to assure her all would be well. More than anything, he wanted to have the right to have her in his life. He pulled the ledger over once more, eyeing its discouraging numbers and columns. There was hardly enough to support those already dependent on this estate.

He had nothing to offer her. Nothing at all.

The housekeeper stepped inside. "Mr. Isley to see you, sir."

Isley? "Thank you."

His friend entered the room, a look of uncertainty on his face. "Tell me if I am unwelcome," he said. "I will understand."

Edward waved that off. "Not at all. Come in."

Isley sat in the chair Father had occupied only a few minutes earlier. He motioned to the ledger open on the desk. "Attempting the impossible?"

"As always," Edward said. "Has your situation *improved* of late?"

Isley's brow pulled in surprised contemplation. "You've not heard the outcome?"

"I haven't." That Isley thought Edward ought to know raised several interesting questions. Was the new Warrick heir someone he knew? Ought Tom to have been home already, and if so, was his continued absence related to the Warricks' decision? "Who was chosen?"

"It isn't my tale to tell," Isley said.

"Then how will I know?"

Isley smiled a little. "You will know."

"You came here to torture me, then?" Edward shook his head even as he grinned.

"I came here to apologize." Isley was in earnest once again. "I behaved abominably. I was unkind and judgmental and dismissive and angry and—"

"—and provoked," Edward spoke over his friend's continued self-castigation. "The Warricks knew precisely what they were about. They dangled salvation just out of reach of the desperate masses, then pulled their strings like puppet masters. I do not blame you, my friend, for needing what they taunted you with and needing it enough to be temporarily blinded by that empty and cruel promise."

"You weren't pulled into it," Isley pointed out.

Edward wasn't certain what to say. He couldn't argue with Isley's logic, but neither did he wish his friend to wallow in regret. "If I were to guess correctly the name of the chosen heir, would you tell me I was correct?"

Isley's expression lightened a little. "No."

"It must be a particularly intriguing result, then."

"Possibly." Isley made a show of examining his fingers, even as a smile twisted his mouth. "Did you and Miss Holmwood depart on agreeable terms?"

"Is that meant to be a clue?" Edward wasn't certain if he wanted Agatha to be the one chosen. She needed the windfall, heaven knew she did, but being chosen likely meant she'd participated in the final, dehumanizing challenge. He didn't want to believe it of her.

"I am not saying a word about the Warricks' decision." Isley settled more comfortably in his chair. "I asked out of genuine curiosity. The two of you were thick as thieves throughout the party, and she seems a good sort of lady."

"She is the very best sort of lady."

Isley shot him a look of empathy. "That was perhaps the cruelest part of that scheme. They must have known some of their guests would grow attached to one another, and yet none were in any position to marry."

It was, indeed, cruel. "Did she seem happy when the party came to a close? Content, at least?"

"Are you attempting to garner clues?"

Edward shook his head. "I am worried for her. Mr. Holmwood had staked her entire future on the outcome of those three weeks."

"She did not seem as light and lively at the end of the gathering as she had at the beginning," Isley said.

Edward had noticed that as well. The pressure of her father's edict had taken a toll. "I hope she is happy," he said quietly.

The housekeeper stepped inside once more. "Begging your pardon, sirs. Mr. and Mrs. Downy have requested Mr. Edward Downy's presence in the drawing room."

"Is anything the matter?" he asked.

Mrs. Jones could be counted on to share what she knew. "Your brother has returned."

Edward caught Isley's eye as they rose. "Perhaps Tom will tell me what you have refused to divulge."

Isley straightened his cuffs. "Perhaps he will."

"Are you saying that the news *is* Tom's to share?"

"I'm not saying a thing," Isley answered.

Edward slapped him on the shoulder. They turned the corner in the corridor. "If you had been this secretive at Eton, the headmaster would never have realized we were the ones who filled the inkwells with tea."

"You ought to have told the Warricks about that bit of ingenious mischief," Isley said. "They would have chosen you without a doubt."

"Or tossed me out even sooner."

Isley stopped just outside the door to the drawing room. "They truly tossed you out?"

"They *kindly* suggested I might be more comfortable at home." He gave his friend a sideways glance. "I couldn't really argue with them. I doubted I could be any less comfortable than I was at their home."

Isley motioned him inside. Edward stepped through the threshold. There, as Mrs. Jones had indicated, stood Tom. *Stood* wasn't entirely the right word. He moved about, leaning forward and backward, bouncing on his feet. Energy spilled out of him like water from an overfilled pitcher.

"There you are, Edward." Tom's eyes darted about, settling on Isley for the briefest of moments. "And Isley. I've not seen you in a few days."

"I came to beg your brother's pardon for being obnoxious these past weeks."

Tom nodded. "You *were* rather annoying."

"I know."

Tom's expression turned more somber. "Did you tell him?"

Isley shook his head. "It wasn't my news to tell."

"Thomas." Mother pulled his name out long as she always did when scolding them. "You have us on the edges of our seats. Do end the suspense."

Tom grinned at them all in turn. "Wish me happy. I am to be married."

"Married?" three voices asked in unison.

Isley did not seem the least surprised.

"Her name is Henrietta Sumner," Tom continued on, apparently undeterred by the shock on his family's faces. "She is an angel. I met her at the Warricks' house party."

"But, son," Father jumped in, "if she was a guest at their party, then she is poor as a church mouse, as, I might add, are you."

"But that is the beauty of it," Tom said. "They chose us."

"They?" Mother asked.

"The Warricks."

"Chose *us?*" Edward motioned to the family.

Tom shook his head. "No. *Us.*" He touched his hand to his heart. "My Henrietta and me. They chose us, as a couple, to inherit their estate. Together. The papers are being drawn up even as we speak. Mr. Sumner is to arrive in Somerset at any moment, only because he must sign the marriage settlement. We also felt it imperative that he know without the slightest doubt that he will have no access to the estate's income or wealth. It will all be tied up neatly. The estate and all that comes with it will remain whole."

"*You* inherited?" Edward pressed. He could hardly believe it.

"We did." Tom was transformed. He'd always had a sunny outlook, but Edward had never seen him so joyous. "And we, *all of us*, are due in Somerset in two days' time. The wedding will be held in a week."

"Good heavens." Mother was all aflutter.

In a moment, the room was filled with the anxious chatter of the housekeeper and mistress of the house making desperate plans, Father and Tom speaking of marriage settlements and the details of the inheritance, Isley offering his genuine congratulations.

Edward remained quiet. Agatha had not been chosen. While that meant there was no hope for a future between the two of them, it called into question her personal future.

What, he wondered in horror, had her father's reaction been? And where was she now?

CHAPTER NINE

"Surely you know the difference between blue and lavender." Mrs. Warrick's slow, patronizing tone grated as much as ever.

Agatha had been subjected to it again and again over the days since the house party ended. What little consideration Mrs. Warrick had displayed during those three weeks had disappeared the moment the final guest had left. The older lady had seemed so pleased when Father had suggested Agatha remain behind as her lady's companion. As it turned out, her pleasure did not translate into kind treatment.

Only self-directed humor had saved Agatha from tearing her hair out. "Lavender is a color?" She blinked as if utterly shocked. "I thought it was a material, like wool or straw."

"Why would I send you to fetch a straw shawl?" Mrs. Warrick's patience was always a bit thin.

"You didn't," Agatha said innocently. "You sent me for a lavender shawl."

"Then why"—she held up the shawl Agatha had just brought to her—"am I holding this? This is blue."

In Agatha's defense, the blue shawl had a strong hint of

purple. "If you will tell me where the shawl you want is, I will happily fetch it."

Mrs. Warrick took a slow breath, then settled her features into a look of patience. "I do not know where it is. I have far more important things to concern myself with. Ask Mrs. Hill or Fanny."

Agatha offered a vague smile and slid from the room. Somehow, it was easier letting her new mistress think she was slow-witted. Perhaps it was a matter of pride. Mrs. Warrick could belittle her all she wanted, but secretly, quietly, Agatha would know she hadn't been bested, not entirely. It was likely wrong of her, but she couldn't help it. Doing so was a matter of survival.

Though Agatha perused nearly the entirety of the second floor, she found neither the housekeeper nor Mrs. Warrick's lady's maid. Truth be told, she was not putting much effort into the search. Taking her time meant avoiding the inevitable haranguing she would receive if she were in Mrs. Warrick's company. She meandered along the corridors and down the stairs, taking as much time as she could reasonably manage.

A few doors shy of returning to Mrs. Warrick's side, Agatha spotted, gazing out the windows of the north sitting room, the one person at the Warrick estate whose company she actually enjoyed. Henrietta Sumner was a quiet sort, but underneath her air of reserve beat a heart as good as gold and as stalwart as any Agatha had known.

She suspected she knew why Henrietta kept so close to the windows overlooking the front drive. "Is your Tom due to arrive today?"

Henrietta looked back at her for only a moment. "At any

moment, actually. I am likely rather pathetic for this, but I have missed him terribly these days he's been away."

Not pathetic in the least. In fact, Agatha felt much the same way about Tom's brother.

"Soon, you will need not be parted," Agatha reminded her new friend. "That must lighten your heart."

"It does, indeed." Henrietta turned and leaned her back against the window frame. "Tom's family is coming with him."

Agatha tried to smile causally, but she could feel the effort fall short.

Henrietta's expression could not have been more empathetic. "I wish we were able to do something for you and Edward, but the Warricks have tied the inheritance up so tightly."

Agatha nodded. "I appreciate your thoughtfulness. And I cannot blame the Warricks for that. They had good reason to make your inheritance all but impossible to draw against."

Henrietta's shoulders drooped. "That reason being my father."

It was the truth, though Agatha was far too diplomatic to acknowledge it. Mr. Sumner had taken his own profitable estate and more than comfortable inheritance and had squandered every last penny. Keeping his daughter's miraculous good fortune out of his hands was crucial, even if it did prevent Tom and Henrietta from helping the remaining members of their families.

"Have you happened to have seen the housekeeper or Mrs. Warrick's lady's maid?" Agatha asked. "I am charged with fetching the mistress's lavender shawl, and it seems they are the only ones likely to know where it is."

Henrietta offered a commiserating smile. "They are avoiding her as much as I am certain you wish you could. I do not know how you will endure her every single day."

"Daily endurance will fall to your fate as well," Agatha reminded her.

"The Warricks leave for London a mere two days after the wedding and do not mean to return here. We will be free of them."

Yes, but I won't. Not for years to come.

Years.

Agatha listened in horrified silence as the sound of new arrivals drifted into the drawing room. Mr. and Mrs. Warrick stood in all their pomp to welcome the Downy family. Agatha kept to her designated corner of the room, wishing she could simply disappear. Not only had her circumstances grown even more desperate, she was seeing *him* again for the first time since realizing beyond a doubt that they could have no future together. She didn't think she could ever have fully prepared herself for that.

Her one source of joy came from watching Henrietta's eager anticipation. The bride-to-be kept herself properly still, but her eyes danced with delight. This would be a joyous reunion for her.

The butler stepped inside. "Mr. and Mrs. Downy, Mr. Edward Downy, and Mr. Thomas Downy."

Edward's parents came inside first. Agatha made a quick study of them and came to the conclusion that the Downy brothers took after their mother's side of the family, though

Edward had his father's smile. She had time to make only that cursory observation before Edward, himself, came into the room.

Oh, how she'd missed him. Seeing him again made her even more aware of the empty space he'd left in her heart. From the first moments of their acquaintance, he had recognized her odd sense of humor, had taken note of her struggles when most of the world would find her too insignificant to bother with, and had cherished their time together as much as she had. Their meeting had been nothing short of fate, though fate had, in the end, proven cruel.

All of the appropriate greetings and curtsies and bows were exchanged between the Downys, Sumners, and Warricks. Agatha was now little better than a servant and didn't warrant any notice. She was grateful for the obscurity. Having her own corner all to herself granted her a moment to regain her composure.

Mrs. Warrick motioned Mrs. Downy to the empty seat beside hers, and the older ladies dove directly into a conversation apart from the others.

"You must forgive my haphazard appearance," Mrs. Warrick said. "My lavender shawl is a much better match for this dress, but I am afraid my lady's companion is not yet very reliable. I've not had time to properly train her."

Mrs. Downy didn't appear to know quite what to say.

Mrs. Warrick patted her hand. "I don't suppose you have ever enjoyed the luxury of a lady's companion."

"I can't say that I have." Mrs. Downy's surprise was obvious, but her manners were impeccable.

"Should you ever find yourself with one, make certain she

has learned her colors." Mrs. Warrick shot Agatha a quick look of smug satisfaction.

Agatha answered with as vague a smile as she could produce.

Mrs. Downy's expression was far less arrogant, with more than a hint of curiosity. "She is young to be a companion. I hope she will be given time for socializing with her own age group."

"She has a job to perform," Mrs. Warrick argued. "I do not pay her to socialize."

That was certainly true. Mrs. Warrick, in fact, hardly paid her at all.

Mrs. Downy's chin raised a notch. "While we are all here, your companion should have ample time to interact with Miss Sumner. I cannot imagine the companionship of Mrs. Sumner and myself should prove insufficient for you."

Was Mrs. Downy offering her, whom she must have considered a stranger, a respite from her employer? It seemed Edward favored his mother in more than just appearance.

"I have only just been showered with the attentions of dozens of houseguests," Mrs. Warrick said. "The presence of merely two—"

"—will, no doubt, be a welcome respite." Mrs. Downy did not permit her hostess to finish what was no doubt the beginnings of an insult. "Allow me to invite your companion to join us, so she can keep company with the young people."

"I do not think she will accept your offer," Mrs. Warrick said, "considering their history."

"History?"

Mrs. Warrick sat ever straighter, a haughty rigidity to her shoulders. "Your younger son, then, did not tell you?"

Tom heard himself being discussed and switched conversations. "What did I not tell my mother?"

"That my companion was, mere days ago, a guest in this house, competing for the same inheritance you and Miss Sumner eventually won."

With that, all eyes turned in Agatha's direction. For the first time since arriving, Edward saw her there. His mouth dropped a bit open. His eyes pulled wide.

"Miss Holmwood," Tom sputtered out her name. "I had no idea you were—I—I have not had the opportunity to thank you yet. Mr. Warrick told us what you did, what you said."

Agatha shook her head vehemently even as she stood. "I do not require a thank-you. I assure you I only did what was right."

Tom did not heed her objection, but crossed directly to her, shaking her hand. "You deserve to be thanked, though I know I could never manage to do it sufficiently."

"Thank her, by all means," Mrs. Warrick said. "It might make her feel less of a fool for throwing away her entire future. We might have actually considered her, if not for her pleading *your* cause. Instead of heiress to a fortune, she is no better than a companion."

No better than . . . Was there no end to the humiliation the lady meant to heap upon her?

For the briefest of moments, Edward's gaze caught and held hers. Agatha tried to smile, tried to summon her sense of the absurd and diverting. But his expression turned almost pitying, and all attempts at humor died instantly.

She was an object of pity. In that moment, despite knowing Mrs. Warrick would thoroughly scold her for it, Agatha could not remain.

Life was simply asking too much.

CHAPTER TEN

E dward required all of half a second to piece together Agatha's past few days. She hadn't been selected as heir. Her father had followed through on his threat not to "continue sacrificing for her," and she'd been handed over to the Warricks as a no doubt underpaid and most certainly ill-treated lady's companion. He required only a half second more to decide to follow her out into the corridor.

"Agatha?" She hadn't gone far. "Please, wait."

She stopped at the end of the corridor and slowly turned back toward him. "I was executing a dramatic exit, Edward Downy. You've ruined it."

Behind her humor was unmistakable wariness. She was using it as a shield again, the way she had with her father the night Edward met her. And, just as he had the night they met, he sensed that joining in the jest was the best means of setting her mind at ease.

"*I* was enacting a heroic pursuit, and *you* have ruined that."

She smiled a bit. "Oh, was I expected to flitter about down the corridor, disappearing around the corner at the last possible moment?"

He nodded solemnly. "Precisely."

"Next time," she said.

He closed the gap between them and reached out for her hands. Holding them tenderly, he asked, "What happened, Agatha? How is it you came to be Mrs. Warrick's lady's companion?" He felt certain he knew the answer, but sensed she needed a confidante.

"My father," she said on a sigh. "He did threaten to stop 'sacrificing' for me, you will recall."

He'd guessed correctly, then. "He blamed you for not being selected as heir."

"He had reason to," she answered quietly.

Edward slipped her arm through his and continued down the corridor with her at his side.

"The Warricks' last requirement, that each guest explain to them why he or she was more deserving of the inheritance than any of the others, did not go well, at least in my father's eyes." She wrapped her arm more closely around his. There was such comfort in her nearness. He had nearly forgotten the soothing influence of her company. "I couldn't bring myself to insist I deserved or needed the inheritance more than anyone else. It simply wasn't true."

Hers, then, hadn't been an objection simply to the task, but also to being required to, in her view, lie. It was little wonder he'd so quickly come to admire and cherish her. She was a good person to the very depths of her heart.

"You told the Warricks that Tom and Henrietta were more deserving?" That was the impression he'd received listening to the stilted conversation in the drawing room a moment earlier.

"I don't know that anyone at the house party was

undeserving," she said. "But what hope, really, did those two have of a future together, of happiness? He is a younger son, which is difficult even in well-heeled families. She is the daughter of a spendthrift who would squander any influx of income the family might have. The Warricks' offered inheritance was a chance neither of them were likely to ever see again."

Edward slipped his arm from hers and wrapped it around her middle. "But missing out on that chance yourself placed you in your current predicament."

She leaned her head against his shoulder as they stepped out onto the back terrace. "Choices are difficult to make when neither outcome is a desirable one. This was a consequence I felt myself better equipped to live with. Doing wrong by Tom and Henrietta for my own gain would have haunted me."

He turned his head enough to press a kiss to the top of her head. "You are a wonderful person, Agatha."

"My father says I'm an unnatural and ungrateful daughter."

"It seems to me any father who would turn away his child for being an extraordinary person is rather unnatural and ungrateful himself."

She turned her gaze up to him. Such sadness touched their depths. "It was something of a blow, yes. I had, until the moment he left, held out some hope that he would see enough value in me to . . . keep me."

Edward stopped their forward progress, despite having only taken a single step inside the garden. He looked more closely at her, worried at the increasing despondency he heard in her voice. "He was wrong, my dear. What he did was wrong. Please do not allow it to consume you."

"My father's unkindness is not what is weighing on me at the moment."

"Then what is?" He brushed his hand along her cheek. He hated seeing her so burdened.

"The terms of Tom's inheritance prevent him from giving any part of it to his family."

She, compassionate soul that she was, worried for *him*. "I know about the terms," he assured her. "Tom told me."

"But you needed the income. You—We—"

He held her face gently in his hands and pressed a light, lingering kiss to her forehead. "*We* will be happy for Tom and Henrietta. And *we* will enjoy the time we have together here. And we will hope that something miraculous occurs."

She set her hands on his chest and leaned into his embrace. He held her, breathing in her warmth, the flowery scent in her hair, the joy of her near to him.

He hadn't been exaggerating; they needed a miracle. They needed one desperately. And he hadn't the slightest idea where to look for one.

❦

Edward's endurance lasted until the next morning. After yet another complaint from Mrs. Warrick about her servants and countless self-congratulatory speeches from Mr. Warrick detailing his tremendous generosity, Edward knew he'd best beat a hasty retreat before he said something he regretted. The Warricks deserved a dressing down, but Tom and Henrietta deserved to not be miserable in the days leading up to their wedding.

The estate was blessedly large, granting Edward ample space to move about uninterrupted. He would have enjoyed Agatha's company, but, alas, her employer demanded her presence at nearly every moment.

Edward's escape took him past the estate's dower house, a modest Tudor-style structure, tucked a bit out of view beyond a bower of birch and ash. The approach to the home was lined on either side with empty flowerbeds. Shrubs sat beneath the front windows, vibrantly green but in dire need of trimming.

He stepped up to the dingy windows and glanced inside. He could only just make out the covered furnishings. The house had clearly been vacant for quite some time, but the exterior, other than the greenery, seemed well cared for. Even the gravel in the drive appeared to have been recently raked.

Should the Downy estate continue to struggle and Edward find himself unable to care for Mother after Father's passing, Tom might be in a position to do so. That brought some comfort.

Edward continued down the lane leading away from the dower house and out toward the vast parkland surrounding the main house. He'd spent enough years evaluating the Downy estate and studying efficient land use and proper planning, to make a detailed assessment of what he saw.

A low-lying section of the east lawn appeared to be draining poorly. Based on the lay of the land beyond, it was likely a problem throughout the eastern portion of the estate. He could make out fields beyond the enclosed lawn. If the land wasn't draining, the crop yield would be relatively poor.

He followed the edge of the lawns, eyeing more outlying fields. He was at too great a distance to make a detailed evaluation, but he spotted a great many things that might be done differently, better. The estate manager didn't appear to be one well versed in more recent agricultural advancements. That came from not being in desperate need of every penny the land could produce.

Desperate need had forced Edward to learn all he could about managing land. He'd felt no particular connection to the Warrick estate during the house party and hadn't paid much heed to the state of it. But this was his brother's land now. He wanted the best for Tom.

As he walked along the winding footpath leading to the back garden, he mentally made a list of the improvements he meant to suggest to his brother. The estate was clearly profitable, but making it efficient would decrease the chances of future generations finding themselves in Edward's unenviable position.

He turned the corner at the far edge of the garden and came upon Tom, ambling about the garden path. Their eyes met, and they both chuckled.

"Couldn't bear it any longer?" Edward guessed.

"Thank the heavens the Warricks will be living year-round in London," Tom said. He lowered his voice and gave Edward an emphasizing look. "We have it in writing."

Edward couldn't help a grin. "Thus, you need only endure them until the wedding."

Tom pushed out a breath. "They are sorely trying my patience." That was something Edward seldom heard from his affable younger brother.

"I've been exploring your estate," Edward said.

"And what are your impressions?" They began a slow circuit of the garden.

"Firstly, you need to think of a name for this place. It is, after all, no longer 'the Warrick estate.'"

Tom nodded. "Henrietta and I discussed that, but we haven't thought of anything yet that we both love."

"You have time. It would, I am certain, be best to delay the rechristening until after the Warricks have moved to Town."

"Indeed." Tom tucked his hands into the pockets of his outer coat. "What else?"

Edward launched into a detailed explanation of what he'd observed, what he inferred based on those observations, and what he would recommend be done. "A great deal has changed in land management in recent years. If I were a betting man, I'd wager the current estate manager has been at his job a very long time and hasn't kept abreast of developments."

"He's ancient," Tom said. "And, quite honestly, looks exhausted. I am surprised he hasn't yet been pensioned off."

An idea formed in Edward's mind, but one riddled with holes and empty spaces. "You need a new estate manager." The statement was something of a question.

"That I do."

"Would you—" Edward hadn't thought this through entirely. The words emerged as broken and half-formed as the idea behind them. "I know a great deal about estate management."

Tom nodded. "Younger sons aren't educated about these things. I feel like I have a lifetime's worth of information to learn overnight."

"What if you had an *older* son nearby? One who knew these things and who cared what happened to you and your family and, therefore, could be counted on to make his best effort?"

Tom stopped walking and turned to look directly at Edward. "What are you proposing?"

It was a fortunate thing Edward had long ago learned to endure humbling moments and circumstances. Asking of a younger brother what he was about to ask would be daunting for most eldest sons in Society. "Would you consider hiring me on as your estate manager? Having a house and income of my own will take a small financial burden off the Downy coffers. Keeping your estate profitable will remove the risk of future Downys facing our current circumstances. And"—his heart thudded against his ribs—"securing employment might allow me to have a future with Agatha. A humble, lowly future, but a future. Assuming, of course, she is willing to accept it."

"I don't imagine she will object to a small income—she has lived that reality, after all—but I've seen the estate manager's cottage, Edward. It is little better than a hovel. Humble does not begin to describe it. Even if you were to make improvements, it would be tiny and cramped and a tremendous step down, even from the circumstances in which she had been living."

Could he, in good conscience, ask Agatha to give up one humiliation, Mrs. Warrick's belittling treatment of her, for another?

"What if—" He paused a moment, allowing his mind to sort through things a bit more. "What if the current estate manager remained in his home and I took up residence in the dower house? It is not large nor extravagant, but neither would it mortify its occupants."

A slow smile spread over Tom's face. "The dower house *is* empty."

Excitement began bubbling inside. "And we needn't

broadcast to the world that I am in your employ. That would save our parents the disapproval of the *ton* and would prevent any of my future children from bearing that stigma as well."

"We are simply so fond of one another that the idea of living on the same estate was too ideal to pass up," Tom suggested with a laugh.

"That will satisfy the toplofty who would hold this arrangement against the family." This would work. He felt certain it would.

"The upkeep of the dower house is the responsibility of the estate," Tom said. "Your income, therefore, would not need to stretch beyond your household needs. There would be enough left over to invest in the Downy estate. Given enough years, you could turn it around as well."

"You must intend to be very generous with my salary," Edward said.

Tom slapped a hand on his shoulder. "I told you when I first decided to win the Warricks' prize that it would benefit us both. This is the only way I know to make that happen. And I mean to make it happen."

"Only one thing remains undecided, then," Edward said.

"What is that?"

"Whether or not I can convince a certain beleaguered lady's companion to take on the life of an estate manager's wife."

Tom pushed him toward the house. "There is but one way to find out."

CHAPTER ELEVEN

"I will require you to be demure in London," Mrs. Warrick said, eyeing Agatha from her wingback chair where she conducted their daily evaluations, which is what she called listing the various ways in which Agatha had disappointed her that day.

"Demure." Agatha nodded. "And 'demure' is not a color, like lavender?"

Mrs. Warrick's expression hardened. "You needn't feign stupidity, Agatha. I have solved the mystery of your profoundly slow-witted declarations."

Oh, dear.

"You may act the fool all you wish," Mrs. Warrick said, "but not when conversing with me, and absolutely never in the presence of company. Am I understood?"

"Yes, Mrs. Warrick." Agatha sighed inwardly. She had lost her one source of escape in this increasingly oppressive arrangement.

"Now." Mrs. Warrick resumed her air of magnanimousness. "We need to discuss a more somber wardrobe for you."

More somber? Agatha had already been limited to her most subdued colors and styles.

The door to the sitting room flew open in that moment. Mrs. Warrick was too startled for any kind of verbal response.

Edward stepped inside, an equal measure of excitement and determination in his stride. His gaze passed over Mrs. Warrick without the slightest pause and settled on Agatha.

"Agatha Holmwood, I love you. I have loved you almost from the first moment I met you."

Warmth stole over her cheeks even as her smile grew ever broader. What had brought on Edward's unexpected but welcome declaration?

"I have little to offer you, but as of this afternoon, I have a small home, a barely adequate income, and the vaguest of hopes that my family estate will not be reduced to a crumbling pile of stones by the time I inherit it." He didn't look away, didn't flinch at the admission of his humble circumstances. "Other than that, I have nothing to give you besides my admiration, my devotion, and my undying love."

"What a pathetic—" Mrs. Warrick got no further than that before Edward's cold glare cut off her insulting evaluation.

"Will you marry me, Agatha?" he asked. "I realize I'd be asking you to give up the company of this sweet-tongued, compassionate angel of a mistress," he added on a mutter.

"Well," Mrs. Warrick huffed.

Agatha ignored her and rose to her feet, barely able to contain the joy rushing through her. She wasn't at all certain what he meant by having a home and an income, but if he had found his situation adequate to support them, then she would have faith that he meant it. She knew him well enough to trust he would explain in greater detail when they were alone.

She crossed the room to where he stood. His eyes danced

with hope and anticipation. Her answer, she realized upon seeing his joy already overflowing, was more of a technicality. But he had asked, and she meant to answer.

"My sweet Edward," she said, resting her hands on his chest, "I would marry you even if doing so meant living in a half-collapsed cabin on the edge of the world."

His lips twitched. "I am relatively confident it won't come to that."

She rose up on her toes and pressed the tiniest, briefest of kisses to his lips. "I love you."

"And I love you," he answered. He pulled her up next to him, and together they turned to face Mrs. Warrick. "Ma'am, I do believe Miss Holmwood's services will no longer be required."

A few sputters followed that announcement. Edward led Agatha out of the room before Mrs. Warrick had a chance to find her voice.

The embarrassment of the house party, the heartbreak of her father's defection, and the misery of fearing she would be separated from Edward forever dissipated as they walked, his arm tucked affectionately around her, down the corridor.

"There is something I must show you," he said, leading her from the house and beyond the gardens. He kept her close even as his pace quickened.

They followed a path that led beyond a thicket of trees. A lovely house in the contrasting colors of the well-known Tudor style sat tucked away among the trees. The scene was beautifully and wonderfully serene.

"What is this place?" she asked.

He turned to face her, then took both her hands in his.

"This, my dearest Agatha, is our 'half-collapsed cabin on the edge of the world.' This is the home I have to offer you. And this"—he raised their clasped hands to his chest—"is the heart I offer you. All of it."

"I accept," she said without hesitation.

"The house or the heart?" he asked, his tone light.

"Both." She threw her arms around his neck.

He wrapped his arms around her and kissed her as he never had before. Gone was the timid uncertainty of their first kiss. This kiss was a celebration.

EPILOGUE

Life was grand at Fromesweir, the name Tom and Henrietta had settled upon for the estate, owing to the fact that the stream running through the grounds resulted from a weir located on the nearby River Frome.

On a warm summer's day a bit more than a year after the Warricks had officially gifted their estate to Tom, Edward, along with Tom and their sister, Caroline, and her husband, George, gathered together to celebrate the family's unexpected good fortune over the past years. They set out a picnic on the now properly drained east lawn. Caroline's young son crawled about, earning the instant adoration of his aunts and uncles. Henrietta held her infant son in her arms, a look of utter contentment on her face.

Edward leaned against the trunk of a tree, watching his extended family. Worry and uncertainty had gripped them for too many years. Caroline had only narrowly avoided a loveless arranged marriage for the sake of the family finances. He and Tom had resigned themselves years earlier to never marrying, never having families of their own. Now, here they all were: happy, loved, with families and futures.

313

He looked up at the sound of footsteps. Agatha. *His* Agatha. Lovely, beautiful, kindhearted Agatha.

"Forgive my tardiness," she said with theatrical regret. "I could not find my lavender shawl."

That had become a jest between them ever since Mrs. Warrick's legendary lecture about the importance of lavender.

Edward hopped to his feet to help her sit. The time for her confinement was quickly approaching, and getting up and down had proven increasingly difficult of late. He saw her comfortably settled, then took his place directly beside her.

"How are you feeling?" Henrietta asked her.

"Ready for this child to make his appearance," was Agatha's wearied response.

"*His?*" Caroline replied. "You believe the baby will be a boy, then?"

Agatha nodded. "But Edward is convinced the child is a girl."

"Not convinced so much as hopeful," Edward answered. Upon first learning they were to be parents, his mind had filled with the image of a dark-haired little girl with her mother's wit and easy smile.

Agatha leaned into his embrace, her hands resting on her rounded middle, his arms tucked gently around her. Caroline and George played with their little one. Tom cooed over the infant in his wife's arms.

"Do you know, love," Agatha said, "I believe I shall write a letter to my father telling him how very wrong he was."

"About what in particular?"

"He insisted I did not emerge from that horrid house party victorious a year ago. He was wrong."

"He was, indeed."

They had found each other at the Battle Royal the Warricks had hosted. They had fallen in love. And, in the end, they had found their happiness.

They had not been chosen as the heirs, but they had, in the end, claimed the greatest prize of all: love.

ABOUT SARAH M. EDEN

Sarah M. Eden is the author of multiple historical romances, including the two-time Whitney Award Winner *Longing for Home* and Whitney Award finalists *Seeking Persephone* and *Courting Miss Lancaster*. Combining her obsession with history and affinity for tender love stories, Sarah loves crafting witty characters and heartfelt romances. She has twice served as the Master of Ceremonies for the LDStorymakers Writers Conference and acted as the Writer in Residence at the Northwest Writers Retreat. Sarah is represented by Pam Howell at D4EO Literary Agency.

Visit Sarah on-line:
Twitter: @SarahMEden
Facebook: Author Sarah M. Eden
Website: SarahMEden.com

Dear Reader,

Thank you for reading *Summer House Party*. We hope you loved the sweet romance novellas! Each collection in the Timeless Regency Collection contains three novellas.

If you enjoyed this collection, please consider leaving a review on Goodreads or any other e-book store you purchase through. Reviews and word-of-mouth is what helps us continue this fun project. For updates and notifications of sales and giveaways, please sign up for our monthly newsletter on our blog: http://timelessromanceanthologies.blogspot.com

We also post announcements on our Facebook page: Timeless Romance Anthologies

Thank you!

The Timeless Romance Authors

More Timeless Regency Collections:

Don't miss our Timeless Romance Anthologies:
Six short romance novellas in each anthology
For the latest updates on our anthologies, sign up on our blog:
http://TimelessRomanceAnthologies.blogspot.com

Made in the USA
Coppell, TX
07 February 2020

15513630R00184